Mountain Time

Trevor & India Reiste

ISBNs
Paperback: 979-8-9990643-0-1
Ebook: 979-8-9990643-1-8

To the couples who turn love into adventure, dream big, and refuse to be anything but unstoppable.

Content Warnings

Dear Reader,

While *Mountain Time* is a light-hearted, funny romance, please take note of the following content warnings:

This book contains emotionally difficult topics like parental death, the discussion of coercive pregnancy, hospitalizations, bodily harm/trauma, and explicit sexual content and language.

We urge anyone who might be upset by the content to consider their well-being before proceeding.

Mountain Time is for ages eighteen and up.

Visit our website for more information.

If you have any questions regarding the content of this book, please contact the authors.

www.thereistes.com/contact

A Note from the Authors

Mountain Time is in no way based on our life, but it is a reflection of our lifestyle. We have loved writing a cowboy romance rooted in firsthand experience and knowledge of the rodeo and ranching world.

Trevor has been a professional bull rider for fourteen years, qualifying for the Wrangler National Finals Rodeo twice and winning many prestigious rodeos like The Pendleton Round-Up. His love for the sport and rodeo lifestyle was the inspiration behind this book.

India was raised on a farm in Iowa working with cattle and horses for many years. Her love of the cattle industry and western lifestyle brings a small glimpse into the realistic view of women in agriculture to this book.

Many rodeo scenes and scenarios in this book are based on real events we have been part of and witnessed. We hope we have fairly represented the amazing world of rodeo and agriculture, but please understand that this is a work of fiction and we have taken liberties to enhance the story. The rodeo lifestyle is full of highs and lows, but everyone who lives it knows it's a damn good life.

This may have started as a single book, but our newfound passion for writing has brought even more stories to life. Stay tuned for many more cowboy romances from the Reistes.

Without further ado, we hope you enjoy Knox and Kacey's story.

Mountain Time Playlist

Listen to the music playing in the background of Knox and Kacey's love story.

Enjoy these songs before you read *Mountain Time,* while you read, in between chapters to stay in the story, or however you choose to enjoy music with your books.

Listen on Spotify:

Listen on Apple Music:

Contents

FROM FIRST TO FOURTH:

OKLAHOMA'S KNOX WARD COULDN'T HANG ONTO NUMBER ONE, FINISHING FOURTH IN THE WORLD

In an unexpected turn of events, the Oklahoma bull rider, initially projected to win the world title, fell short. Ward rode just two out of ten bulls at the National Finals Rodeo, falling from first to fourth place, leaving fans wondering what went wrong.

*Knox Ward refused to comment.

Chapter 1

Kacey

April, Four Years Later

Groaning, I roll over, away from the sun burning through the windows and right into my retinas. I mentally scold myself for forgetting to close the blinds last night.

As I climb out of bed, I can hear people outside, telling me the work for the day is starting on the ranch. I get dressed, throwing on a long-sleeve button down, a pair of jeans, and my jacket. Dragging my feet, I slowly make my way into the kitchen for coffee. I pour some in a to-go mug, grab a protein bar, put on my boots, and walk out the door.

From my front porch, I have a perfect view of the brown and white horse barn and south pasture where the mares and foals live. With the Rocky Mountains in the distance, it really is picture perfect. I love this ranch. It's been in my family for four generations and I couldn't imagine being anywhere else. I take a deep breath and one last look before I head to the barn to saddle my horse.

I walk about halfway down the barn alley and stop.

Where is my dog?

I whistle loudly. "Oh Rein," I singsong.

From around the corner runs a little half-breed Red Heeler, Australian Shepherd mix dog. At only thirty-five pounds, she looks innocent, but don't let her looks fool you, she has a wild side a mile long. I bend over and give her some scratches behind the ears, her soft red and white speckled fur flying up and sticking to my sleeve.

After I've paid Rein's pet tax, I walk down a few more stalls, grab a halter, and open the stall door. Inside, ears perked forward, stands my horse—a little sorrel gelding named Hooch. He's 14.2 hands tall with a white blaze and four white socks. Most girls want a more colorful horse, like blue roans, buckskins or palominos, but that's not me. I like red dogs and red horses. Other girls also like pink and sparkle tack, while I prefer the classic suede-like appearance of plain, rough out, tan leather.

With Hooch saddled, I whistle at my wild child and ride out of the barn. April mornings in Colorado are always chilly. In the crisp morning air, with dew on the grass, the foals like to race across the pasture finding their legs. So even with the chill, spring is always my favorite season on the ranch.

Nothing is better than foaling season.

About 100 yards into the pasture, my dad is sitting on his horse talking to our ranch foreman. Dad is a third-generation rancher—and he's good at it. He saved this ranch by talking Grandpa into starting the cattle feedlot, which then turned into adding a butcher shop and selling meat directly to high-end restaurants. Located southwest of Denver, The Diamond Hart Ranch consists of roughly 45,000 acres and is the most successful, diverse, and well-operated ranch in the state. And in my opinion, it's the prettiest ranch, too.

Today, we're going to the mountain pasture, my favorite place to ride. It's always a beautiful ride, like something you would see in a magazine or movie.

The ranch foreman, Chester, mostly known as Chet, was brought on a few years ago and we don't exactly get along. He's sitting by Dad, wearing his gray silverbelly cowboy hat that always looks a little crooked. He's pretty smart when it comes to cattle health, and he does great with the pairs on pasture. So much so, Chet has a bit of a chip on his shoulder. As for training horses, not so much. He doesn't have the patience for it.

I still don't understand why my dad hired him—he never even asked me if I wanted the job.

The men turn when Hooch and I get closer.

"Why is your hat always crooked?" I tease Chet.

He reaches up, adjusting it. "It is not."

I smirk at the fact that he checked.

My father chuckles behind his thick beard. "Please be nice to the cowboys, we have a long day ahead of us."

Chet holds his tongue, but the way his face flushes is priceless.

"Well, one of you holler at the boys. We got cattle to gather," my father says.

Chet whistles and seven nearby cowboys heed his call, riding up on their own horses. With that, we all head up the mountain.

After about two hours, we reach the top. My father sends two cowboys and me down the north side—the closest side to the corrals—while he and two others take the south. Chet and one cowboy take the east, while Carson and another take the west.

Carson is my favorite of the cowboys. He's in his mid-thirties with blonde shaggy hair and a scruffy face under a ragged old black Resistol cowboy hat. He's the best ranch hand we have. He can rope, train horses, fix about anything, and he's tougher than nails. I've seen him get kicked in the ribs, saddle the same horse and ride away on it like it never happened. He's quiet, reserved, maybe even a little grumpy, but he's as loyal as they come—you definitely don't want to mess with someone he cares about.

Carson has been on the ranch since I was eight and he's more of a big brother than a ranch hand to me. I know he sees me as a sister, too. He started teaching me to train horses when I was twelve. He's helped me ever since, including Hooch. He really should be the foreman, not that Dad hasn't offered him the job, but every time, Carson just says he likes his current position.

I'll never understand it.

Everyone disperses in their assigned directions, but before I head down the mountain, I take a second to soak up the view. It's breathtaking. Each time I see it is like the first. I can see all of the main parts of the ranch, the stone house and big, old wood barn with white trim my great-grandparents built. Just north of the old barn is the horse barn with an indoor arena Dad built for me. To the west of the arena is the house my grandfather built—which I now live in—and southwest of it is the ranch foreman's house. Although it's not where Chet lives, Dad made Carson take it when he turned down the foreman job the third time.

I smooch at Hooch and begin our descent down the mountain. Twenty minutes later, I spot a group of the yearlings.

I look at Rein and give her the cue, "Ssksskssk."

She speeds through the trees, barking as she gets close, nipping at their heels, effectively pushing them into a group. A few rebels head to run up the mountain, but we're quick to cut them off on our horses. They spin around, all of them now running in the right direction.

I call off the feral red hound.

She lays down, her tail wagging like, "*Look what I did, Mom!*"

I chuckle at her.

We locate more cattle after another fifteen minutes and direct them down the mountain. Within about three hours, the trees start to clear, signaling we're near the bottom. Everything is going smoothly until I turn my head to the right to see a single yearling break off into a dead run back up the mountain.

I holler at the closest cowboy, "Open your eyes, your future isn't that bright!"

He looks up in time to watch the steer run right by him.

"Stay with the herd!" I yell as I kick up Hooch and shake out a loop in my rope. Rein is reliably at my side. We run back into the woods where I can see the black calf weaving between trees. In my pursuit, I'm dodging branches. Everyone gave me hell for keeping Hooch, but riding a short horse means I don't have to duck near as many branches.

I give Rein her command and she takes off like a bolt of lightning. She heads off the steer in a small clearing. The calf cuts back left, but not before I throw my loop. It goes perfectly over its head as one front leg slips directly into it. I pull the rope's slack and wrap it around the saddle horn, dallying off.

I whistle, calling off Rein while Hooch pulls the calf back toward the herd. As soon as we exit the trees, I ride around the calf and un-dally. I give it a little push toward the herd now that it can see them.

By midafternoon, we get about thirty-five head of cattle back to the ranch and into the corral. The others are an hour or so behind. Except for Dad, he'll be about five hours on that south side and I know that's why he took it. He's always watching out for me.

I was seven when my mom died. Since then, it's just been me and Dad. Growing up, he was my superhero, and I guess he still is. It didn't matter what function it was, my dad was there. Whether dance recitals, tea parties, or ropings, he always made time to be there. Half the time at school events it was him and thirty-five moms in the room, but it never seemed to bother him.

The two cowboys and I ride back to the barn to untack. I put my saddle and bridle away and walk Hooch out to the wash rack to spray him down. After tying him up, I grab a hoof pick and pick up each of his feet to clean them out, making sure no rocks are stuck. I work my way around him, and when I get to the last foot, I notice the shoe is gone.

"Damn it, Hooch, you pulled a shoe," I reprimand like he can talk back.

Thankfully, it came off clean. He didn't break out any of the hoof wall, but I'll still be calling the farrier.

I put him on the walker to cool down while I pick his stall. I give him some hay and top off his water bucket, then I do the same for Dad's horse's stall.

Pulling my phone out of my pocket, I dial the farrier. It rings until I get his voicemail, and I leave a message.

"Hey, Jack, it's Kacey. Hooch lost a shoe today. I know it's short notice, but I have a jackpot next weekend. If you can make it over before then, that would be great. Call me back when you get a chance. Thanks."

As I put Hooch away for the day, I can see four cowboys in the distance with about thirty head in front of them. I relax when moments later, I see Dad accompanying the last thirty-five or so.

I'm latching the gate behind Hooch when my phone rings.

"Hey, Kacey, it's Jack. I'm sorry, but I won't be able to make it out. A horse kicked me today and broke my shinbone."

"Oh no, I'm sorry to hear that."

This is not good. I not only need a shoe back on, but I have other horses that will need to be reset in a few weeks.

"Ah, it'll buff. I'll be back at it in six weeks."

"Okay, well, get healed up. If you know any other farriers, please let me know."

"Yep, I'm going to call around and see who I can get to fill in that doesn't suck."

I snort. There are a lot of farriers who suck. "Thanks, Jack. Take care of that leg."

"I will. I'm going to the Fort Worth Stockyards with some buddies this weekend. I'll have to crutch my ass around, but at least I won't have to drive."

"Well, have fun and stay out of trouble down there."

"We will. Tell your old man hi."

"I will. Bye, Jack."

Click.

Fuck.

I might have to ask Carson to put on this shoe and he *hates* farrier work.

Chapter 2

Knox

Oklahoma

The crowd roars with laughter after the rodeo clown finishes his act. It's one I've seen a hundred times but still chuckle at.

"Lawton, Oklahoma, y'all are great," the clown says, walking back to his barrel.

"Hey, Knox, don't be a pussy!" Trey yells at me from two chutes down. His navy blue chaps swing around his legs.

"You just worry about keeping your hand shut," I holler back, standing above my bull.

"Ladies and gentlemen, the chutes are loaded for the final section of bull riding. ARE YOU READY!?" the announcer hypes up the crowd.

"Fifty dollars to whoever places higher?"

Seems like Trey just can't help himself tonight.

I raise a single brow at him. "You're on. You sure you got an extra fifty bucks? I only accept cash."

Trey has been my traveling partner for the last two years. I'd seen him around at some rodeos and he was improving steadily. One day he asked to hop a ride from one rodeo to the next and I thought, *Sure why not. What could it hurt? He seems like a nice kid.*

He. Never. Left.

Trey's like a stray dog I fed and now can't get rid of. He moved in with me a month later. All jokes aside, he has become my best friend. Though a few years younger and still on the wild side, he's as loyal as they come. Since getting in with me, he's riding better and even made the finals last year.

Trey hollers something back, but I've zoned out—or rather, *in.* I take a deep breath. It's the final section, and no one has covered a bull. I have a new bull I know nothing about. He doesn't even have a name yet, just a brand, "025." I'm guessing he's a four-year-old. That wouldn't put him in his prime yet, but that doesn't mean he's going to be easy to ride.

Six guys before me. I take another deep breath, repeating my usual affirmations.

Whatever it takes, keep moving. I came to win. I deserve to win. Over and over in my head.

Three guys before me. I pull my helmet over my head and snap the chin piece in place. Sliding my glove onto my right hand, I have someone behind the chutes pull it back so it's tight before I pull athletic tape out of my vest pocket and start wrapping my wrist with it to hold my glove in place.

One guy before me. I climb into the chute and tell the guy pulling my rope to pull it tight. I run my gloved hand up and down the tail of the rope in a quick jerking motion to heat up the rosin—a mixture of pine sap, soap, and glycerine—until it's good and sticky. I can smell the familiar scent of the hot rosin mixed with the smell of dusty ol' bulls.

The announcer and clown talk over the mic and the crowd cheers as the guy before me calls for his bull, but I can't make out a word they're saying, nor do I care. I'm completely in the zone.

"Whatever it takes, keep moving. I came to fucking win," I say and let out a growl as if to become just as animalistic as the 1,500-pound beast I'm about to tie my hand to.

I see the latch men move to my chute as I slide my hand in the handle of my rope.

CLANK! KABOOM!

My bull kicks up in the box. I see an arm fly out to catch me, but it's too late. My head crashes into the slide gate. Before I can grab something solid or get caught by the guy spotting me, he kicks up again, sending my head into the slide. I feel my ankle twist and my knees bounce off every rung of the chute before I finally catch the top rung of the chute and pull my knees up. I hold my position.

As soon as he settles, I look up at the flank man. "Well, that felt fucking good. Nice to see you chute broke him before you brought him to town."

He looks at me pissed at first, then realizes who I am. We've been friends for a long time—two of his sons are close to me in age. "Sorry, Knox, we'll massage his neck with a rope, that will keep him calm. You want this one, you'll win on him."

I want to tell him I can't win shit if he kills me in the chute, but I keep my mouth shut.

They get a rope over his head and lightly run it back and forth around his neck. Most guys here would get scared and try for the re-ride bull. Not me, it's personal now.

I can hear the announcer in the background. "They'll get this bull calmed down folks, and it'll be worth the wait. This is four-time National Finals qualifier Knox Ward, a home state boy from right here in Oklahoma. He finished fourth in the world last year and has already started this year out strong!"

The crowd cheers as I get my breathing under control and warm my rope back up.

Putting my hand back in the handle, I tell the guy, "Pull . . . pull . . . pull." Taking the tail of my bull rope from him, I run it over the top of my hand and around it, then run the tail back over my palm. I close my hand and take one more deep breath as I slide up to my rope, grit my teeth, and nod my head.

The gate flies open and everything becomes a blur, but at the same time, I can see everything, feel everything. My mind is running a hundred different scenarios at once.

Then I feel the first kick. I stick my chest out and lift on my rope. The bull comes into a rear and I climb up over his hump, driving forward with my legs. He kicks again and I feel him in the left lead, so I lower my free arm and tilt my head to the left.

He rears and kicks. I match him perfectly. When I feel him stutter step, I stick my chest out again and raise my free arm slightly. He rears higher than before. I climb out over him, pushing a little more on the handle of my rope, then we're floating in the air. Time stops.

I feel the next kick coming, and I know it's going to be a big one. Gritting my teeth, I set my hips lifting on my rope and pull my knees up. His front feet hit the dirt, still in his left lead. Lowering my free arm, I keep my shoulders square.

He does this three more times around to the left before I finally hear the whistle blow. I ride him one more jump before I grab the tail of my rope with my free hand, then all at the same time, I yank on the tail and rotate my hips to the right. He kicks, flinging me off like I'm getting ejected from an airplane.

I look down.

Yikes.

I got some airtime on this dismount. I stick both heels in the dirt and stumble forward onto my hands and knees. I jump up and run to the bucking chute so I'm out of the way of the bullfighters and safe from getting run over.

"How about 90 points?!" the announcer roars.

The crowd erupts.

I smile and start giving the surrounding guys high fives.

"Good bull ride!" I hear.

"Way to be a hand!" someone yells.

"You're one sticky dude!"

Guys all around me are excited about the ride and score.

That was one wild four-year-old.

I walk back to the chutes. I high five the returning bull fighters as I pick up my rope out of the arena dirt.

Climbing over the chute where Trey is standing over his bull, I challenge him. "Your turn."

"Shit, they loaded your ass. You do make it look pretty though; I'll give you that," Trey says with a lopsided grin, flipping his blond hair out of his eyes.

I roll my eyes at him. "Shut up and ride your bull so you can pay me my $50."

The gate opens, and the next kid is immediately bucked off. The bull runs around the arena trying to hook anything and everything.

Trey looks at me. "He sure is an angry feller."

"Just focus and get in the chute. You joke around too much." I wave my hand, motioning for him to get to work.

Trey has a black and white spotted bull I rode last year in San Antonio. He's just a good bull, should be one or two jumps out, then go in either direction. About 83–85 points.

Trey slides up and nods. The bull kicks out two jumps, turns back to the right, into his hand. He rides him like it's just another day in the office. Pulling his tail, Trey steps off, sticking the dismount before walking to the fence, and waits for the bull to leave the arena. Once the bull has left, he gives the crowd a dramatic bow. Always one to show off.

"86 points for the cowboy!" the announcer calls over the mic as Trey walks behind the chutes.

"Look who got loaded now." I laugh in response to his glare.

"Oh, fuck off. Go do your interview so we can get out of here."

"On the plus side, we're the only two qualified rides. It's going to be a good payday."

Trey perks up like a little kid getting offered a cookie at that news. "Really? Hell yeah. To the bar we go!"

"Nah, man, I'm good." I outgrew the bar scene years ago. I've never been a big drinker, and I'd rather get some sleep or hit the gym. Trey knows this but still tries anyway.

"Oh, come on, old man. Live a little. You can go to the gym tomorrow."

"Fine, but you're coming with me," I tell him.

"Deal!"

I do a quick TV interview as the winner of the event, then we pack our bags and head to the after party.

Trey orders a bucket of beer and I order a Pendleton Whiskey and Coke. The bar is packed, but we manage to snag a spot at a standing table between the pool tables and the dance floor. A live band is playing an old George Strait song, and the dance floor is full of couples swing dancing.

I grab a pool cue and crack my neck as I make my way to the table.

Man, I'm going to feel those hits on the bucking chute tomorrow. I'm not as young as I used to be.

Trey grabs a cue as I rack them and break. When I stand, there's a dark-haired woman in a miniskirt next to me, her tits hanging all but out.

"I hear you won the bull riding?" she purrs.

"Yes, ma'am, I did." I try to walk around her.

"And I took second." Trey puffs his chest and smiles at her from across the table.

Good, he can have her. I have zero interest.

I move away, but she clearly isn't taking the hint. "You should buy me a drink, and we can hit the dance floor. Maybe later you can show me if you can go for longer than 8 seconds." She giggles.

Yeah, pass. "I'm good, thank you. I'll be leaving after this drink anyhow." My tone is friendly but firm—I'm not interested.

"He thinks he's a hardass. He doesn't like fun; *I'm* the fun one. I'm also the one with all the dance moves." Trey flips his cowboy hat to impress the girl as he moves to step around me toward her.

I lean over to him. "Dude, she's just a buckle bunny."

He looks at her, then back at me. "Well, I used to show bunnies in FFA, and I was great at it. I wouldn't mind showing this one some of my winning moves, if you know what I mean." He winks at me, then walks up to the girl and introduces himself.

I see him wrap his arm around her shoulders as they head for the bar.

I chuckle. Damn kids these days.

Without a pool competitor, I decide to make a lap to see if there are any familiar faces at the bar. That's when I see a man on crutches trying to hold his beer and crutch his way around.

Jack Lockwood. What on earth is he doing here?

Jack is an old family friend and last I heard, lived in Colorado.

"Hey, you broke old blacksmith, would you like a hand?"

Jack wobbles around to face me. "Hey, Knox! Good bull ride tonight."

"Thanks, Jack. What did you do? Bust the bull rope back out?"

"Hell no." He laughs. "A horse broke it. Always love when clients don't work with their horses."

Isn't that the truth? I like to say I'm a parttime farrier. I don't really need the income, but I've known how to shoe a horse since I was a kid, so I've always thought of it as a good backup gig.

"I hear ya. I'm just thankful I still ride well enough that I don't need to be bent over slapping on iron all day."

Jack laughs. "Lucky bastard, keep at it and you'll be back at the big show for the fifth time."

"That's the plan. So, what're you doing down here? Thought you were in Colorado these days." I take a sip of my drink.

Jack leans one crutch on the railing next to us so he can drink his beer. "Oh, I am, but since I broke my leg, I figured I'd head to the stockyards with the boys for a few days. When we heard Lawton's Extreme Bulls was tonight, we decided to hop over here on the way down."

"Well, hopping is all you'll be doing for a while." I grin.

"Hilarious." He squints at me. "Hey, are you busy the next few weeks? I know April and May are your slow months."

"I've got a few weeks off. What's up?"

"Well, I've got some clients who need horses shod. I'd pay for your fuel and you can stay in the apartment above my barn if you would cover for me."

I take a drink to give myself a second to think through my schedule. I know I don't have any rodeos coming up soon and I'm not against helping Jack out.

I'd be breaking colts and probably putting shoes on at the local ranch I day work at, anyway. Plus, I know he'd do the same for me—he's supported me and helped me out a lot over the years. "Yeah, I could do that. A little hard labor will only make me want to win that much more at the next rodeo," I joke.

"Atta kid. Thank you, Knox. I'll call you Monday; I'll be headed back north and we can work out the details, but the sooner you can head west the better."

"Yessir. I can drive out Monday or Tuesday. Good seeing ya. I'm going to head out before it gets too rowdy here." I set my empty glass down on the railing.

"You, too, and congratulations on the win!"

Turning toward the door, I see Trey with his arm around the buckle bunny at the bar, and I chuckle.

No way he's going to the gym tomorrow.

Good thing we drove separately tonight.

It's a three-hour drive back to Savanna, Oklahoma. I don't mind it, though. I've never had an issue being alone. I actually prefer it. Chasing women, alcohol, or drugs doesn't do it for me. I prefer to stay focused on my goals.

Chasing a gold buckle is what I live for. I've come close a few times, finishing third and fourth in the world. Now at thirty, older for a bull rider at my level, I have to stay fit to prolong my career. I feel like I've gained wisdom I didn't have when I was twenty-two at my first National Finals and I know this will be my year. Maybe shoeing a few horses first will be the perfect reset before the summer run.

Chapter 3

Kacey

My phone rings, I see it's Jack.

"Hello!"

"Hey, Kacey, I wanted to let you know I have a friend coming up from Oklahoma to cover for me for a few weeks. He'll be here Tuesday and should be able to fit you in Wednesday afternoon."

"That's perfect. The jackpot is on Saturday. Thank you, Jack."

"Good deal. I'll have him call or text you when he knows a rough time."

"Sounds good."

"Bye, Kacey. Have a good one."

A sigh of relief rushes out of me, and I head for Dad's house. This works—I can continue to ride Hooch in the arena until he gets the shoe back on. Just no riding on rocks so he doesn't bruise his foot.

"Hey," I say to Dad when I spot him in the living room, "Jack has some guy coming to put Hooch's shoe back on this Wednesday."

"Good. If he has time, see if he'll trim those broodmares."

Ha, yeah right. No one wants to trim broodmares. Broodmares—female horses, specifically used for breeding—are known for being moody and a royal pain when it comes to trimming their feet.

"I'll ask, but I doubt he does."

"Either he will, or he won't. No big deal." Dad never gets too worked up about things. He takes a sip of his whiskey and continues to watch TV. "Any new foals today?"

"Nope. There are only a few mares left; we should be done in the next couple of weeks."

Broodmares, foals, and colts starting are my areas of expertise on the Diamond Hart. I could talk for hours about which colts show promise, which don't, and how we can improve our breeding program.

"Good. Have you picked your favorite yet?"

Dad gives me a knowing look.

I scoff. "I do not pick favorites . . . this early." I'm lying and he knows it. "There is a really nice red roan stud colt, though."

The truth is, these horses saved me. When I was drowning in grief, they were there. Forcing me to get up and get going. They have been the constant in my life I needed after my mom passed.

Dad chuckles under his breath. "Show me tomorrow."

I stand and exit the stall. One of my mares decided this morning's unseasonable warmth was the perfect weather to go into labor. I stayed back, monitoring her while the cowboys went to move more yearlings to the feedyard. Now, it's only 10 a.m., and we have a new, perfectly healthy foal.

Ding!

Unknown

> Hi Kacey, this is Knox. Jack said you need a shoe put back on. I can be there around noon.

Kacey

> Great, thanks. I'll have him out and ready for you.

Two hours later, I'm leaning on the fence watching the new foal stumble around on shaky legs when a third generation black Dodge pulls into the drive. I push off the fence and head toward the barn as he backs up to the open doorway. I almost trip on my own feet when a man several inches taller than me, with a *very* fit build steps out of the truck. Light brown curly hair peeks from underneath a flat-billed ball cap, and what looks like week-old scruff accents a face fit for a movie star. His Carhartt sweatshirt with the sleeves pushed up his forearms and cinch jeans are *definitely* working for him.

I caught myself thinking I could request to completely reset the shoes on Hooch, just for the view. Sure. I might not be interested in dating, but a girl can window shop.

When he shuts the truck door and says, "Hi, I'm Knox," in a deep, smooth voice, I almost swallow my tongue.

I clear my throat. "Hey, I'm Kacey. Thanks for coming all the way out here. I really appreciate it."

His eyes scan me quickly. He's checking me out, but not in a creepy way, more of an appraisal, like I wasn't what he was expecting.

Then, Knox removes his hat and shakes my hand.

Oh gosh, I hope he can't feel my sweaty palm. Get it together, Kacey, you've met attractive men before. Granted, those men don't look like I designed my dream man on a computer, but still.

Shit. I held onto that handshake way too long.

Focus, Kacey.

"Uh, Hooch is up here in the crossties. Need help carrying anything?"

"Yeah, could you grab my hoof stand?"

I reach for the hoof stand on the tailgate. From the corner of my eye, I watch as he pulls off his sweatshirt, which accidentally pulls up his t-shirt in the process.

Damn, his abs look like they were carved from marble—this man is absolutely shredded. And did I see a tattoo on his ribs?

I blink twice, realizing my mouth is wide open. *Oops.*

Knox doesn't seem to notice. He throws his sweatshirt on the tailgate and reaches for his shoeing box.

"You must work out more than any farrier I've met."

What the fuck? Why did I just say that? Shut up, shut up, shut up.

He laughs. "I shoe horses but it's not my full-time gig."

His laugh makes me blush. Why am I acting like I'm four-teen, and this is the first boy I've had a crush on?

I have got to start getting off the ranch more.

"What is your normal gig?" I ask.

He doesn't answer right away, like he's trying to think of what his actual job is, or he doesn't want to answer. That's when I see the sun reflect off something on the front of his jeans. It's a buckle, but not just a buckle—it's a bull riding buckle.

Oh great, I'm standing here drooling over a bull rider. *You've lost your mind, Kacey.*

"So, you're a bull rider?" I point down at the buckle; he looks down at his buckle then back up at me.

"You checking me out or sizing me up?" He grins.

Is he flirting with me? "Oh, uh, no. It's just hard not to notice the buckle," I say awkwardly.

"I'm messing with you. Yes, riding bulls is how I pay my bills." He turns slightly, looking over my head and nods. "New foal?"

"Yeah, born two hours ago. She's a strong one, on her feet in less than an hour," I say as I grab the hoof stand, he grabs his anvil and holds it under one arm, then picks up his shoeing box.

Whoa, those things are not light, and he's acting like it weighs nothing.

"Isn't that heavy?" I ask.

"It's only seventy pounds," he replies.

So apparently, he's truly a gym rat.

We walk down the alley to the crossties where Hooch waits. His box and anvil scrape on the concrete as he sets them down before walking up to Hooch and rubbing his forehead. "Hey, red, you ready to get that shoe back on?"

Knox moves over to the front right leg. Picking it up and putting it between his legs, he sets to work cleaning up the foot. When he's finished, he sets it down gently.

"Well, he's got good feet. No cracks, solid hoof wall, and no thrush."

"That's good. I clean his feet every chance I get. So, where did you learn to shoe horses?" I don't think Jack would have someone fill in for him who isn't good, but I'd rather not risk Hooch coming up lame because some bull rider doesn't know what he's doing.

He smirks at me like he knows exactly what I'm asking. "Family business. My grandpa and my dad both did it for a living. I was shoeing horses shortly after I broke my first colt."

"Oh, so you're not one of those bull riders who can't actually cowboy?"

He chuckles. "I've worked cows plenty, and I can rope, but I consider myself more of a horseman. I like to see a horse develop as I train it every day. If I wasn't here helping Jack, I'd be breaking colts back in Oklahoma all spring."

Okay, so if I wasn't crushing earlier, I'm definitely crushing now. This guy seems perfect; *except* the fact he's a bull rider. It's widely known that bull riders—or rodeo cowboys in general—do not have a good reputation when it comes to women. A lot of them are self-proclaimed womanizers and most of the time, they aren't wrong. They have no issues picking up women and then leaving them on read when they head to the next rodeo.

"I understand that. I've worked with Hooch since the day he was born. He's a heck of a heeling horse." I stroke his neck, feeling his shiny coat under my fingers.

"I bet. He's the perfect size and build," Knox replies as he looks Hooch over.

"He gets the job done," I say modestly. Hooch and I have won a lot of money in the last couple of years, but I don't like to brag.

Bending over, he grabs a shoe from his box and begins shaping it on the anvil. I'm not sure if there is anything sexier than a man sweating as they're swinging a hammer, the sound of metal on metal ringing in the air.

Things around here just got a little more interesting.

Chapter 4

Knox

I stand, checking my shoe to make sure it's level. I'm trying to keep my eyes focused on the job and not the gorgeous woman watching my every move.

The way Jack talked, I was expecting to show up to put a shoe on a horse for a woman who was meaner and tougher than the bulls I rode. He made it sound like she'd be chewing tobacco and arm wrestling the ranch hands when I got here.

Instead, the first thing I see is a head turner. She's petite, a few inches shorter than me, with long blonde hair and a sweet smile. The Kimes Jeans she's wearing might be the death of me and her tight long-sleeve shirt with a vest shows off her toned arms and slim waist. It's not the build of a woman who spends all day in the gym, but of a woman who works hard every day. She's beautiful. And she has no idea who I am, which is a breath of fresh air.

I'm no stranger to beautiful women. On the road, the barrel racers, breakaway ropers, and even some photographers and timers catch my attention, but this girl has something different about her.

Thanks for the heads up, Jack.

On the other hand, after I leave today, I'll probably never see her again.

I grab eight nails, put them between my lips, and roll my box back to the front right hoof. I pick the foot up, put it between my legs, and set the shoe on the foot to position it. Holding the shoe in place, I start driving nails. After I drive the last nail, I grab my nail block to block the nails. Then, I pull the foot forward onto the hoof stand, clinch my nails and rasp the hoof wall down to the shoe.

"Well, looks like my work here is done."

When I face her, her magnificent sea green eyes lock on mine. I've never seen eyes this color—it's like looking into a sunlit ocean, where blues and greens swirl together in endless depths.

"What do I owe you?" She reaches into her pocket, snapping me out of my trance.

"Nothing, this one's on Jack." It's his client, and the asshole is probably sitting at home laughing at me right now.

It's clear she isn't comfortable with that answer. "No really, I insist."

"It's all good, it took me less than fifteen minutes." I smile and pick up my anvil, pinning it under one arm and grab my shoeing box with the other hand.

"Well, thank you." Her lips form a perfect smile. She picks up the hoof stand for me, and we head back to my pickup.

"No problem."

As I set my anvil on the tailgate, I hear something scurrying behind me. When I turn around, a flash of red hurls itself in my direction. I step to my left, avoiding impact as the ball of red goes rolling into the truck box.

"What the hell?" Turning back around, I see a red heeler regaining its feet and coming right to the edge of the tailgate, tongue hanging out, tail wagging as fast as it possibly can.

"I'm so sorry—that's my little nightmare child. She thinks she's going for a ride," Kacey supplies as she sets the hoof stand down.

"Well hi, NC." I reach out to let the dog sniff me. Within a couple seconds, it shoves its nose under my hand encouraging me to pet her. I reach out with my other hand, placing one on each side of her neck and massage behind her ears. "You're not really a nightmare, are ya? You just want attention." She throws herself to her side to demand belly rubs and I oblige.

Kacey smiles. "Come on, Rein, he doesn't want you up there."

"She's fine, I'm a dog guy. I'd have one if I was home more." I bend over to grab my shoeing box and the little red dog hops on my back, balancing herself on the top of my shoulders. I can't help but laugh. "You are one crazy little dog, aren't you?"

Kacey bursts out in laughter. "I can't say I've ever seen her do that before."

Note to self: If I ever see this girl again, make her laugh, she's even prettier when she's laughing.

"Okay, Rein. Down, girl." The red heeler hops off my back. "Sit." She sits, staring at me, tail still wagging, tongue hanging out. "Good girl," I tell her, scratching her behind the ear. I can't help but notice Kacey's jaw drop.

Wide eyed, she says, "She must like you. She never listens to anyone but me and Dad."

A cocky smirk slides across my face. "Looks like I've got a new number one fan, huh, Rein?" I might not know much about life, but I know if a woman's dog doesn't like you, she won't either. By the look on Kacey's face, I'd say Rein just did me a solid.

I load my tools into the truck and put up the tailgate. "Well, if you lose another shoe, give me a call. I'll be here for a few weeks, filling in for Jack."

"I hope I don't lose any more. I have a jackpot this weekend, and I need him ready to win." She gives me a small smile, then quickly looks away.

I wonder if she's single . . . I'm not looking for a relationship—not after my last one—but I'll admit this girl has caught my attention. Besides, there's nothing wrong with a little flirting.

She shifts on her feet. "But in that case, my dad did want me to ask you if you have time to trim some broodmares."

"How many?" Trimming broodmares is normally as fun as getting a root canal, but I wouldn't mind doing it so much if it means I can see her again.

"There's eleven—"

ELEVEN? Call the dentist, I'd rather get a root canal.

" . . . *this* round. But I want to warn you, no one enjoys trimming them, not even Jack. He normally ends up with vertigo, a bad hangnail, or some other nonexistent ailment when he's supposed to come do them." She laughs like she's joking, but I know she's not.

"Dad and Grandpa always made me trim the broodmares. This week is pretty booked for me, but I can do them early next week if that works? Say Tuesday?" I hear myself say.

What is this woman? Some kind of witch? I met her twenty minutes ago and I'm agreeing to trim eleven broodmares just to see her again.

She looks surprised. I can't blame her. No one in their right mind wants to trim eleven broodmares, but I have ulterior motives. Stupid and pointless motives that might get the shit kicked out of me by a bunch of mares, but I've done dumber things in my life.

I'm just glad Trey isn't here to see this—he'd give me so much shit. I can hear him laughing, saying, "*There are easier ways to get laid, dude.*"

"Yeah, that'll work, but if you don't want to do them, I completely understand."

She's giving me an out. And of course I don't *want* to do them, but I do want to see her again.

"I can handle a few broodmares. I'll be back next week. Nice to meet you, Kacey." Then I do something I know shouldn't: I wink at her before turning on my heel and leaving.

Great. Fucking broodmares.

I stop at two more farms before heading back to Jack's. I'm staying in the apartment above his barn while I'm here. I've known Jack since I was a kid. He used to try and ride bulls but lacked the natural ability, so when it didn't pan out, he learned to shoe horses from my grandpa. He's always moved around—he'd be in Oklahoma or Texas for a few years, then

Kansas. Now, he seems to have settled in Colorado for the time being.

I walk in the back door to his kitchen without knocking and holler, "You owe me $50, old man!" The screen door slams behind me. I hear Jack before I see him—his crutches squeak against the floor as he shuffles into the room.

"What are you going on about? I ain't givin' you $50. You'll just spend it on entry fees and then fall off."

He's not wrong, not about the entry fee part, anyway. But I don't fall off . . . that often.

"You sent me over to The Diamond Hart Ranch to put that shoe on with no warning. Actually, with the opposite of a warning. The rancher's 'rough and tough daughter' you said. She was raised by her single dad and 'will run that ranch soon' you said. The way you talked, I was expecting to meet Teeter from *Yellowstone*, but I got Bella Hadid instead." I give him a displeased look.

He laughs. I knew it—he knows exactly what he did. Since I got here, he's been going on about how I'm getting older and need to be thinking about my future. You know, the usual; get married, settle down, have a pack of kids, and grow old with a good woman. Ironic coming from him, considering he's an old bachelor himself.

I tried to tell him it's not worth the time and effort. After Megan and I broke up at the finals a few years ago, I swore off dating. Things were great when I was home, hard and confusing while I was on the road, but we made it work.

Until the National Finals.

When I didn't ride well and lost the world title, she left me—publicly—for another national finals qualifier who placed better than me that year.

And while I wouldn't say I was devastatingly heartbroken, it stung. I was already in a rough headspace and her betrayal sent me into a spiral. The only thing that pulled me out of it was a swift kick in the ass from Trey and my love for bull riding.

When I finally got my shit together and went back on the road, I swore I was done dating. Don't get me wrong, I'm no monk, but I'd rather focus on my career; winning a world title is the goal. I can worry about relationships when I retire.

It's every cowboy's dream to be a world champion, and I've come so close so many times. This is my year, I can feel it. I don't need a girlfriend messing with my mental game . . . but that nagging voice in the back of my head keeps saying, *what's the harm in a little flirting?* Kacey seems cool and it could be fun to have someone to hang out with while I'm in Colorado.

Jack sits at the table. "Who the fuck is Bella Hadid?" When I glare at him, not giving him a response, he continues, "Nothing I said was a lie. She is tough and when Cody slows down someday, she will run that ranch. As for anything else about her you might have found . . ." He pauses, considering his words. "*Pleasing* . . . that's on you." He accents his speech with a smirk.

I give Jack the fakest smile I have. "Even if that's true, I didn't charge her, I told her it was on you. So you owe me $50." I'm fully aware I'll never see the money and to be honest, I don't really care. I just like to give the old man a hard time. It keeps him young.

Jack gives me a look, letting me know I'm 100% right about never seeing that money. "How were your other stops? Did any of the horses give you trouble?"

I pull out a chair and sit across from him at the table. "Nope, everything went well. That filly over at the Johnson's had a touch of thrush, a bacterial infection in the hoof, but I got the frog trimmed up and bars cut out. That should open the foot up to keep the thrush from forming."

"Good. The Johnsons are nice people."

"Yeah, they seemed like they were on top of it. I did, however, sign up to trim eleven broodmares next week . . ." I say slowly, waiting for his response.

He chuckles. "Eleven broodmares you say? That's interesting. I can't imagine anyone who could talk you into doing that many fire breathing drag— Oh, wait a minute . . . The *Diamond Hart Ranch* has broodmares. Huh. Wonder who asked you to trim those. I guess you'll see Kacey again next week."

I get up, heading to the fridge to grab a drink and hide my smile. "Yep, I guess so."

Chapter 5

Knox

I get my third horse shod for the morning and start packing up to head to the next stop when Jack calls.

"Hey, buddy, we got a change of plans. There are two horses at a jackpot that lost a shoe. I rescheduled your other appointments so you can go tack those back on. I told them $100 each since it's last-minute."

"Define jackpot . . . like barrel racing jackpot—"

"Oh no, not can chasers," he cuts me off. "A team roping jackpot. I wouldn't subject you to the barrel racers. Being you're a famous heartthrob bull rider, they might eat you alive."

"I'm going to pretend you didn't say that last bit with sarcasm and just thank you for acknowledging my success and not subjecting me to barrel racers. This works though, this way I can hit the gym later this afternoon." I put my tools in the truck and shut the tailgate.

"Boy, you don't work hard enough, or you'd be too tired to go to the gym." He chuckles over the phone. "On second thought, come pick me up. I'm sick of watching TV."

I'm pretty sure he's at home watching team roping or some other rodeo event on TV, so why not crutch around watching it in person? Makes sense. "Yes sir, a little daylight wouldn't hurt ya. See you in a few."

I picked up Jack, and we rolled into the fairgrounds an hour before the event is supposed to start.

It's your typical small town rodeo arena. Rusted old bucking chutes, two small sets of bleachers and some pens for cattle. We pull into the back gate where the contestants enter and drive across a grass field toward the stock pens. There are trailers parked everywhere—no rhyme or reason to how any of them parked. It's like no one can stand the thought of having someone park next to them. Once we're close to the pens, I find a spot nearby with a tree that will supply some shade, and it's out of the way from the contestants warming their horses up.

"I'll let them know where we're parked." Jack pulls his phone out of his pocket as he cracks a beer he'd placed in the cup holder.

"Easy there, old timer." I open the door of the pickup. "Start too early and you'll forget how to operate those crutches."

"Don't tell me ho—"

I close the door, cutting him off just to rile him up.

The horses are brought over to shoe and I get started. Before I finished with the second, two other people showed up wanting full resets, which Jack, of course, hiked the price up on. That old geezer cracks me up—he's always trying to up the price when he gets an excuse.

I get halfway through the first horse when Jack decides to crutch up to the arena to watch the start of the jackpot. "I'm going to watch for a bit. Come find me when you're finished."

"Alright, find somewhere to sit. You need to keep that leg elevated," I tell him.

"Yes, mother," he grumbles as he crutches away.

These team ropings can run on for hours, so he better enjoy it while he can, because once I'm done, we're out of here. I need a good workout. It's been a few days since I've been able to hit the gym and with the summer run coming up, I need to be as fit as I can be.

The summer rodeo run is grueling, to say the least. It's nonstop rodeo from June to October. I typically get on five or six bulls a week and that might not sound like a lot, but trust me, it takes a toll on your body after a few weeks. Not to mention the hours spent driving and the lack of sleep and good food. We rarely get to ride in the same place two nights in a row—we're always loading the truck and heading to the next town. That town might be two hours down the road or twelve. That's why we travel with partners. You have to split the driving, or you'd never sleep.

We pack our gear after the rodeo, and by then, all the restaurants are closed. Our campers aren't set up for cooking; they're meant to drive fifty thousand miles in a few short months, which is what we do. Truck stop food or whatever snacks we've stocked up on at the grocery store is what we survive on.

While technically the rodeo season is October 1st to September 30th, most of the big money is earned from June through September each year. I had a good winter at the stock show rodeos and currently sit sixth in the world, with Trey not far behind in ninth. But we have a lot of season left, we'll both need to ride at our best to make the finals in December. It's always been my goal to win the World, and this year is my year. It has to be. I'm not getting any younger and bull riding is a young man's sport.

By the time I'm done with another horse, I see a white truck and trailer pull in—someone running late. Then, I see the Diamond Hart brand on the side. Through the windshield, I see long blonde hair and know instantly who it is.

I wonder who her partner is . . .

I can't help but smile and shake my head. Of course she's here. I get started on the next horse as I contemplate pushing my workout back an hour and sticking around a little longer.

Chapter 6

Kacey

Chet is an idiot. He took off this morning in *my* truck to get horse feed and we need to leave in fifteen minutes. The flatbed had a flat tire, and he's too lazy to change it. Dad's off somewhere working, and I could have Carson change it before we leave, but I don't trust the spare to make it ten miles down the road, let alone an hour to the jackpot.

I'm going to kill Chet.

Thirty minutes later, Chet shows back up. After unloading all the feed and a good ass chewing from me, he heads out to doctor some calves. Carson gets the trailer hooked up while I grab the horses and we leave, running forty-five minutes behind schedule.

I hate being late. It stresses me out.

"We'll still have plenty of time. We aren't one of the first teams. Just take a deep breath," Carson says, knowing I'm highly irritated right now. I don't reply and after a minute he asks, "So you got that shoe back on Hooch this week, right? Who came out for Jack?"

"Yep, some bull rider buddy of his from Oklahoma came out. I guess he's here for a few weeks covering for him."

"Oh, he's got a Sooner kid doing his bidding? Good for Jack." He smiles. Carson normally doesn't talk much unless he's around Dad and me. Most people think he's grumpy, but he's not, at least not with me. He's just quiet; always has been.

After my mom passed, my dad tried his best to balance taking care of me and the ranch, but it was hard. When Carson showed up a year later asking for a ranch hand job, my dad hired him, but unbeknownst to him—and Carson—he'd just hired a babysitter. I followed Carson *everywhere*. I was a sad kid, and he seemed a little sad, too. I didn't want to talk about my mom, and he didn't make me.

Carson also never mentioned anything about his life before he came to the ranch, and I never asked. We all have things that haunt us; it should be our choice when and if we share those nightmares with others. I have a feeling Carson has more than one nightmare from his past.

When I was sixteen, I wanted to start roping. Carson taught me to throw a rope, and Dad got me an old grade bay gelding that was already trained. Carson would drag the roping dummy for me every night. I'd get home from school, and he'd have my horse saddled and the dummy hooked up.

The next summer I started roping live cattle, and we quickly discovered I was a much better heeler than I was a header. Carson has been heading steers for me ever since. He's never once complained or left me hanging. I'm ten years younger than him, but that's never mattered to us. Even though I don't have any siblings, I have Carson and know I can count on him.

I realize Carson said something, but I was too in my head to listen. "What?"

"So, is that bull rider any good?" he asks again. "Or is he a bull get'er on'er, not an actual bull rider?"

I laugh because it's true, there are a lot of guys who get on bulls, but very few who can actually ride them. "Well, he's shoeing horses instead of riding at a rodeo, so I can't imagine he's very good."

He huffs in amusement. "Fair point. I wouldn't think a top bull rider would want to shoe horses all day."

Being a farrier is hard work. Horses don't stand; they try to kick, bite, or strike you. They'll lay most of their weight on the one leg you're trying to work on. Not to mention there's always flies biting them, making them waller around on top of you. Most of the blame is on the owners not working with them—they think it's the farrier's job to train them. It's not. You don't hire a mechanic and then expect them to teach you how to drive.

"Does anyone really want to shoe horses all day?" I ask, turning on the radio.

We rolled into the rodeo grounds twenty-five minutes later.

We showed up just in time to warm up our horses and rope our first steer. Thankfully, we were further down the draw list. Our time was 5.3 with no penalties. Not bad. We have two steers left to run; we'll be here all afternoon.

There are several different formats for team roping jackpots. Some of them you can rope as many times as you want to pay the entry fee for. But this format only allows you to enter once as a header and/or once as a heeler. Then, it's the fastest time off your aggregate. Entry fees are $100 per man.

Team roping is pretty simple; one person ropes the head—preferably just the horns of the steer—then one person ropes the two hind legs. If you miss a hind leg, you get five seconds added to your time. Another penalty is breaking the barrier. The barrier is a rope at the front of the roping box that is tied to the steer through a pulley system. When the steer reaches a certain distance known as the score—a head start, if you will—the rope will come off and the barrier will break free. If you break the barrier before the steer has reached its score, you will have ten seconds added to your time.

Carson and I sit on our horses, watching the preceding teams make their runs while waiting for our next steer, but we have a while yet. Carson looks around, then picks up his reins to ride over by the end of the small set of bleachers. I see crutches leaning on the end. Jack sits above them, leg propped up next to him. I smooch at Hooch, and we follow him over.

"Hey, Jack, how's the leg?" Carson asks.

He waves at us. "Hey, Carson, Kacey, good first run you had. The leg is pretty good. Doc says I should be back in another five weeks."

Does that mean Knox will be here for five weeks? I get it's the slowest months of the rodeo season, but that's still a long time to take off. He either really isn't good, or he's *really* good and can afford the time off. Most top rodeo athletes take off April, May, October, and November. Since their season is technically all year, they have to find a break in the season somewhere.

"That's good news. I'm sure your clients will be more than ready to have you back. I hear you have a bull rider filling in for you." Carson continues talking to Jack as I attempt to look around discreetly, but don't see Knox.

Jack laughs. "Yep, sure do. He's an all-around hand, really. I've seen him break colts, work cattle, and ride ranch broncs and bulls. He's doing great filling in for me. He's actually around here somewhere; he came to tack on two shoes and got roped into a couple resets."

I can't help but smile. "Yeah, that sounds like a bunch of team ropers, showing up to the roping half falling apart and hungover." That makes Carson and Jack laugh.

"Sounds like a decent kid working for ya," Carson says.

"Well, he ain't much of a kid anymore, he's thirty now. I keep telling him he needs to think about his plans for the future. You can't ride bulls forever."

Carson scoffs. "Well, I'm not sure bull riding is a great career choice at any age."

"We should go warm up," I interrupt. "They're getting close to us. We'll see you later, Jack." We aren't really that close to being up, but I don't need crabby Carson offending my ex-bull riding farrier. Good farriers are hard to find, I'd like to keep mine.

We rope our next steer, he was a fast one, but we made it work for a 6.8 second run. As long as we get one more clean run and speed it up a little, we should pull a decent check. As we're riding back toward Jack, I see Knox has shown up. He looks good—*really* good. Even with dirt and horse hair all over his blue Henley shirt.

He's leaning on the end of the bleachers with his arms crossed, grinning at me. "Keeping those shoes on, speedy?"

"Yeah, so far it seems like my farrier knew what he was doing." I can't help but give him a smile back. Something about him puts me at ease, like I've known him forever.

I don't trust it. But it's nice to pretend for a little while.

"Hey now, what about me? Three of those shoes were put on by me," Jack says with mock offense.

"Well, so far she's lost one of yours and none of mine, so odds aren't looking good for you, old man." Knox laughs, raising his brows at Jack. He has a genuine smile when he laughs, and I can't help but stare. His dark blue shirt makes his bright blue eyes pop. He seriously could be a model.

"In your defense, Jack, she was chasing cattle all over the side of a mountain when she lost it." Carson helpfully chimes in as he steps off his horse, walking up to Knox. Carson stands over six feet tall causing him to look down at Knox as he reaches out a hand. "I'm Carson, you must be the bull rider. Or bull get'er on'er; no one has told me which one yet."

Oh my gosh.

I can't believe he just said that to him. I can feel my face turning red with embarrassment, but Knox just chuckles and shakes his hand. "Yes sir, that's me. You know the game, sometimes you're the windshield, sometimes you're the bug. The trick is being the windshield most of the time."

Carson gives him more of a grimace than a smile. "I prefer being in the saddle of a broke horse, but to each their own."

"So, which are you most of the time?" I ask, genuinely curious.

"Well, maybe you'll have to come watch sometime, then you'll find out." He looks at me with a grin, but is that cockiness or confidence?

Jack pipes up. "He'll be in Greeley and Estes Park. Neither is all that far of a drive."

"Really? I love Estes Park. My best friend and I take a trip there every summer, but we've never gone to the rodeo." I glance at Knox and see he's fully focused on me. I can feel my cheeks turning red again and I glance away. I'm not normally this awkward around men. I don't know what it is about this one, but he makes me nervous.

"We might be too busy at the ranch, we'll see how it lines out." Carson says while he gives me a look. That big brother look. Like, *you are not getting involved with this bull rider.*

He has always been a little protective, but especially after my last relationship disaster. I dated Garrett for two years, only to find out he didn't really want me, just our ranch. And he would do anything—and I mean anything—to get it. When Carson found out, he was livid. I honestly don't think I've ever seen him so mad. He knew how I felt about Garrett, and I was really upset. That was two years ago, and I haven't dated since.

Knox smirks at Carson before turning to me. "It's in early July. Let me know if you can arrange a couple of nights away from the ranch. It's a great rodeo and I'm sure I could get you tickets."

Before I can reply, Carson cuts me off. "I think we're up soon; we should go warm the horses back up." He climbs on his horse then narrows his eyes at Knox. "Nice to meet you. I'm sure we'll see you around." We are most definitely not up soon, but I get on Hooch to follow him anyway. It's not like

I'd ever go to Estes Park to play buckle bunny for some bull rider. That's not who I am.

"Yeah. You, too. See you Tuesday, Kacey."

Right, the broodmares.

By the way Carson is looking at me, he will also be helping trim the mares now.

Great.

Chapter 7

Kacey

Coffee tomorrow morning?

Jessie

Please. I'll be coming off a 14 hour shift.

Kacey

Perfect, meet you at Plot Twist at 9.

Jessie

Okay. How was the jackpot?

Kacey

Not over yet but it's been interesting. I thought Carson and my farrier were going to whip them out and measure. I'll explain tomorrow.

Jessie

HA isn't your farrier like 60 years old? I can't wait for this story.

T he next morning, I meet my best friend, Jessie, at The Plot Twist Café, our favorite coffee and book shop. It's in an old brick building in downtown Cottonwood Valley. The owner, Lainey, has done a fantastic job with it. When you walk in, the first thing you see is the huge, petrified tree where she has glued used book pages in place of leaves. It looks like it grows right into the ceiling. There are floor-to-ceiling bookshelves with eclectic decor, stained glass lamps and mismatching vintage furniture everywhere.

She added the coffee shop to make sure it always made a profit, but her actual love is books. Jessie and I both went to high school with Lainey, and we've stayed friends; meeting up once a month to discuss the different books we're reading. It's less of a book club and more of Jessie telling us how many unhinged smut books she's managed to consume in the given month.

She really needs a boyfriend.

I beat Jessie here. She's an ER nurse at the local hospital and often runs late if a trauma arrives. I'm sitting at a small table near the tree waiting for my caramel macchiato and muffin when she comes barreling in.

"Okay, I'm here. Tell me all about Carson's small dick," she announces a little too loud.

Yep, people are definitely looking.

Typical Jessie, but I expect nothing less.

"Can you please sit down and lower your voice?" I laugh at her. "No 'Hi, Kacey. Good to see you. How are you?' You're just concerned about Carson's dick—which not only grosses me out but concerns me about your lack of a sex life."

She plops in the seat across from me. She's wearing standard blue scrub pants, but her top is a blue and purple leopard print. Her dark red hair is French braided down her back, with stray hairs loose around her freckled face from work, giving her an effortlessly beautiful look.

"Fine. How are you, my love?"

I roll my eyes at her heavy dose of sarcasm. "I'm wonderful, thank you for asking. We won a good check at the jackpot yesterday. How was your shift?"

"That's great, it was great. Now about the dick measuring contest . . ."

I shake my head. She's like a dog with a bone.

Ever since middle school, Jessie has been the wild child, class clown, and every boy's crush. Where I was quiet and reserved, she was the outgoing life of the party. Sometimes I wonder how much of her firecracker personality is a shield guarding her against the world.

She had a rough home life and was mostly raised by her grandmother, so she spent a lot of time at the ranch. My dad treats her like a second daughter, always including her in events, getting her flowers for her birthday, all the things her dad has never once done. I'm not even sure she's talked to her dad in years.

"Okay, okay," I say. If I don't tell her, she'll just keep at me, and we won't catch up on our lives. I haven't seen her for a couple weeks; she's been pulling double shifts at the hospital. "Jack broke his leg, so he has a guy from Oklahoma filling in for him. For reasons unknown to me, Carson didn't take a liking to him. You know how he can be."

When I followed Carson around as a kid, Jessie followed me, therefore following Carson. I'll just say he tolerated her and leave it at that. They bicker and pick at each other nonstop, but I know Carson still thinks of her as a sister and he's the closest thing she has to a brother.

"Okay . . . Carson can be grumpy, but if he truly dislikes someone, there is normally a reason. Is this guy a dirtbag or something?" she asks as the waitress approaches our table. She places my coffee and muffin down and takes Jessie's order. I take a bite of my muffin and moan.

Lainey's baked goods are *amazing*.

What I will not tell Jessie is Carson's and my conversation in the truck after the jackpot. He for sure noticed the flirting and was not impressed. He told me in no uncertain terms that a bull rider is the last guy I should date, and I have a feeling Jessie would advise the exact opposite. But it's a moot point, they both know I don't date. Not anymore.

"Uh . . . he may have flirted with me a bit. But I'm not interested," I rush to say. "He's only here for a few weeks to fill in for Jack. I'm sure he's just looking for some fling while he's in town."

I'm not lying to her, I do think he's just looking for a fling. But I'm also not sharing all the facts. Like the fact that he is the hottest man I've ever seen. And how I could feel his eyes on me yesterday after we rode off. It's like there is a string tied between us; I can feel when his attention is on me. When I would turn around and catch him watching me, he wouldn't even try to look away. It made my stomach flip.

I pick up my coffee and take a sip, hoping Jessie will change the subject.

I should know better.

"He flirted with you? How old is this guy? What's he look like? Is he a good bull rider? What's his name? I'll find him on social media." The rapid-fire questions come so quickly I can't even answer.

Once she pauses for a breath, grabbing her phone to start hunting the man down on social media, I explain. "It's not a big deal. Like I said, I'm not interested. And I don't even know his last name, so let's please move on to other subjects."

She huffs, setting her phone down. "Fine, if you say so." Then I hear her say under her breath, "He must be ugly." I try not to laugh at that.

"So, tell me about the hospital. Has it been busy?"

We spend the next hour getting caught up before I head back to the ranch.

Chapter 8

Knox

I drive under the steel Diamond Hart Ranch brand sign above the entry gate, then follow a long gravel driveway lined with redbud trees on both sides. I didn't pay much attention last time, but I do today. The driveway is over a mile long, with pastures and hay fields on both sides of the drive. The ranch is situated in a valley with mountains surrounding it on three sides.

I drive past what looks like the main house on my way to the horse barn, but I can see two other houses off to the side and what looks like a bunk house attached to an older barn. Everything is brown and white, even the ranch trucks are white with brown DHR logos on the sides. It's all perfectly maintained—this ranch is clearly extremely successful and probably one of the largest in Colorado.

As I back my truck up to the same spot where I parked last week, I take my last swig of my morning coffee. I step out and drop the tailgate. When I reach for my hoof stand, I spot Kacey and Carson walking up with four brood mares.

I watched the two of them at the roping. They never acted like a couple, but Carson didn't like it when I invited Kacey to Estes, that's for sure. There is a clear age gap between them, and I've wondered for the past three days what their relationship is. I'd concluded he must work on the ranch.

To be honest, I'm not sure why I keep flirting with her. Yeah, she's beautiful, and it's been a while since I've been with anyone, but she doesn't seem like the type for one night stands. I don't know her at all, but I can just tell she's a relationship girl and I'm the last thing she needs.

But I can't help myself.

"Morning," I say, looking toward Kacey. She's wearing those damn jeans that fit her like a glove again, with a three-quarter zip sweatshirt and a Kimes ball cap on, her blonde hair pulled back. I remind myself not to check her out with Carson nearby.

Damn, she's beautiful.

"Morning, Knox." She smiles.

Carson walks past with two of the horses to put them in the barn. Instead of saying hi or good morning, he just grunts.

What is this guy's problem with me? Or is he like this to everyone?

"Well, isn't he just Mr. Sunshine this morning?" I can't help but mumble once he's out of earshot.

Kacey smirks. "He'll warm up to you. He just doesn't know you."

I hear his spurs jingle behind me as he walks back toward the truck. Behind Kacey, I see a big man approaching from the direction of the main house.

"You must be the stand-in farrier for Jack," he says gruffly through a thick beard.

"Yes sir, I'm—"

"Knox Ward," the man cuts me off. "I know exactly who you are, I watch you ride on TV all the time. You're a damn handy bull rider. Looks like you're heading back to the finals again this year."

The look on Kacey's face is pure shock and confusion. Her eyes flick back and forth between the man and me.

The man extends a hand to shake mine. "Cody Hart, nice to meet you."

Hart. This must be her dad.

I shake his hand. "You, too. This is a nice spread you have here." I glance at Kacey and her face has just gone from shock to something else . . . annoyance maybe? *That's weird.*

"Thanks, I think my grandad picked a pretty nice spot when he started this ranch."

I turn back to Cody, and I think I can make out a smile behind his beard. He clearly hasn't noticed the change in Kacey's body language.

Carson clears his throat from behind me. "So, I guess you must be the windshield more than the bug? At least you're modest."

I just give him a nod.

His eyes have a look to them, like he has some sort of plan running through his head.

Kacey hasn't said a word.

He looks past me to Cody. "Boss, that three-year-old gelding isn't coming around. We've wasted enough time with him, he needs to go to town."

Yep, he definitely works here.

Kacey's head snaps around to look at him. "No way, we aren't taking him to the sale barn. I know Chet worked with him, but he's an idiot. Can't you spend a little more time with him?"

"I've spent time with him, more time than I have for him. And you *will not* be spending time with him," he says sternly. "This is the same horse that ran you down and took three grown men to halter at weaning. He bucks every time you saddle him. He's a liability and needs to go. I'm sorry, Kacey."

Her face falls, I can tell she knows he's probably right.

"Think he'd make a bucking horse?" Cody asks. "I could call that stock contractor over by Denver."

"Well, there's one way to find out. What if Mr. Bull Rider hops on him?" He looks at me with a challenge in his eyes.

"You do realize this kid's sitting at the top of the standings right now, and he's trying to make his fifth trip to the finals, right? He doesn't want to get hurt climbing aboard an outlaw. Do you, Knox?" Cody looks at me, giving me an out.

My eyes shift to Kacey; she looks crushed about this horse. Out of the corner of my eye I can see Carson, with a big smirk on his face. I'd think he was an asshole if I didn't agree with him. It sounds like Kacey shouldn't be anywhere near this horse until he's calmed down. He probably thinks my ego's big enough I'd actually say yes to this stupid endeavor, but I wasn't born yesterday. Not that I can't ride the horse through whatever he throws, but that won't really teach it anything.

"Well, sir, I'm not much for the old bronc-busting ways. I do have an idea though. How about you let me work with him for a few weeks and we'll see if I can straighten him out? I could use a project while I'm in town." Honestly, starting an outlaw colt is the last thing I need—I'm busy enough with Jack's clients and trying to get in the gym before the season starts. But something about the sadness I can see in her eyes has me offering to at least give the colt a chance.

First the broodmares and now a bucker. This girl might *actually* be the death of me.

Kacey looks at me like I'm an interesting artifact.

"Are you sure you have the time?" Cody asks, giving me another out.

This colt must be a handful.

I nod. "Yeah, I've got time."

"I guess it doesn't hurt to try. What's a few more weeks of feed when I've been feeding him for three years? You get these mares done, then Kacey can show you where he is. I'm off to check the feedyard—y'all have fun. Carson, play nice." He gives the ranch hand a look.

The joke is on Carson though; I've been training horses for a long time. I'll get him calmed down.

I'll be spending a lot more time around The Diamond Hart Ranch.

And Kacey Hart.

It's taken me most of the day to fight through the heavy old broodmares. It's late in the afternoon now—their feet were long, so it wasn't a fast job. I'm sure the ol' girls feel a lot better now.

It's safe to say I'm definitely not going to the gym today, my lower back and legs were starting to shake on that last one. I stand and straighten my back out.

Carson unhooks the crossties. "Well, Champ, I guess now you know why no one likes trimming these mares." He chuckles, but I can tell I've earned a little respect from him. "You're a go-getter, I'll give you that much." He almost cracks a smile and leads the mare toward the barn door.

I'm calling that a win for the day.

"You ready to see what this outlaw is all about?" Kacey announces as she walks up, halter in hand. I lean against a stall, trying to give my legs a break without letting her see how tired I am. "Sure, let me pack up real quick and we can go see him."

"You probably just want the hell out of here after doing those ol' nags." She half laughs but is also serious.

"Ah, they weren't that bad. At least I never got kicked or bit." I grin, even though one of them didn't want me working with her back feet and did in fact try to kick me. I thought she was going to get me a few times.

Out in the round pen is a big, stout, 15.3-hand buckskin colored gelding. He has a wild look in his eye, and I already know he's going to be a fun one.

"He'll let you catch him, but he throws a fit if you do much else. Carson's been working with him on and off since he was two, and I'm pretty sure Chet's dumbass has been throwing a saddle on him and trying to ride him, although he spends more time in the dirt. Now that he has size to him, he can put up a pretty good fight. Got any bright ideas on how to go about him?" She raises a brow, and I get the feeling this is some kind of test.

"The same way I've gone about every horse I've trained." I unlatch the gate and walk in.

I walk up slowly and halter the big three-year-old. I slowly reach toward his forelock, he bobs his head up like he's going to fly backwards. But after a second, he lowers his head, realizing my hand isn't that scary and I rub his forehead for a few minutes.

I lead him around the round pen, making sure I do both directions, and walk on each side of him. Most people don't realize that a horse sees out of each eye separately, so you have to work both sides for them to be comfortable on each side.

Next, I step around him, smooching to him, letting him know to start lunging. He quickly takes off at a lope, hitting the end of my rope but keeping pressure off me.

Okay, so he's done this before.

I turn him around and he goes the other direction perfectly. After that, I tie him to the big post in the center of the round pen—"the thinking post" I like to call them—and I start patting my hand on his back. He flies backwards, shaking his head when he hits the end of his lead rope.

"Woah, woah," I say calm, deep, and slow, but loud enough he can hear me. He quits and stands straight. I repeat my same action, but this time I'm moving at a snail's pace. He jumps a little but doesn't freak out this time. I do this for the next few minutes, just patting him everywhere. His chest, neck, belly, and rump. After I can pat him anywhere and he doesn't flinch, I untie him and turn him loose again.

"That's all you're doing with him today?" I was so focused on the horse, I completely forgot Kacey was watching. That's one reason I like training horses—I can tune everything out and focus. I don't have to talk to anyone. It's just me and the horse.

"Yep, it's not a race. I need him to trust me. Once he does that, he'll want to start learning."

She smiles. "Sure you don't just want to cowboy him?"

"I think he'll learn a lot more a lot faster this way." I smile back at her, unlatching the gate to leave his pen.

I can't explain it, but I really want to get to know her better. Yes, she's beautiful, but there is something else about her I can't seem to put my finger on. She's quiet and reserved, but I can tell there is more to her . . . she just won't let me see it yet.

"Want to go get some dinner? I'm starving." I blurt without thinking.

"Uh." Her eyes go wide. I caught her off guard. "I think I'll take a rain check. I still have some things I need to do around here before I can call it a day. Thanks for the offer, though." She seems sincere.

I'm slightly relieved at her answer. I didn't think before asking her. Flirting is one thing, dinner is another. I don't date, and I don't want to give her the impression that I do.

I bend to pet the little red dog who just showed up to greet us. Rein had been in and out of the barn all day while I trimmed the mares. "Alright, no worries. Bye, Rein. You're a good girl." I give her one more pet and her owner a smile before walking to my truck, calling, "I'll see you tomorrow."

"Tomorrow?" she questions.

"Yeah, tomorrow. I've got Buck here to work with." I can see the moment it clicks in her brain. I'll be at the ranch almost every day now.

A shy smile comes to her lips before she heads back into the barn.

I barely know her, but I can already tell Kacey is an amazing woman. One I need to keep my distance from, and distance is the opposite of what I just signed up for.

Fuck.

Chapter 9

Knox

Trey

You've been entering us right?

Knox

Yes Trey, I got it covered.

Trey

Thanks dad. I'm ducking bored. Can you enter me in Red Bluff?

Knox

Going to do the Wild Ride? If you do get a video.

Trey

Hell no, you know I don't mess with horses.

Knox

Be funny if you did.

Trey

When are you coming back to the house? We need to hit the road. I'm chomping at the bit here.

Knox

Oh calm down, you should be training. We've got a busy summer ahead of us. I'll be back for the Weatherford run.

Trey

I am training. Chasing these women in Southeast Oklahoma is a workout. Lots of cardio!

Knox

That's far more than I needed to know . . . less cardio, more reps kid! The summer run will be here soon.

The saddle creaks and Buck twitches his ear at me. I'm putting weight in the stirrup for the second time and he's handling it really well. I haven't swung my leg over him yet. First, I want him comfortable with my weight all on one side, like I'm going to sit on him. I haven't worked with a horse this jumpy in a long time. It's a fun challenge to show him new things in a way that doesn't freak him out.

"He looks like he's starting to come around," Cody says from the round pen gate. His face is hidden beneath the shadow of his black cowboy hat.

I didn't see him walk up. Pulling my foot from the stirrup, I turn toward him. "Yeah, I think he's starting to trust me. He hasn't thrown any fits today, and he's been taking the bridle and ground driving well."

He runs his hand down his beard. "Looks like you've got a knack for horses."

I chuckle. "I don't know about that. I have a lot of patience for them, I guess."

"I've seen men with patience who couldn't train a horse to walk forward if they wanted them to. You look like you know how to think like a horse." Cody's stern in his words, but they're words of respect.

I've noticed Kacey watching me, but maybe she isn't the only one.

"Ah, they aren't that tough to figure out. Most of them are just scared of what they don't know. People aren't much different."

"Son, those words are wiser than you realize." He unlatches the gate and walks in. Again, I'm shocked at how tall he is while Kacey is so small. She must take after her mom, and I haven't met her yet.

In a few strides, he's standing next to me, and reaches out to rub Buck's neck. Then he starts patting the saddle, making a loud *fwaap* noise as his big hand hits the saddle. "It's only been a few days since you started working with him and before then this horse would have flown back, bug eyed, bucking around this pen. You're doing really good work."

"Thank you, sir."

He gives Buck a couple more pats before fully turning to me. "I spoke to Jack, and he vouched for you, but I still need to say this. On this ranch, there are no drugs, fighting, or stealing. We're a pretty laid-back bunch, but those three rules are nonnegotiable."

The way he says it isn't hard or judgmental, it sounds like something he's said to many men before me. I won't say it isn't intimidating, though. It doesn't help that he is a mountain of a man looking down to meet my eyes.

"Understood. I respect that. I know I'm a bull rider and we have a bit of a reputation, but I've never been one for any of that."

He pauses for a second and runs his hand through his beard. "Good. Jack said you're focused on your career and take it seriously, but anyone can see that in your riding."

Thank you, Jack. He can keep the $50 he never gave me now.

"Yes sir, I believe if you want to be the best in the world, you better train like it and live like it."

Buck chooses this moment to shake the dust off.

Cody looks him over. "I don't know what my daughter's attachment to this horse is, but she seems to see potential in him. Did she tell you about haltering him as a weanling or him running her down?"

"Not the full story, but it's been mentioned. While he's coming around, I do believe he will always be a little jumpy and have a strong will, but that can be used to a good cowboy's or cowgirl's advantage."

It's almost a full minute before he replies, and I'm starting to feel awkward when he says. "You know, Kacey's pretty good with a horse, too, but she's never worked with one like this guy. She's learned some from me, but mostly from Carson. He's good, but I think she could learn a thing or two from you as well. You should ask her to lend a hand with Buck here."

"Yes sir, I can do that." Not sure what I can teach her that she hasn't already seen me do. Her green eyes have been fixated on me and Buck every day. I'm sure she thought she was being discreet by poking her head around the corner or acting like she was spraying a horse's legs off, but it was pretty obvious. It made it hard to keep a straight face and act like I didn't see her. Especially since I was watching her, too.

"Don't let her know it was my idea. It's better if you ask her to help."

"I can do that. I'm sure it will be good for Buck to have someone else working with him."

Cody nods. "Keep it up and I might have to hire you to break all the colts around here."

Cody heads for the gate as a big grin forms on my face. "Wouldn't that make Kacey my boss?"

"Yes, yes, it would." He chuckles. "Very few men can handle her, but I have a feeling you'd get along alright."

Yeah, I have a feeling we'd get along great, if she'd ever give me the time of day.

Chapter 10

Kacey

Jessie

What are you doing today? I have the day off.
Want to annoy Carson until he snaps?

Kacey

No, you're mean. But come to the ranch, I'm
at the barn.

Jessie

Coming. I still plan to annoy him, with or
without you.

Kacey

Whatever, I'll saddle a couple of horses.

Knox has been working with Buck for five days. So naturally, I've been discreetly watching him for five days. He's good with him—great, actually. Not to mention the way his biceps flex has my mind imagining things I never knew biceps could make me imagine.

I really need to charge my vibrator. Apparently, it's been too long since I've used it if biceps alone are about to push me over the edge.

Knox is quiet and patient with him, more patient than I've seen anyone be with a horse. He has a way of getting Buck to understand what he's asking of him, so he doesn't freak out about every new thing. On day two, he spent the entire afternoon desensitizing him to the saddle blanket. He'd toss it onto his back, pull it off, toss it under his belly, then onto his butt and repeat. Every time Buck would freak out, Knox would wait for him to calm down, rub his forehead and neck, then start the process over again until Buck no longer cared.

I'm standing in the barn door watching Knox and Buck in the round pen when Jessie pulls in the drive. I immediately recognize my mistake: she's going to see him.

This is about to get interesting. At least I'm saving Carson—now she'll be annoying me.

I head to her SUV, hoping to cut her off and redirect her toward the barn, but she climbs out too fast and turns to look right at the round pen. She starts walking that way.

What the hell? Why is she walking over there?

"Jessie, come into the barn. I have Hooch and Bear saddled. We'll go for a ride and find Carson," I call out. Now I have no problem using him as my scapegoat; I'll annoy him with her if it gets me out of this situation.

"In a minute," she hollers back and keeps walking. Her dark red ponytail sways to the rhythm of her hips.

"Hey, I'm Jessie. I haven't seen you around before. You new on the ranch?" I hear her say once she reaches the fence. I watch Knox turn away from Buck to look at her.

Here we go. Jessie is every guy's dream girl. With long, dark red hair, a curvy body and the sass to match. I've never really cared much that most guys go for her over me, but for some reason, her trying for Knox's attention doesn't sit right with me.

"Hi, I'm Knox. Not new here, just working with Buck." He turns back to the horse. Jessie's head whips around to me so fast it has to hurt her neck. And he didn't even check her out.

Is he blind or dead?

"Knox, you say? I've heard of you. Kacey said—"

I walk up just in time to kick her in the back of the calf and cut her off. "Sorry about her. We won't bother you; we're just heading out for a ride." I drag her away by the arm.

Knox turns around with a smirk on his face. "I'd kind of like to hear what you say about me." He winks at me.

What is with this man and winking? It makes my cheeks flush red, and I hate that.

Jessie, also known as The World's Worst Best Friend, hollers back, "Come with us and I'll tell you!"

I'm going to kill her. I bet Carson would help me bury her. There are plenty of places to bury a body on a ranch.

"I don't think Buck's quite up to it yet, but thanks anyway. Maybe some other time." He laughs and goes back to work.

I have a feeling this is going to be a long ride.

Jessie at least has the courtesy to wait until we've ridden out of earshot to lay into me.

"You lying little bitch! And I quote, '*He's ugly.*'"

"No, I did not lie. You said, 'he must be ugly,' and I just never disagreed. That's not lying."

"*Semantics.* God took extra time making that man and you know it. What is going on between you two? I saw him wink at you and your face turned bright red, so spill it. Now."

I was afraid she saw that. "Nothing is going on. He's flirted with me a few times and may have asked me to dinner, but I said no. End of story."

We turn the horses toward the mare pasture.

"Uh no, not end of story. Kacey, why did you say no?" Her tone has changed, and she looks at me like I'm a puppy someone just kicked.

I hate that look and it's part of the reason I don't even try to date anymore. After Garrett stomped all over my heart, everyone treated me like I was made of glass for months. I'm not made of glass; I just have no interest in repeating that particular experience.

I sigh. "You know why. My situation hasn't changed and I'm not going through that again." And by situation, I mean the ranch. I'm grateful my dad owns the largest and most successful ranch in the state, but it makes dating and making friends difficult. It's hard to know who likes me for me, and who likes me because of the fact that I stand to inherit all of this. Most people say I won't be inheriting a ranch, I'll be inheriting an empire.

Jessie looks straight ahead while we ride in silence for a few minutes. "You know I love you," she says, breaking the silence.

"When Garrett did what he did, I wanted to kill him. In fact, if I saw him crossing the street today, I would hit him with my car. But honey, you have to move on. Maybe this Knox guy is the perfect opportunity to get back in the game. He's only in town for a few weeks, right? You'll probably never see him again. What's the harm in going out and having some fun? No pressure, no expectations, just get back out there and knock the rust off. Figuratively speaking. Or not . . . I wouldn't blame you if you climbed that man like a tree."

My eyes are watering, but I can't help but laugh.

"I know you get lonely," she continues, her words hitting me right in the chest. "You may be an introvert, but you've always wanted to find love. You, Kacey Hart, are not the woman who dies an old bachelorette with fifty cats. I won't allow it. You want and deserve to find love. Maybe spending time with Knox will help you get back out there to find that."

Jessie might be wild, but she can make people feel loved and understood like no one else I've ever met. And she's right, I've always wanted that. True love, a partner, even kids someday. It wasn't until Garrett that I gave up on that dream. Maybe I let him steal more than my trust, maybe he stole my hope.

"Thanks, Jessie. I think I needed to hear that. I'm not sure I'm ready to go all in, but maybe spending some time with Knox couldn't hurt. That's if he's even interested." Just because he's flirted with me a couple times doesn't mean he actually wants to spend time with me. He looks like a Greek god and he's a professional bull rider—most women would walk across hot coals for a chance with him.

She smirks at me. "Oh, he's interested, trust me. I'm also now invested and expect daily updates."

"Ha, of course you do."

"Oh, did you get his last name? Is he any good at riding bulls?"

"Yeah, about that." I hesitate to tell her. It only helps her prove her point. My family has money, but from what I read, Knox doesn't need it. He has a very successful career and huge sponsors.

"Do tell, do tell."

"Oddly enough, Dad knew exactly who he was. I guess he sees him on TV all the time. I looked him up after I found out and he's sixth in the world. He's been to the finals like four times. So, safe to say he doesn't suck."

Jessie's eyes go wide. "Wow . . . that just made him even hotter."

I burst out laughing, because she's not wrong.

When we get back from our ride, I see Knox putting Buck away like he's done for the day.

I look at Jessie. "Hey, I'm gonna—"

"Yeah, yeah, ditch me for the world's hottest cowboy. I'm going to stop by Gran's on my way home anyway." She dismounts and hands me Bear's reins.

"Sounds good. Tell her I said hello."

She heads for her SUV as I steer Hooch in Knox's direction, bringing Bear along with me.

"Hey, want a tour of the ranch?" I ask and he looks at me like I've grown two heads. That's fair, I haven't exactly reciprocated his interest. In fact, I've avoided him the last few days.

"Yeah, that would be great."

I figured now was as good a time as any to get to know him a little better. I'm always more comfortable on horseback and this way, I don't have time to chicken out.

Knox rubs his palm down Bear's neck, adjusts the stirrups and climbs on. "So, where to first, tour guide?"

"Let's head for the working facility. I think Carson's doctoring some cows."

As we ride toward the working facility, you can see part of the broodmare and foal pasture.

"It seems like you handle a lot of the horses here," he says.

"Yeah, I've always loved horses, and it came naturally. We've always had horses, but I started our breeding program ten years ago and typically keep thirty to thirty-five broodmares on the property. So, if you ever want more broodmares to trim, just let me know," I say jokingly.

That makes him laugh. "Well thanks, if I start falling off and need entry fee money, I'll give you a call."

After our stop at the working facility to check on a grumpy Carson, we head for the feyard. While we ride, I give him the rundown on the ranch—how many head of cattle and horses, the feedyard, plus the hay ground production. I tell him how we train the young horses we breed and then sell them as finished horses after using them on the ranch for a couple of years.

I'd rather bring it all up now and gauge his response. I heard what he said to my dad about the ranch, but that could've been a normal compliment. He wouldn't be the first to say it. I'm probably just paranoid.

"Originally, Dad bought calves to fill the feed

yard but once he and Grandpa brought in new genetics to the herd, we started producing super high-quality meat. That allowed him to open a locker and sell directly to high-end restaurants and ski resorts around Denver. We might have lost the ranch if Dad hadn't started that program."

"Wow, you all have a lot going on. Where is the locker?"

"It's on the far side of the yard. We can't see it from the side we were on." I turn toward my favorite pasture at the base of a mountain, and we ride in silence for a while. I've been so busy on the ranch and with roping, I don't remember the last time I rode this pasture. The grass is that bright green you only get in the spring and wildflowers are starting to sprout in the fence lines and under trees.

Knox clears his throat and looks a little nervous. I'm starting to wonder if he's going to ask me to dinner again when he says, "So I could use a second set of hands with Buck for the next few days. I want to get him used to another person and get some weight in the saddle. Do you think you could help me?"

Oh, that wasn't what I was expecting. "Yeah, of course." I've seen him working with Buck, and I actually have a few questions about his training method. "Just let me know what time you think you'll be over tomorrow, and I'll make sure I'm around."

He gives me a crooked smile. "Great, will do."

I point out a few more things about the ranch, but for the most part, we settle into silence the rest of the ride. I expected it to be awkward, but it's not. I've always been more of the quiet, introverted type. Maybe he is too—the silence doesn't seem to bother him.

He hasn't made me uncomfortable with any of his questions about the ranch, he never asked about money, or even how many employees we have. He seems more interested in my role on the ranch and what I enjoy about it.

Maybe Jessie is right, and this will work. Knox seems relaxed around me and hasn't flirted or asked me out again on our ride. Maybe we could be friends. I could do that. We can work with Buck and shoe horses, maybe I can even convince Carson to give the guy a chance and we can go rope some steers. I remember Jack said he can rope.

Once we return to the main barn, Knox helps me unsaddle the horses, and I walk him out to his truck.

"Thanks for the tour," he says.

"You're welcome. I'll see you tomorrow?"

"You bet. Have a good night, Kace." He smiles, and as I watch him walk away, I notice I'm biting my lower lip. He called me Kace, and I like the sound of the nickname on his lips.

Friends. Just friends, Kacey, I remind myself.

No chance of heartbreak with a friend.

Chapter 11

Knox

Three missed calls from Trey.

"**H**ave *kids*," they say. "*It'll be fun*," they say. Well, I have Trey, and I'm not having fun. This morning sucked, none of the horses stood, so it took way longer than planned, and I want to get to the ranch and see Kacey. But if I don't call him back, he'll just keep trying me.

Trey picks up on the first ring. "Can I come to Colorado?"

"What? No." I climb in the truck and turn the key. My phone connects to the truck speakers that I had blaring this morning, so at full volume I hear, "But Daaad—"

"Stop it," I cut him off. "What do you want? I've been shoeing asshole horses all morning and have somewhere to be."

"Wow, someone's crabby. You need to get laid. I know a girl in Denver, she does this thing with her—"

"*NOPE*. Stop right there. Any girl who has done anything to you, with you, or for you, is a no go for me."

"You don't even know her. She's a nice girl, could be the future Mrs. Ward, for all you know."

I sigh and put the truck in drive. "Again, I ask, what do you want, Trey?"

"I'm soooo bored. There's nothing fun to do here," he whines.

"Life isn't always fun. Have you tried going to the gym, or I don't know, get a part-time job?"

He laughs like I'm joking. "When you ride and look this good, you don't need a job. In fact, *you* don't need a part-time job. I still don't understand why you went out there."

"Jack is a friend. And maybe I like this job."

He scoffs. "Yeah, it really sounds like it, crabass."

"Listen, if you don't need anything, I'm running late to meet Kacey. She'll be waiting . . . uh—"

Shit, I shouldn't have said her name.

"Wait a minute. Who's Kacey?" Trey might be dumb, but he isn't stupid. There is no chance he'll drop this subject now, but there is a zero percent chance I'm discussing Kacey with him. There is nothing to discuss, anyway.

"Uh, no one. I really have to go. Go hit the gym or something. I'll be back in a few weeks."

"WEEKS—"

Click.

————————————

Kacey and I spend the next few days working with Buck together. Cody was right, she's good with horses. Buck took to her right away. Yesterday I got on him, and he never flinched, even when I shifted my weight all over the saddle.

Today I'm going to have Kacey keep him on the lunge line while I ride him. Since this is what Buck already knows, he just needs to learn to do it with the weight on his back. I step into the saddle and swing a leg over him. He doesn't react—*good, he remembers*—I start to lightly tap him with the heels of my boots as I smooch to him to move forward.

He takes one step, and I can feel him hump up under the saddle, I prepare for him to go rogue. I smooch to him again, and he takes a few more steps before I feel him relax. We let him walk in both directions, then got him to trot and lope, never once offering to live up to his name.

While we've worked with Buck, I've asked Kacey some questions to get to know her better. She's quiet, and I can tell she's keeping me at a distance. But every once in a while, when she laughs at something I say or Buck picks up on something new, I can see it—the real Kacey poking her head around the wall she seems to have built, keeping everyone out.

I love it when she laughs. I have a new goal now: make Kacey laugh at least twice a day.

Carson has stopped by a few times and didn't growl at me, so I consider that a win. I learned that he's ten years older than Kacey and the closest thing she has to a brother; his dislike of me makes a lot more sense now. I have a sister and if she got hit on by some bull rider, I probably wouldn't like it either. Thankfully, she's married to a great guy, so I don't have to worry about it.

"I think he's had enough for today," I tell Kacey as I swing out of the saddle. It's almost dark and I'm starving. I shod four horses before coming here and all I've had is a protein shake today.

She gives Buck a couple of pats and starts leading him to the gate. "Yeah, he's been great today, though. I think he's ready to ride without a lunge line. What do you think?"

Some of her blonde hair has fallen out of her ponytail through the day, framing her freckled cheeks and sea green eyes. There has been more than one time over the last few days I've had to shake my head, clearing the thoughts of her from it. Just standing this close to her has my blood heating in my veins.

"I think that's a good next step. We'll have to wait a day though; I can't come tomorrow. I have too many horses scheduled to make it over."

I see her face fall slightly before she masks it. "Oh, that's okay. I'm sure he'd appreciate a day off."

"Or he'll wander around his pen missing me all day." I smirk at her.

"Ha, yes, I'm sure he will."

"Ya know, if you're going to miss me, too, it's okay to say so. I'd totally understand if you struggle to go a day without seeing me, I'm pretty—"

She laughs, a real laugh.

Check. Laugh one for the day, complete.

"I think I'll survive a day without you, but I applaud your confidence."

I've been trying not to flirt with her like before. It seemed to make her uncomfortable, but I see the way she looks at me sometimes and I can't help myself. I love making her cheeks turn pink and it's so easy.

I let out a dramatic sigh. "Alright, if you say so."

We take Buck into the barn, and I start to unsaddle him. I've worked in some nice horse facilities before, but this place beats most of them. The fourteen-stall barn has every bell and whistle, including an indoor arena large enough to team rope in. You can tell they put some money into this. If I was a betting man, I'd say Cody built that arena strictly so Kacey can rope in the winter.

When I let him out into his paddock next to the barn, I turn to see Kacey looking at my ass. Her eyes snap up and cheeks flush red, again.

Yep, you're busted, sweetheart.

I don't mind. She can look all she wants.

Rein comes running into the barn, straight for me, making Kacey scrunch her nose. "I raised you, feed you, and give you a warm place to sleep at night, and you don't even glance at me. You just run straight to him. What a little traitor."

I chuckle at the dog while it pays no attention to her owner's rant. Me and ol' Rein have been sneaking in some pets when Kacey isn't looking.

"She knows I haven't paid my pet tax today."

When I first heard Kacey call it a pet tax, I cracked up. It's so true though, just like the government, you have to pay up, or Rein will come and take them by force.

I decide now is a good time to give dinner another shot.

"I'm starving; I'm going to head into town to eat. Do you want to come with me? And before you say no, this would not be a date. Just two people getting dinner together. I haven't been anywhere in town, so I don't know what's good or bad. You'd be doing me a favor by going with me."

I didn't say "not a date" to trick her. This isn't a date—I don't date—but I wouldn't mind getting to know her better. She wrings her fingers in her hands and glances away from me. She's going to say no.

"Uh, yeah, sure. I know a good café in town—"

I knew it. "That's okay, I totally underst—" *Wait, what did she just say? A café? She said yes?* "I mean, great, let's go to the café. I'll drive." Shit, now my face is turning red.

She looks down at her jeans and t-shirt. "Do you mind if I change quick? A calf got me pretty good earlier today." She points to the shit splattered all over her jeans.

I've shod horses and worked with Buck today, so I hardly smell like roses, but at least I don't have calf crap all over me. I'm pretty sure I have some cologne in my truck.

"No problem. I'll grab my truck and meet you at your place."

She nods and takes off toward her house, practically running.

Chapter 12

Kacey

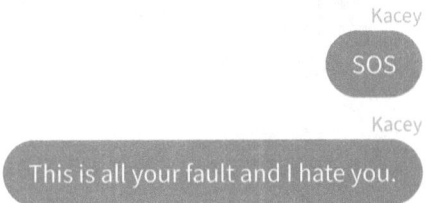

Kacey

SOS

Kacey

This is all your fault and I hate you.

I fly into my house and scramble for some clean jeans and a long-sleeve shirt. I don't have time to think about what I'm wearing; I just need clean clothes. I can't believe I just agreed to go out with Knox. He said it's not a date, but that isn't stopping me from having a panic attack. I feel like I'm in a crowded Costco—chest tight, palms sweaty, breathing in short panting breaths.

I'm pathetic.

Kacey

HELLO? Did you not see the SOS??!

I run into the bathroom to brush my teeth and throw on some mascara. Finally, my phone vibrates.

Jessie

> Good lord woman, what has your panties in a wad?

Jessie

> I hope it's Knox. Please tell me it's Knox.

Kacey

> My panties are not in a wad. You convinced me to get to know him, and I have been. At the ranch, with a horse between us. Until now.

Jessie

> Ooo what's between you now?

Kacey

> Jessie! I'm serious, I'm freaking out here. He asked me out to dinner again, and I said yes. I'm in my house changing right now.

Jessie

> Okay, just take a deep breath. He's obviously interested in you, so just be yourself. Eat a burger, have a beer, no pressure, right?

Kacey

> Right. No pressure. He just pulled up, gotta go. Thanks!

Jessie

> Details! I want details after!

I walk out of the house and run down the stairs to Knox's truck before he can try to come inside. In the middle of the living room is a pile of unfolded laundry next to a stack of romance books. I'm good with him *not* seeing that. I'm stressed enough as it is.

As soon as I climb in, Knox rushes to say, "Sorry about the mess. I don't clean my work truck near as much as the rodeo truck." He sounds frazzled, and for some reason that makes me feel slightly better. I guess I'm not the only one who's stressed about this "not a date."

I look around, and it's clean. There might be some dust and an empty bottle here or there, but if he thinks this is dirty, he'd have a heart attack if he got in one of the ranch trucks.

Mr. Fancy Pants here with two trucks.

"You have a separate truck for rodeo?"

"Yeah, most guys do. With the miles we put on and having a Capri camper on the back, it just makes sense."

That's fair, I never thought about the camper.

I spend the drive to town answering Knox's questions about Cottonwood Valley and the surrounding area.

At the café, we make small talk until after we've ordered our food, then he takes a sip of his water before asking, "So, have you always wanted to be a rancher?"

For this not being a date, that is very much a first date question. I knew I should've picked a restaurant that served alcohol. "Yeah, I have. Even before my mom died, I was always out with Dad checking pairs or feeding the horses. I loved it all, even as a child. I never see myself leaving the ranch."

Knox's eyes go wide. "I didn't know about your mom. I'm sorry. When did she pass?"

Right. Because he doesn't know me, not really anyway. He's tried to ask a few questions while we work with Buck, but I haven't given him much.

"It was a long time ago. I was seven. It was a car accident." I pause when he gives me a sympathetic look before changing the subject. "Are you close with your parents?" If he wants to play twenty questions, he'll have to pony up a few answers, too.

"I am with my mom. She and my sister don't live far from me. I was close with my dad growing up—he taught me how to be a cowboy. But when he and Mom divorced, and he remarried, all his focus turned to his new family. We rarely talk anymore."

I watch his facial expressions closely. He doesn't seem upset discussing this. He says it like it's just facts and not his relationship—or lack thereof—with his dad.

"I'm sorry, that must be hard. I don't know what I'd do without my dad."

"I've noticed you two seem close. Although, I'm not sure how close you can be when he knew who I was, he's watched me ride. You, however, had no idea who I was," Knox says playfully. With a smirk on his face, I know he's messing with me.

"Yeah, yeah, Mr. Hot Shot bull rider. How long have you rode for, anyway?"

"Since I was eight. My dad put me on a steer thinking I'd fall off, it'd hurt, and that would get it out of my system. Jokes on him—twenty-two years later it's still not out of my system."

"Eight?! That's insane. I know you said steer, but I still can't imagine putting an eight-year-old on one."

He laughs. "Yeah, it sounds a little young, but you'd be surprised how young most of today's professional riders started."

His phone vibrates on the table. I glance at it and see it's a photo of him and a pretty woman in her fifties, with the same hair as Knox, and a little boy around six years old. He catches me looking.

"It's my mom. Do you mind?"

"No, of course not. Answer it."

I take a drink of my water and look away, trying not to eavesdrop. The café is empty though and I can hear every word.

"Hey, Mom," he says as he takes his ball cap off, to smooth his curls. It does nothing—they bounce right back and it's cute.

"Hi, Knox, honey. Are you still in Colorado? The dishwasher is leaking all over the floor. I got it pulled out and the water shut off, but I can't figure out where the leak is coming from."

"Yeah, I'm still out here. Is Logan gone? I can call Trey in the morning and send him over. He needs something to do, anyway."

"Yes, he's gone until next week. If Trey could come, that would be wonderful. I'll bake him some cookies."

I fight to hide my smile. She sounds so sweet.

"Ha, I'm sure he'd appreciate that. You're okay now though? It's not leaking anymore?" The way he talks to her makes my heart flutter. It's sweet, you can hear how much he loves her in his voice.

"No, no, it's shut off. There is no hurry."

"Alright, good. Hey, Ma, I'm at dinner with a friend. Can I call you tomorrow?"

"Of course. Have fun, honey. Love you."

"Love you, too." Knox sets his phone down right as our food comes.

What I wouldn't give to be able to call my mom. It's been years, but I still miss her. I see other girls out shopping or getting coffee with their moms and my heart breaks all over again.

Most people think of the big things you'll miss them at—birthdays, graduation, your wedding—and they aren't wrong. But often times, it's the small moments you see other people getting to have with their moms that make you hold your breath through the wave of grief.

Knox clears his throat. "Sorry about that. She lives alone, so my brother-in-law Logan and I help out a lot, but he's out of town for work."

"It's nice of you both to help her. Is Trey your brother?"

He smiles. "No, it's just me and my sister. Trey is my traveling partner, and we live together. He's a lot, very dramatic, and a little on the wild side, but he's a good friend. The best, actually. He can fix just about anything and is always helping friends out. He even takes tools on the road with us."

We eat our burgers and fries while he tells me more about him and Trey meeting and becoming friends. He even tells me a couple of stories about Trey and the wild things he's done on the road.

"He sounds like Jessie. She's wild and has zero filter. Drives Carson insane sometimes and I swear she does it on purpose."

"Well, heaven help us all if Trey and Jessie ever meet."

"I don't know . . . the way you describe him, I might pay a pretty penny to see him give Jessie a run for her money."

"How long have you two been friends?"

"As long as I can remember, she's been my best friend. We are polar opposites personality-wise, but I think that's why we work."

We finish our food while I tell him stories about Jessie and me growing up.

I'm relaxed until he asks, "So, Carson . . . you guys seem pretty close, and I get the feeling he doesn't like me very much."

I try to swallow the lump in my throat. Carson doesn't like any man who looks at me, not since Garrett. But I can't tell Knox that—I won't discuss Garrett with him.

"He's just protective and a little grumpy sometimes. He came to the ranch when he was eighteen, a year after my mom died. He became more of a babysitter than a ranch hand for my dad and we've always been close. He's the closest thing I have to a sibling."

"That makes sense. I'm pretty protective of my sister, too. I bet you and Jessie ran him ragged as kids." He laughs and shakes his head when I nod vigorously. "Oh yeah, he got his first gray hair at twenty-six and blamed us."

The waitress brings our check, and Knox refuses to split it. He said this wasn't a date, but I could tell this was an argument I wouldn't win. After he pays, we head back to the ranch, and I'm starting to think Jessie was right. This was fun. The longer we talked, the more comfortable I became. Knox seems genuinely interested in my life and the people in it, not just the ranch. Not that I'll ever tell Jessie she was right—she'd be insufferable.

Chapter 13

Knox

We're halfway back to the ranch and I feel like dinner went well. Kacey actually talked about something other than Buck and looked more relaxed around me. The more I get to know her, the more I like her. She's beautiful, but she's also smart and compassionate. I know I shouldn't be thinking about her like this right before the summer run, but I can't seem to stop myself.

I need to get it together.

I said this wasn't a date, and that's probably the only reason she agreed to go. It's clear she has reservations about me, but she seems to be slowly letting her guard down. I enjoy spending time with her, I want to get to know her better, and I'm not sure why she is hesitant to let me. I know she's single, and I've seen the way she looks at me. Hell, she's even flirted with me several times. So why is she so hesitant?

Maybe because I'm a rodeo cowboy, and we have horrible reputations? Or because she knows I'm only here for a few weeks?

"So, when's your next rodeo?"

Her voice snaps me out of the spiral of questions I shouldn't even be asking myself. I'm not looking for a girlfriend. I shift in my seat and release the death grip I had on the steering wheel.

"I'd have to look at my schedule, but I think it's Mount Pleasant, Texas in early June."

She turns in her seat to face me fully. "Are you ever afraid? When you get on a bull."

This isn't an uncommon question, and my answer has always been the same.

"There is a quote by Will Smith that's always stuck with me. 'Fear is not real. The only place that fear can exist is in our thoughts of the future. It is a product of our imagination, causing us to fear things that do not at present and may not ever exist. That is near insanity. Do not misunderstand me, danger is very real but fear is a choice.' That said, I believe the day a man fears riding bulls is the day he should stop."

She scrunches her brows together, and I can tell she doesn't fully understand me. That's okay, most people don't.

"Don't get me wrong, there are bulls out there that'll make a guy's mouth go dry. They may have a bad reputation, or they buck so hard that no one's ridden them, but bulls don't scare me. I know there is a level of danger there, but I see them as an obstacle or a challenge, and I have always expected myself to rise to the occasion."

She slowly nods. "I guess that makes sense. It's all about how you perceive things. Some people are terrified of horses, but even as a child, I was never afraid of them. Have you ever been seriously hurt before?"

I have zero plans of sitting here and listing out all the shit I've broken, torn, or had stomped on. "All bull riders get hurt. I've been hurt badly enough to take a few months off, and I've been hurt when I only take a few days off. It's all part of the sport," is all I say. I don't really talk about this stuff with anyone, but especially not with women. She'll probably think I'm insane for continuing to ride. I just got her to talk to me; I'm not going to scare her off now.

I change the subject as I pull into the drive of the ranch.

"Thanks for coming with me. This was fun." I smile at her as I pull up to her house.

"It was, I'm glad I came." Her cheeks turn a little pink as she makes eye contact with me and I sense she means it.

She climbs out of the truck, and I make the snap decision to walk her to her door. My mom raised me right. This might not be a real date, but I'm not just dumping her at the curb.

"Oh, you don't have to walk me up," she says when she sees me coming around the front of the truck.

"Now, what kind of gentleman would I be if I didn't walk you to your door?" I put my hand on the small of her back as we walk through the small gate into her yard.

"Well, thank you. I can honestly say no one has ever walked me to my door." She lets out a huff of a laugh.

Wait—what? No man has ever brought this girl home from a date and walked her to her door? What kind of douchebags has she been dating?

The worst part is she doesn't seem bothered by this fact. Does she have no clue how a man should treat her? I don't have much of a temper, but this has me wanting a list of names. Maybe Carson knows, and we could use this as a bonding tool for us. He'd love me by the end.

We reach her porch and climb the steps. At the top, I lightly pull on her forearm turning her toward me because I can't help myself. I reach up and rub a strand of her silky blonde hair between my fingers.

She sucks in a breath and meets my eyes. I've never seen green eyes this beautiful before. I'd stand here all night looking at them if she'd let me.

"Sweetheart, you deserve to be walked to your door. You deserve to be told how breathtaking you are. I don't know what kind of men you've been dating but find better ones."

I drop her hair and run my hand down her arm. She doesn't reply. I'm not even sure she's breathing.

"Goodnight, Kacey." I let go of her arm and start walking back to my truck.

I hear her say softly, "Goodnight, Knox."

I don't even make it past the gate of the ranch before I have to fight the urge to turn back around and knock on her door. Imagining her dating someone who isn't me makes my stomach churn, but I'm not what she needs. Besides, I need to focus on my goal: win a world title.

So why can't I stop thinking about her?

Chapter 14

Kacey

Jessie

clears throat Hellooo? I'm waiting for my update on last night.

Jessie

How did it go?!

Kacey

Good.

Jessie

Good? That's all I get? I basically facilitated this entire date and all I get is 'Good'?

Kacey

First of all, you are the most dramatic person I know. Secondly, it was not a date. I'm busy working cows, I'll fill you in later.

Jessie

First of all, I take pride in that title, thank you. Second, fine, I'll be patient—but barely. Meet me at Gran's for dinner tonight.

After Knox got in his truck and drove off last night, I promptly went inside to hyperventilate. His whole "not a date" definitely felt like one by the end of the night. I'm trying not to overthink it or read into anything, but the way he touched me, the things he said, replay in a constant loop in my mind. And never in my life has a man looked at me the way he did. Like he wanted to cherish me, yet at the same time, pin me against the wall and prove exactly how breathtaking he thinks I am.

I'm helping Chet, Carson, and two of the other cowboys work cows, but all I can think about is the hungry look in Knox's eyes. He wanted to kiss me, I could see it. And to be honest, I'm not sure I would've stopped him if he—

"Kacey! Wake up!" Chet yells, right as a cow we need runs past me.

Shit.

"Sorry, I'll grab her!"

Carson follows me. "What's up with you? You've been out of it all morning."

"Nothing's up. Just tired is all."

There is no way I'm telling Carson about Knox and me. Not that there is a Knox and me to talk about. I know there is no future for us—he's leaving in a few weeks and doesn't even live here. Not that the butterflies in my stomach seem to understand that. I've never felt so drawn to a man, and it terrifies me. And even worse, just for a few minutes last night, I let my guard down.

We get around the cow and head her back toward the chute. Once we get her in, Carson stops his horse next to mine.

"Stay up late reading again?" He rolls his eyes at me under his black cowboy hat. One time, he found out what Jessie and I read, and he gagged. Now, he uses that information to mock us.

"No, for your information, I went out last night."

"What? Where? With who?"

I realize my mistake too late. "Uh, it looks like Chet needs help." I spur Hooch and leave Carson with a scowl on his face.

I don't even get through the door at Gran's before Jessie is on me.

"I've been waiting all day. Spill it!"

I sigh and move through the kitchen to greet Gran. I love Jessie's Grandma Dorothy. All my grandparents have been gone a long time, so she's the only grandma I have. After Jessie moved in with her, we started having what we called "epic sleepovers" where Gran let us eat junk food and watch scary movies.

She's lived in the same little house on Columbine Street in Cottonwood Valley my whole life. The kitchen and dining area is an open space with pale yellow walls and a daisy wall-paper border. I remember when she let Jessie pick it out when we were nine. She's never changed it.

"Hi, Gran," I say as I give her a hug. Her tiny but strong frame squeezes me tight as her signature scent of vanilla and moth balls hit me. She has her long, white hair braided down her back and a flower-printed dress on.

"Hi, sweetie. Go on and sit down. I'm making chicken and noodles. It'll be ready soon."

Oh, bless her heart. I love Gran's chicken and noodles.

"Helloooo? My update! I'm on the edge of my seat here," Jessie calls from the table, still in her scrubs. She must have picked up an extra shift. I frown, concerned by the hours my friend has been working.

Now Gran is the one who sighs. "Jessie, honey, please just let her come in and sit down. What is this update you're wanting about, anyhow?"

Jessie smiles like the cheshire cat. "It's about Kacey's new man. He's the world's hottest bull rider."

"Oh, you don't say? Good for you, sweetie." And with that, she returns to the stove.

I sit down at the table and glare at Jessie. "He isn't my man. He's just a friend, and he's only in town for a few weeks."

Gran turns from the stove and looks at me like she's waiting for me to say more. When I don't, she says, "I noticed you didn't dispute the 'hot' part."

Jessie busts out laughing. This is where she gets it from; Gran might be pushing eighty, but she's sharp as a tack and has no filter.

I smirk at her. "When I was a kid, you told me not to lie. You said liars go to hell."

She lets out a cackle. "That's my girl. Now, tell us what happened last night with the hot man who isn't your man."

I drop my head into my hands and groan. I knew this was how tonight would go.

Gran sets out plates and utensils, unfazed by my obvious annoyance. "Dinner is ready. Make your plate and we can chat at the table, girls."

We make our plates and sit down. I fill Gran in on who Knox is and why he's in town. Jessie gives a *very* detailed physical description before finally looking up his Instagram and showing her a photo.

Gran releases a low whistle. "I have to agree with Jessie, he is *very* good looking. There's just something about cowboys."

I finally give Jessie her long-awaited recap of last night. I tell them about our conversation at dinner and the drive back to the ranch. However, I fail to mention the way his touch sent heat through me or how I found myself leaning into it.

"Then he walked me to my door, and I went to bed," I finish as I blow on my fork full of noodles to cover up the fact that my face is turning red just thinking about what he said last night. And the way his fingers felt running down my arm . . . .

Jessie looks up from her plate. "That's it? No kiss? No 'can we go out again?'" She frowns at me.

"No, it wasn't a date. He just walked me to the door."

I chance a glance at Gran but quickly look away. Her eyes are narrowed at me from her seat to my left. As a child, I swore she could read minds. As an adult . . . well, I still think she can. I can feel my face is red, so I look down at my plate.

"Bullshit," Gran calls me out. "I wasn't born yesterday, dear. I can tell when there's more to a story. Let's have it."

Jessie busts up, almost spitting her food out. I thought she was going to choke for a second. My cheeks turn even redder, and I curse my pale skin. I should have known better than to hide anything from Gran.

"Alright, fine." I lean against my seat's back with a huff. "When we got back to my house and he started walking me to my door, I told him he didn't need to do that. No one has ever walked me to my door. When we got to the door, he turned me to face him, picked a lock of my hair to rub between his fingers and said, '*Sweetheart, you deserve to be walked to your door. You deserve to be told how breathtaking you are. I don't know what kind of men you've been dating but find better ones.*' Then he left and I went into the house and hyperventilated."

Jessie's jaw is on the floor. It's been years since I've seen her speechless. Leave it to Knox to finally shut her up.

Gran, however, is not speechless. She blows out a long breath. "Honey, back in my day I would've melted against him like wax on a burning candle for talking like that—especially one as good-looking as him. Hell, I would lock him in the basement 'till he gave me a ring if I were you."

Jessie snorts. "Well . . . you don't have a basement. So what are you gonna do?"

Closing my eyes, I let my head fall back. A sad laugh escapes my lips. "I have no idea."

Chapter 15

Kacey

Kacey

Hey, I'm running behind. I'll be about 30 minutes late to hold those horses.

Knox

No worries. I'm almost to the ranch, is there a horse you know stands well? I can put it in the crossties and get started.

Kacey

Yeah, go ahead and start on the dun horse in stall 12. Thanks!

Carson, Chet, and I were moving some cattle to the feedyard and got behind schedule. We're headed back to the ranch now so I can hold some horses for Knox to reset shoes on, but I'm really late.

We pull up to the barn to see Knox's truck backed up to the door like normal. It's colder today, so I have the barn doors closed and the heaters on. We unload from the truck and walk in through the side door. I hear the clang of a hammer striking steel as I walk around the corner. When I look toward the cross ties, I find Knox at his anvil stand shaping a shoe . . . shirtless.

Oh, wow.

I instantly halt and take in the sight. Every swing of the big hammer, sweat running down his body, and the quick flexing of every muscle in his arm, shoulder, pecs . . . and those abs—those sexy, chiseled abs. Next thing I know, someone is crashing into me.

"Oof. What the hell? Don't just stop in front of someone like that." Chet catches me with a hand on each of my arms so I don't fall. I don't even turn to look at him, no way I'm missing a second of the show.

"Carson didn't run into me, how 'bout you just watch where you're walking?"

Carson stands slightly in front of me wearing a facial expression I can't read and glancing between me and Knox.

Chet looks over my shoulder and narrows his eyes. "What the hell is this guy doing?"

"Looks like he's shoeing a horse to me," I reply sarcastically.

We walk down the alley closer to the crossties.

"This is a ranch, not Magic Mike. Put a fucking shirt on," Chet chides as Knox inspects the shoe.

He looks up, wearing a shit-eating grin. "If one of you threw a couple dollar bills my way, it could be."

Chet looks like steam is about to come rolling out of his ears.

I laugh and even Carson lets out a snort.

Carson steps up to hold the dun. "Chet, you act like you've never seen a shirtless man before, yet you live in a bunkhouse full of ranch hands. Why is it so hot in here?"

"No idea," Knox answers, before turning to face Chet. "I'm Knox, by the way. You must be Chet, the foreman." He grabs eight nails, puts them between his lips, picks up a back foot and nails the shoe on. He clearly doesn't care what Chet has to say.

"Yes, I am. And I'll turn the heat down in this hot box if you'll put a shirt on."

Tink tink tink. Knox hammers the nails. "Whatever you say, boss."

It *is* hot in here. I turned on the heat but must have forgotten to check the temperature it was set to. On second thought, this worked out really well for me. I'm enjoying the show immensely—maybe more than I should be. *I haven't been this attracted to a man in a long time.*

Scratch that. I've never been this attracted to a man.

I watch Knox nail on the shoe and notice he has a cross necklace hanging from a chain around his neck. There is a scar going down one of his pecs and the tattoos on his ribs are back numbers, his national finals back numbers.

Could this man get any sexier?

He finishes with that foot and moves to the next. I'm fixated on the way his muscles flex and—

A throat clears. I blink and look up. I'm not sure how long I've been staring at the man, but he's definitely noticed.

Oops.

"You okay there, Kace? You look a little warm."

I can feel it now, my face *is* red. On instinct, I bring a hand up to my cheek and can feel it's on fire.

He gives me a smirk that would make the devil weep, and I have to stop myself from clenching my thighs together. I should not be this turned on—he hasn't even touched me.

"Um, yep. I'm good. Here, Carson, I can take over." I take my coat off and walk up to the dun.

Carson looks at me, then he looks at Knox, shakes his head, and walks away.

Great. I'm sure I'll hear about this exchange later.

Knox finishes the dun, and I get another horse out for him. Chet has left and Knox still hasn't put a shirt on. I guess it's my lucky day.

"So, how was yesterday without me? Lonely? Depressing?" he asks with a smirk.

I scoff. He is so full of himself.

I've been reserved around him until now, but he's about to find out I can give it right back. I was raised on a ranch full of cowboys, after all.

"Actually, it was great. We worked some cattle and, in the evening, I had dinner plans." I watch him swing his hammer and miss, nearly smashing his thumb in the process. His shoulder muscles tense.

He doesn't look at me. "Dinner, you say?"

If I didn't know any better, I'd say he's jealous.

I hear the side door open and shut.

"Holy hell, it's hot in here!" My dad yells as he walks in. "You expecting Satan to come to town or what?"

"Sorry, I had the heat turned up a little high. Knox was complaining about it being cold. The Okie can't handle anything under seventy degrees."

Dad looks him over and says, "Son, I don't mean to tell a man what to do, but you probably wouldn't be so cold if you had a shirt on."

I snort a laugh.

"I was not—" Knox shakes his head and sighs, giving me a sideways glance. "Never mind." He grabs his shirt to put on.

Bummer.

Dad walks up, looking at the gelding's feet and bends over to pick one up as he says, "These look real pretty. You do a good job. Maybe better than Jack."

Knox laughs. "Thank you. I cannot wait to tell him you said so."

"Well now, don't go ratting me out. You're only in town for a few weeks. I'll need him to come back after you leave."

He sets the foot down and heads for the door. "Family dinner tonight, Kacey. I'm grilling steaks. You come, too, Knox. You might want a jacket though, the house is only set to sixty-eight." He doesn't give either of us a chance to reply before he walks out the door.

What. The. Hell. Why did Dad just invite Knox to dinner?

"Umm, sorry about him. That was less of an invitation and more of a demand. You don't have to come if you don't want to."

"I want to," is all he says before going back to work.

I pull out my phone to text Jessie.

Kacey

Please tell me you have tonight off.

Jessie

I'll be getting off a long shift. I plan to head home and fall into bed. Why?

Kacey

Knox has been shoeing horses shirtless all day and my father just invited him to dinner. I need you to come.

Jessie

Hot. Take a picture.

Jessie

I'll be there. Make me a pot of coffee.

Jessie

And hide his shirt until I get there.

Kacey

I am not taking a picture or hiding his shirt. You're insane.

Kacey

Best I can do is make sure there's coffee.

Jessie

Fine, I'll text Carson and ask for a picture.

Kacey

Good luck with that.

I put my phone away and check on Knox's progress. He's bent over working on a back foot. I have the perfect view of his ass in his Cinch jeans from this angle. I guess this is a good consolation prize, since he put his shirt back on.

After we finish the horses and work with Buck for a while, Knox heads back to his apartment to shower. I finish chores before running to my house to do the same, hoping to beat Knox back to my dad's.

I spend far too long picking an outfit. Normally, I could give two shits about what I wear, but Knox has me on edge. He's lodged himself in my mind, and I can't shake him loose. Working shirtless today and the way he smiles at me when we're working with Buck doesn't help. This is supposed to be a no-pressure, just-for-fun, kind of thing, but I'm starting to feel like I could have feelings for him and it's scaring the shit out of me.

On the bright side, he's coming to family dinner, and our family isn't exactly normal. With Jessie and Carson bickering, they're bound to scare him off.

It's not far from my house to Dad's, so I decide to walk, and Rein jumps off my porch to follow me. The walk gives me a few minutes to think, and of course, I think about Knox. It's honestly annoying how much I've been thinking about him. It's not just the fact that he's good looking—like, really good-looking—but he's one of those people who draws you in. I feel comfortable around him. I've never felt like he was judging me or putting me up to some standards I'll never measure up to.

I'll admit, when Carson said no to the foreman job—*again*—I really thought my dad would ask me, but he didn't. He didn't even tell me he was looking at hiring someone off the ranch, Chet just pulled in one day with no warning. If I'm being honest with myself, I think a lot of my insecurities come from that. I do a good job on this ranch and wasn't even given the opportunity for foreman. My trust issues with men, on the other hand, are all Garrett's fault.

The foreman job isn't something I've ever brought up to my dad. I probably should, but I don't know how to say it without sounding like the spoiled rancher's daughter who expects things handed to her. I've never wanted anything handed to me—I'm willing to work for it. Maybe there is something I should be doing that I'm not. Maybe I need to take more responsibility on the ranch, but I just can't see it.

When I walk in the back door to Dad's kitchen, Carson and Jessie are standing by the coffeepot and Chet is sitting at the bar.

"What is Chester doing here?" I ask no one in particular.

"Your dad invited me. Is that a problem?" he replies snarkily.

Carson steps in to buffer, as he often does. "Can you two just not for one night? Knox is going to think you're all feral."

Oddly enough, he's never seemed to have any issues with Chet. Hell, they almost act like friends half the time, as much as two grown men who speak in half grunts and cowboy lingo can be.

Just then, we hear someone walking up the back porch steps. When Jessie catches sight of Knox, she immediately grumbles. "Damn. He put a shirt on."

Carson sighs and rubs his eyes with his thumb and forefinger. "Like I said, *feral*."

Knox opens the screen door. "Sorry, I wasn't sure what door to come to and I heard voices."

Pushing off the counter, Carson replies. "You're good, come on in. Just leave the door open in case Jessie needs out. She isn't quite house broken."

Chet smothers his laugh behind his hand, but I don't attempt to smother mine.

"Me?! That's rich coming from you. I remember your thirty-third birthday when you—"

"Steaks are on," my dad announces, cutting Jessie off.

Thank god, because I also remember Carson's thirty-third birthday.

"Knox, how do you want your steak cooked? I know how the rest of you kids like it."

"Well done, please," is his quick reply.

The entire kitchen goes silent. I'm pretty sure Rein just whimpered from outside. It is so quiet for so long, I can hear the wind outside in the trees and—yep, that's a cricket.

"I'm messing with you. Rare to medium rare, please." Knox finally says with that same shit-eating grin.

Everyone talks at once.

"I was going to throw him out."

"First the shirt, and now the steak."

"Who invited him?"

Dad laughs while he grabs two beers out of the fridge, handing one to Carson. "Anyone else want one? We have beer or whiskey."

"Ooh, pour some whiskey in this coffee," Jessie says before turning to Knox. "Hi Knox, nice to see you again. I heard you don't handle the cold well."

Dear lord. She is about as subtle as a foghorn. Why not just say, 'Hi Knox, Kacey texted me and told me she was drooling all over you today'?

Dad picks up the whiskey to hand it to her, but Carson intercepts him. "Oh no, this is the last thing she needs."

Knox ignores Jessie and holds out his hand. "I think I might need it." This makes my dad and Carson laugh. It looks like Knox will be able to handle Jessie just fine.

She frowns. "Rude. I just worked a thirteen-hour shift that included an old man running down the hallway butt ass naked screaming 'the aliens are in the ocean!' If anyone needs that, it's me."

Carson and Chet talk at the same time.

"You're an alien from the ocean," Carson grumbles, naturally.

Chet is dead serious when he says, "There are aliens in the ocean. I watched a Netflix documentary about it."

We all look at Chet like he's grown another head, except for Knox, who doesn't seem bothered while pouring himself a drink.

This, Jessie notices. "Knox, you're pretty quiet over there. You know something about the aliens?"

"Nope, only the same thing Chet knows. My traveling partner made me watch that documentary while we were on an all-night drive. Supposedly, we have their bodies and technology, but I don't buy it considering Southeast Oklahoma still has no cell service."

"I wonder if they're hot." Jessie tilts her head, pondering.

Dad looks at Carson and says, "You were right about the whiskey," before walking outside to flip the steaks.

Jessie and I get the side dishes ready while the boys set the table and move everything into the dining room. When we all sit down to eat, I end up sitting next to Knox after Jessie practically threw me on the floor when I tried to sit by Carson.

We've all started to eat when he leans over and whispers, "Is this dinner better than last night's?"

Ha, I knew he was jealous. "Oh, I don't know, last night was pretty good," I say nonchalantly.

"What was pretty good?" Carson asks from across the table.

"Her dinner last night," Knox answers him before I can.

Jessie, who apparently has *elephant ears* at the other end of the table, chimes in, "Oh yeah, Gran makes *the best* chicken and noodles. Plus, she made us cookies to go."

"Gran made cookies, and you didn't bring me any?" Carson says with a frown.

"Gran?" Knox questions me with an eyebrow raised.

Shit. Busted.

Thankfully, my father, who is clueless to this conversation, interrupts. "The Smiths are hosting an open rodeo next week. They're raising money for the local women's shelter. I figured a few of us should enter. It's for a good cause."

I give my full attention to my dad, purposefully not making eye contact with Knox, but I can feel his eyes on me, and I know there is a smirk on his face.

Chet swallows. "I can calf rope. Carson, Kacey, you want an afternoon off to rope?"

"Yeah, we can do that," Carson answers for us. He knows my answer will always be yes to a roping.

What I don't expect is Knox. "It's been a while, but I can team rope if I've got a partner. Cody?"

Chet glances at him, definitely not buying what he's selling.

However, my dad is. "We could do that. I'm best on the heels, are you good with heading?"

"Yep, I'll turn 'em, you heel 'em. We should probably practice before."

Dad chuckles. "Yeah, we wouldn't want to ruin your rodeo star cowboy reputation."

Now that I think about it . . . "I'm pretty sure Lainey is serving coffee and pastries at the event, so at least we'll have good snacks."

Carson swallows his beer down the wrong pipe and starts coughing. He must have swallowed a lot, he's practically choking.

Dad looks at him, concerned.

Jessie laughs. "You're supposed to drink the beer, not inhale it."

"Who's Lainey?" Knox asks.

I'm still watching Carson choke when I reply, "She owns Plot Twist in town. She sells coffee, pastries, and books."

"Oh that does sound good. Sounds like it will be a fun day."

"Shirts are required, though," Chet quips.

Knox smirks but doesn't reply.

Jessie snorts. Literally *snorts*, like a pig. "You sure know how to suck the fun out of something, don't you, Chester? Maybe I'll take the day off and join. Mix things up a bit for you."

He sighs. "Please don't."

But she most definitely does.

Chapter 16

Kacey

I'm the last one at Dad's. I wanted to stay and help him clean up. We're hand washing and drying the last of the dishes when he says, "You and that bull rider are spending a lot of time together."

Oh great, here we go.

I shrug. "I mean, he's our temp farrier and training Buck, so I don't really have a choice."

He gives me a look that says, *"I'm your father—don't bullshit me."* I think because my mom died when I was so young, my dad picked up some of those extra mom senses. It's not like I'd ever go into detail about men I'm dating, but we're close—closer than most fathers and daughters.

I sigh, relenting. "Yeah, we've spent some time together. He's nice. It's been nice. Okay?"

"Okay, Bug. That's nice." He chuckles, using my childhood nickname.

"I know I haven't really dated since, well, you know. And I don't plan to date Knox, but it's nice having someone to spend time with."

"You know, if you want to date Knox—or anyone—you can, right? Not everyone is like Garrett."

It took a while before my dad found out what happened between Garrett and me. I finally told Carson he could tell him. I was too broken-hearted and embarrassed to tell him myself, so I wasn't there, but I know he didn't react well. What father would?

I take a deep breath before replying. "Yeah, I know, but he's leaving soon, anyway."

"Just for a few months. He could always come back if he had something worth coming back for. And you, my girl, are worth coming back for." He wraps one arm around me, giving me a quick hug.

I walk out the back door and notice Rein isn't here.

That's weird. She always waits by the door for me. Maybe she got bored and headed home.

When I round the corner of the house, I see exactly where my traitor of a dog is. Right next to *him*. \

He's leaning against his truck, wearing his signature Cinch jeans, black henley shirt, and ball cap. He looks like a cover model for one of those cowboy romance books Lainey reads all the time. His muscles are pulling at the shoulders and sleeves of his shirt. As his light brown curls—like always—peek from under the hat, curling up around the band.

I want to run my fingers through them.

"I thought you left," I say as I walk up, bending to pet Rein.

"It's a nice night. I figured I'd walk you home, like a gentleman." His tone is cautious, and he's watching me, trying to gauge how I feel.

"Oh. Okay. That would be nice." The butterflies in my stomach have me stumbling over my words and regretting that last glass of whiskey.

Who does this, though? What man stands outside, waiting for a girl, so he can walk her home when it's her family ranch and she lives a quarter mile away? This man, apparently.

He says nothing, just whistles at Rein, and we head toward my house, gravel crunching under our boots. Moonlight is the only source of light on the lane.

The walk is quiet. We don't talk, but we don't need to. The sky stretches wide above us, but the open air does nothing to steady my quick, nervous breaths. I can feel his body heat next to me in the cool night air. I feel his eyes flick over to me every few seconds. When the wind shifts, I smell bergamot with a touch of leather and sandalwood. I suppress a moan.

Damn, he smells good. Has he always smelled this good?

I feel myself leaning toward him before I catch myself and jerk away.

Knox tenses and puts his hands in his pockets but says nothing.

I refocus on the gravel lane winding ahead of us.

Rein, oblivious to the tension, runs ahead of us, then circles back, then runs ahead again.

He walks me all the way to my door before I finally find some words. Not the words I was expecting, but words, nonetheless.

"So, what would a gentleman do now?" I turn to face him, coming a step closer than I should. I blame the two glasses of whiskey and whatever heaven-made cologne he's wearing.

He gazes down at me, always looking into my eyes like he's searching for something. "You want me to tell you what a gentleman would do? Or what I would do?" His voice has a raspy edge to it.

I attempt to swallow my nerves, and his gaze drops to my throat. His eyes flare as he tracks the movement.

"Are you saying you aren't a gentleman?"

He smirks, drawing my eyes to his mouth. "Oh, sweetheart, you have no idea what I am."

"What would *you* do?"

Ye*p, it's definitely the whiskey making me this brave.*

He reaches out, his fingers lightly grazing my wrist, setting my skin on fire. "Well, first, you would invite me inside." He starts to run the pads of his fingers up my arm, painfully slow. "Then, I'd ask you how your day was. You'd tell me all about the things you did and what happened." His hand has reached my shoulder now, and I have goosebumps that have nothing to do with the chill in the night air.

"Then what?" I ask, my voice sounding breathier than expected.

His fingers inch toward my neck. "Then I would pull you into my arms, tell you how beautiful you are, and kiss you. You'd moan into my mouth and push your hips into my hardening cock."

Oh my gosh.

I thought men only said things like that in books. It's like a switch has flipped in this man and this isn't a game I'm going to win. I'm not sure I want to win if losing means his hands stay on me. I'll gladly lose all day.

His other hand comes to rest on my hip, and I hear my breathing speed up. I start to lean into him. I'm clenching my thighs together and feel the moisture building between my legs.

"Then what?" I'm like a parrot repeating the same question over again, but I can't help myself. For as much as I've tried to keep my distance from this man, I'm failing miserably tonight, and I'm not sure that I care.

He cups the back of my head. "Then, I'd tell you good night." He drops his hands as a smirk crosses his face. "Goodnight, Kace."

Uh, excuse me? My brain must be short-circuiting. Wait, what just happened?

He turns and walks down the steps as I huff out an angry breath. He just turned me on, then walked away.

Fine. Fuck. Him.

I don't respond as I go inside and slam the door.

Joke's on him, because I don't need him.

I march to my bedroom, rip open my nightstand drawer, and pull out my favorite vibrator.

Heading back into the living room, I find my favorite smut book in one of the stacks of books. I rip my jeans off and lay down on the couch. I don't need him. I haven't needed a man in a long time. I'm perfectly capable of fulfilling my own needs.

I open the book and flip to my favorite part; I know the chapter by heart. Turning on my vibrator, I start reading and working it up and down my clit. I slide it inside and moan when I hit just the right spot.

But when I close my eyes, it's not the book character I see, it's Knox. I imagine him shirtless, his arm muscles tightening as he grips my hips and slams into me. He whispers how perfect my pussy is, and heat consumes me. He picks up his pace as I beg for more. I reach up and pull his face down to—

Knock, knock.

I yelp—loudly—dropping my book and jerking the vibrator out. It slips and falls on the floor. I flip over onto my side to reach down and grab it, but I didn't realize how close I was to the edge of the couch. I fall onto the floor with a thud and a very unladylike grunt.

Knock, knock.

"Are you okay?" I hear Knox ask from outside.

I curse and sit up to grab the vibrator. Only it's not there, I can hear it, but I can't see it.

Oh shit, oh shit.

It's under the damn couch! I'm scrambling onto my stomach, trying to reach under and grab it.

Bvvvvt. Bvvvvt. Bvvvvt.

It's like this is the world's loudest vibrator.

Surely, he can't hear it through the door, right?

"Kace? What's that noise? Are you okay?"

Okay, apparently he *can* hear something through the door. "Uh, yeah. One sec!"

What is he doing back here, anyway? Did he change his mind? Because I can leave this vibrator under the couch if he wants to—I got it!

I pull it out and shut it off. Throwing my jeans back on as I jump across the living room toward the door, cursing my open floor plan house.

"Yeah. Hey, hi," I say breathlessly as I barely crack the door open, holding the vibrator behind my back. I know my face is beet red, I can feel it.

"Um, you okay?" he asks, trying to peek behind me into the house.

All I can do is nod.

"Okay, well, I forgot to ask if you wanted to trim more broodmares this week. I should have some extra time."

Well, that totally could've been a text. "Yep, that would be great. Anything else?" I brush some hair out of my face with the non-vibrator hand.

This is what my life has come to. Perfect.

He glances down at the arm tucked around my back and smirks at me.

The man *smirks*. I have a sinking feeling in my gut that he knew exactly what I was just doing.

"Nope, that's it. Have a good night," he says, but he doesn't turn to leave. He just stands there, smirking at me.

How has this gone from one of the best days—shirtless, sweaty Knox—to the worst day—vibrator under the couch—in a matter of a few hours? I'll never be able to show my face around him again.

"Okay, night." And with that, I shut the door and leave him standing on my porch.

I head back to the couch, only to find my mood has drastically changed.

So much for fulfilling my own needs.

Chapter 17

Knox

I back my truck up to the barn and drop the tailgate so I can unload my tools.

We're trimming more broodmares today and I think Kacey is avoiding me. I haven't seen her for two days. She texted me two lame excuses for why she couldn't help with Buck, and I probably shouldn't find it funny, but I do. I don't know what went on behind that front door the other night, but I have a pretty damn good idea. She was adorable answering the door, hair messed, cheeks red, and clearly flustered.

I'm not playing games with her. I didn't leave her standing on her porch clenching her thighs, eyes burning with desire for fun. I want her to admit she wants me as badly as I want her. I could feel the tension as I walked her home. We've spent a lot of time together, and I feel like I've gotten to know her better over the last few weeks. I don't know if she could handle the rodeo season, but I like her enough to see where this goes.

As I walk around my truck, I hear the crunching of gravel and look up to see Kacey walking in my direction. A red flash comes out of nowhere and flies past her, headed right for me.

I crouch. "Hi, Rein." I pat my palms on my knees as the red dog barrels toward me and jumps in my lap, almost knocking me over as I rock on my heels.

"I don't know why, but she seems to like you."

"I mean, what's not to like? I think I'm great." I smirk up at her, noticing the glare she's already directing at me and her dog.

"You sure don't lack confidence, do you?"

"Nah, confidence is key. You know, being a bull rider and all." I give Rein one last pet before turning to face her owner.

"Buck switched leads smoothly in a figure eight yesterday. You'll have to ride him later; he's really coming along. How was hauling cattle with Carson? Everything go smoothly?" That was one of the excuses I got. And I bought it. Until Carson walked by the arena, heading to work on one of the ranch trucks. Kacey was nowhere in sight.

"It was fine."

"That's good. Hope he got that truck fixed he was working on all afternoon, too. Busy guy." I raise a brow at her.

She shuffles on her feet before looking up to see the grin split across my face.

She scoffs and hits my upper arm, shoving me to the side. "You're an asshole."

I can't help but laugh, which seems to only irritate her more. "What did I do?"

"You know what you did." She glares at me, crossing her arms.

"I am completely innocent. I'm practically an angel."

"So was Lucifer," she grumbles under her breath. "Pull a stunt like that again, and you'll regret it."

She's cute when she's mad. Her nose is scrunched up, her eyes flashing with a mix of frustration and determination.

"Oh, is that so, sweetheart?" I cross my arms back at her and step into her space.

"Don't 'sweetheart' me," she huffs, but leans into me, our arms touching now. "You think you're so smooth, don't you?"

I say nothing, only giving her a crooked grin and a wink. She sidesteps to walk around me, but I grab her waist and pull her in until we're chest to chest. "Sweetheart, I never think about myself when I'm around you. There's no time with all the thoughts of you running through my mind."

I can see the heat flare in her eyes when she looks up at me. Right before they flick to my lips.

Then, she jerks away from me. "Ugh! Why do you always smell so good?" she yells as she stomps toward the barn.

I throw my head back and let out a roar of a laugh.

This is going to be a fun afternoon.

Kacey gets the first mare out to trim.

"You sure are cute when you get fired up, you know that?" I ask before I bend to pick up a front hoof.

"Speaking of fires, you know you shouldn't pour gasoline on them, right?"

"Yeah, but I like to live on the wild side." I smirk up at her before I get to work, pulling my hoof knife through the frog of the foot.

Several hours and a couple of very angry broodmares later, we're finally on the last one. Suddenly, the sound of rustling in a stall and hooves hitting boards catches my attention.

"Sounds like a horse is trying to roll in their stall. Do you want to go check and make sure they aren't cast?"

I've seen a few horses get cast. They'll lay there, stuck on their side or back, thrashing around, until they finally kick themselves away from the wall they rolled too close to so they can stand. Or until someone finds them and pulls them away from the wall.

"Yeah, I probably should. Last thing I need is a hurt horse." Kacey hands me the lead to the mare and walks down the alley. "It's just Hooch trying to roll." She smooches at him and he must get up because she comes back and takes the lead again.

I finish the foot, and as I set it back on the concrete, we hear Hooch trying to roll again.

Kacey leads the mare to an empty stall. "Can you go look at him?"

I walk down to his stall, put his halter on, and lead him down the alley to her. He's a little gaunt and the droop in his ears is noticeable. "Think he's colicky?"

"He kind of acts like it. I agree that he isn't feeling good; I better treat him. I don't want him to twist a gut from rolling too much. I'll go get some Banamine if you want to walk him around until I get back?"

"Yeah, no problem." I walk him out to the round pen, and he tries to lie down as soon as we step into the sand. I pulled on his lead. "Come on, bud, you have to keep moving."

Kacey returns, and we give him the medicine. She tries to convince me I don't need to stay, but there is no way I'm leaving her here with a colicky horse by herself all night. We take turns walking him around, stopping every ten minutes to see if he wants water.

I hear the gate to the round pen open.

Kacey suggests, "We can probably put him on the walker now. We'll just keep an eye on him."

I walk him out to the walker and clip his halter to a lead coming off one of the arms.

Kacey flips the switch, and the machine turns on, leading Hooch around and around.

We both climb a nearby panel and sit on the top rung right as headlights shine around the barn, landing on us.

Cody pulls up and holds out two paper bags. "Figured you two might want some burgers. How's Hooch?"

"He drank a little water. We're just waiting now."

"Good. Well, if you need me, let me know." He drives off and we both inhale our burgers.

It's late, and after trimming those mares I've been starving.

We wait another hour before putting Hooch back in his stall. It's late now, but I grab a hay bale and place it across from him so we can keep an eye on him. Thankfully, the barn is warm. We both drop onto the bale with heavy sighs. I can tell Kacey is exhausted. I know she worked all day before we trimmed the mares, and she did chores earlier while I walked Hooch.

She leans her head back onto the stall behind us. "You didn't have to stay all night, but thanks."

"I don't mind. I enjoy spending time with you. Helping you isn't a chore, Kace. It's something I want to do."

"You mean that, don't you?" Her voice is quiet as she turns to face me.

"Every word," I reassure her.

We slip into silence, and a few minutes later, I hear her breathing slow. She's fallen asleep. When her head softly leans into my shoulder, I slip my arm behind her, gently holding her. Even though her hair is messy and her clothes are dirty, she's beautiful. Her blonde lashes rest on her cheeks; her lips sit slightly parted.

She catches me off guard when her arm crosses over and she slips her hand into mine.

I don't move, I don't even breathe for several seconds, but she doesn't stir. She's sound asleep. I don't think she's even aware she did it. I could sit here like this until the sun comes up. The more time I spend with her, the more I want—her attention, her thoughts, her body.

And a few minutes later, right before I start to fall asleep, I come to the startling conclusion that even though I said it, I don't want her to *find someone better to date*. I'm ready to take my no-girlfriends rule and chuck it out the window.

I want Kacey Hart, and I'll do whatever it takes to get her.

Chapter 18

Kacey

I'm warm and comfortable. That's the first thing I think when I begin to slowly come out of my sleep haze. As I open my eyes, I realize I'm still in the barn, facing Hooch's stall where he stands, sound asleep. The sun peeks in the windows as I lift my head off—Knox?

Oh shit. I fell asleep on Knox. And he stayed here, holding me. *All night.*

I look down and see we're holding hands. *When did that happen?* He's like a furnace with his other arm wrapped around me, keeping me warm.

He's still asleep, his breaths deep, body completely relaxed. I take a moment to study his facial features. It feels funny to say a man is beautiful, but he is. His defined jawline with his short, trimmed facial hair, eyebrows and lashes a shade darker than his hair. Curly hair that flips up around the band of his baseball cap. Now that I think about it, I've never seen him in a cowboy hat, but I'd like to.

There is something about a man in a cowboy hat.

Gently, I start to pull my hand from his, but he stirs.

"Hey, what time is it? How's—" He doesn't finish when he looks up and sees Hooch standing in his stall sleeping. It's a good sign; he's feeling better.

Clearing my throat, I pull my hand from his and sit up. "Sorry, I didn't mean to fall asleep. I can't believe we slept here. You should have woken me up."

He cracks a yawn and stretches his arms out before smiling at me. "It was worth it."

I don't know how to respond to that. I've never had a man who cared enough about me to stay up half the night taking care of a sick horse, then hold me while I slept outside of the stall.

When he told me he was staying to help me last night, my immediate reaction was to make him leave. I've walked and medicated colicky horses by myself before. I'm not saying it's fun to manage by myself, but I can do it. I know he knew that. He knew I could handle it alone, but I didn't have to because he's here. He wants to be with me, no matter what we're doing.

His patience and kindness doesn't just extend to horses; he's also extended it to me. I've built up my walls and kept him at arm's length since he's gotten here, but he still shows up every day with a smile on his face, excited to see me. He hasn't pushed me for more; he lets me set the pace of whatever this relationship is between us.

I don't know what to make of it. He's only here for a few weeks... *but he could come back.* That's what my dad said. And when I gave in and Googled him, I learned he's not just a good bull rider, he's a *great* bull rider. With his regular season earnings and sponsors, he's financially set. I'm starting to wonder if he isn't like Garrett. Maybe he doesn't just want me for the ranch and my family's money. Maybe he wants me for me.

It's a startling realization, and I don't fully trust it. Then again, I don't fully trust my own judgment when it comes to men in general. But waking up next to him felt safe; it felt like I belonged there. I stand up from the hay bale to put some distance between us and gather my thoughts.

Hooch opens his eyes and flicks his ears forward to me when I reach his stall. When I don't move to open his stall door, he turns his ass to me, ready to go back to sleep. Pretty ungrateful considering I stayed up most of the night making sure he didn't, you know, *die*. From a tummy ache, of all things. Horses are ridiculously high maintenance.

Hay crunches as Knox stands and joins me. "Looks like he's feeling better," he says from behind me, and I nod my head in response.

We stand in silence for several minutes, watching Hooch doze off again, before Knox's boots scrape across the barn floor and he comes up so close behind me I can smell his bergamot and leather scent wrap around me.

"Your thoughts are pretty loud. Want to share them?"

I turn around to face him, finding his blue eyes studying me. "Not really. I don't think what they're wanting is very wise."

Because what I *want* is to kiss him. What I *want* is to feel his hands on me again. Most of all, what I *want* is to stop having a sinking feeling in my stomach every time I think about letting my guard down around another man. And how Knox might be the one to take that feeling away.

He cocks his head to the side, confused by my statement. But understanding flares in his eyes when my eyes flick down to his lips, and my tongue swipes out to wet my own. His hands are on me in less than a second—one sliding around my hip, one coming up my neck to cup my jaw.

I don't think. I grab the front of his shirt, pull him to me, and kiss him.

He meets me in the middle, his lips finding mine.

And I feel like I've never been kissed before. This is what I've been missing my entire life. His fingers thread into my hair and a rush of heat runs through me. He tilts my head, giving himself better access, before his tongue runs along my lower lip, seeking entry.

I jerk back, breaking the kiss. "Oh my gosh. I'm so sorry. I probably have morning breath, and I just *slept in a barn*." My cheeks turn red with mortification.

Why did I make this our first kiss? I am such an—

His hands move to cup my face, halting my thoughts. "I've been waiting to kiss you since the first day I met you, when I saw your kind smile and green eyes. I don't give a *fuck* about morning breath," he growls before pulling me back in for a searing kiss.

I melt into him and his words. He kisses me like I'm the air he breathes and I kiss him back. This time feels less like discovery and more like an all-consuming need.

If this is how Knox kisses, what would it be like if I surrendered entirely?

We hear a truck pull up outside of the barn, and Knox pulls away. He tucks loose strands of my blonde hair behind my ears. "I better go. I have appointments this morning."

My heart pounds as I try to catch my breath, but my mind catches up far before my body. Before I can stop myself, I blurt, "I don't date."

Knox's eyes go wide for a split second before he masks his surprise with a wicked grin. "I agree. You don't date—anyone but me." He winks as he heads for the door, leaving me stunned in silence. "Whenever you're ready, sweetheart," he calls back before disappearing out the door.

What? That is not what I meant. I can't date him. The sentiment behind his words *whenever you're ready* has a swarm of butterflies taking off in my stomach. I don't know what to do or think. Knox seems genuine, but I can't take the heartache; not again.

But the little voice in the back of my head asks, *what if he doesn't break your heart?*

Chapter 19

Knox

I'm pulling away from my last shoeing appointment for the day and I can't stop thinking about her. I haven't kissed Kacey again, and she hasn't brought it up. I'm trying to be patient. I thought after that kiss, we would turn a corner, and she'd start opening up to me more. And while she isn't keeping her distance from me, she's still holding her thoughts just out of reach. Meanwhile, I can't stop replaying that kiss in my head. I've never felt a connection to someone like that before, and I know she felt it too.

The way her body responded to mine. If someone hadn't pulled up to the barn, I don't know far we would've gone. I'm not sure either one of us could've stopped it. The tension between us has been stretched to the limit for weeks, and we're going to snap. It's only a matter of time.

Today is the open rodeo where I'm roping with Cody. Jack got his cast removed last week and is back to work. so tomorrow, I'll head back to Oklahoma before the summer run starts this coming weekend. If Kacey's going to let me in and try to keep whatever it is we're doing going over the summer, she's going to have to do it soon.

I see the rest of the crew pull into the rodeo grounds right behind me. We all had work to do this morning, so I'm meeting them here and we only have fifteen minutes before the event starts. I climb out of my truck and look around. The arena is set up like most rodeo arenas. Your bucking chutes are on one end with back pens for rough stock; on the other end of the arena are your roping boxes and roping steers.

The smell of horses, cattle, and fair food float through the air. It doesn't get much better than a rodeo in my book. No matter how big or small, for a few hours, it's always the best place in the world.

I walk over to the truck and trailer right as the back door to the truck opens and I hear, "All I'm saying is you sound a little insecure about your masculinity. There is nothing wrong with men barrel racing, but if you can't handle it just say so, it's okay." This, of course, comes from Jessie.

Kacey climbs out next, followed by a very annoyed-looking Chet.

"I am not signing up for barrel racing and it has nothing to do with my masculinity," he grumbles.

Cody gets out of the driver's seat and Carson comes around the front of the truck. They're pouring out of this thing like it's a clown car and with Jessie in it, it just might be.

"Fun ride to town?" I ask no one in particular. Four heads turn to glare at me while one just has a smirk on her face.

"Before Chet, she wanted *me* to barrel race. Watch yourself, she's on one today," Kacey says as she heads for the mid tack on the trailer. Carson passes me without a glance, heading to unload the horses.

Jessie, who apparently came today solely for the purpose of causing mayhem, turns to me. "Hey, bull rider, I hear they're doing a wild cow milking today. I'll go get you, Carson, and Chet signed up."

It's official, this woman is insane. "Whoa, whoa, whoa, there will be no wild cow milking for me. I ride the beef, I don't milk it."

Wild cow milking is an event with teams made of three people. There are haltered wild cows loaded in the bucking chutes, every team already holding onto a long lead when all the cows are released at once. Two guys try to hold the cow still while one guy milks the cow and runs the milk across the finish line. Fastest team wins. It might not sound too hard, but it's normally a complete shit show of people getting kicked, stomped on, and run over. Often only one or two teams get their cow milked. People don't watch it for the milking; they watch it for the wrecks.

Cody sighs loudly as he walks by. "Jessie, he doesn't want to get hurt before the summer run starts and unless you plan on filling in for Carson or Chet on the ranch, they won't be milking anything, either." He gives her a firm paternal look. "Why don't you go find Lainey and get some coffee? We'll meet up with you after the team roping," he instructs.

She lets out a dramatic huff. "You guys are no fun. But I don't ranch, so I guess I'll go find the coffee. I could use an energy boost, and I know she keeps some Bailey's in the back." Jessie skips off toward the stands on the other side of the arena. Her long red hair flicking behind her in the sun, like a waterfall of flames.

Carson ties the last horse to the trailer and turns to Cody. "Good job, the last thing that tornado needs is more caffeine."

"You want to milk a cow? I can call her back," Cody says as he starts to saddle his horse.

I get to work saddling the dun I'm borrowing.

Once we're saddled, we head for the warmup pen. I can hear Cody Johnson's "Where Cowboys Are King" playing over the sea of cowboy hats. Everyone is laughing and having a good time. It seems like the Hart crew knows every single person here. After shoeing horses around here for six weeks, I even know a few.

The Diamond Hart Ranch and Cottonwood Valley have started to feel like home without even realizing it. Spending time at the ranch every day, meeting the locals, and participating in community events feels good. This isn't something I've ever really felt back in Oklahoma. Outside of my family and the few rodeo friends I have, I don't have any strong ties to a community.

We're stopped by a dozen people to talk before we finally get warmed up for the team roping. As we head for the boxes I ride up next to Kacey.

"Hey, how about we make this a little more interesting? Care for a wager?"

She turns in her saddle, her blonde braid flipping behind her. She has a gleam in her eye when she grins at me. "What'd you have in mind?"

"Three questions, three honest answers. No half answers and no passing on a question."

"Alright, you're on. You're going to lose though you know that, right? You and Dad have roped together twice, Carson and I do this all the time." She sounds confident, but I can tell by her face she's taking this seriously. I've done my share of heading and Cody is just as good of a heeler as Kacey. She watched us practice last week—we have a real shot at beating them if we have a good steer.

"May the best roper win," I say with a smirk and a wink I know will turn her face red.

Kacey and Carson are up first. Cody and I watch, sitting on our horses, as she backs into the box, more focused than I've ever seen her. She really doesn't want to lose. Carson calls for the steer and gets out clean, takes three swings and catches both horns. Kacey is right on its heels when Carson turns the steer. She swings and catches both hind legs. They pull their ropes tight, and the clock stops at 5.3 seconds.

That's a damn good time. I turn to Cody. "No pressure or anything, but I would really like to beat them. How does five seconds flat sound to you?"

Cody laughs loudly and replies. "I like the way you think."

Kacey and Carson trot back to us, and before she even gets into ear shot, I can tell by the look on her face that she has something smart-mouthed to say.

"Well, boys, second place is all yours if you want it," she says confidently.

I like this version of her. I still want to beat her, and I will, but I like seeing her in her element.

Carson is wearing a bigger smile than I've ever seen. Smug bastard.

I look at Kacey. "We'll see about that. I have old age on my side."

"Hey!" Cody exclaims, feigning offense.

"I mean *experience*, it's a compliment." Everyone chuckles as Cody and I head for the box.

Over the last week, I spent time with Cody getting ready to rope. I have a lot of respect for him and what he's built at the ranch. He shared with me how he had to think outside of the box and build other streams of income to keep the ranch going. I can see where Kacey gets her critical thinking.

I never talk to my dad, so it was nice to spend some time with Cody and discuss life. He asked a lot about my career goals, and life in general. You can tell by talking to him he cares about the people around him—his daughter, most of all. He mentioned more than once how proud he was of her for her roping and work on the ranch.

Cody and I back our horses into the box. I look over to make sure he's set and ready, then take a deep breath, just like I do before I nod my head on a bull. I call for the steer.

Shit, I'm late.

Fuck it, I swing twice and reach, throwing the loop out over the steer. I catch both horns, pull my slack and turn the steer.

Cody, being the old pro he is, was not late. He has thrown his loop before I can even glance back. He dallies off and I turn to face, stopping the clock.

5.1 seconds.

No way.

Kacey must be fuming. I was late leaving the box, and we still beat them.

This is a great day.

Chapter 20

Kacey

You've got to be fucking kidding me.

Not only was I right about the cowboy hat—the man could make a vegan crave beef—but it was 5.1 seconds, and he was *late* leaving the box? My dad will never let me live this down, and I'm terrified of what three questions Knox will ask. Maybe he'll stick to basic stuff like "When's your birthday?" and "What's your favorite food?"

I audibly groan and lean back in my saddle. It definitely won't be questions like those.

"It was a lucky loop; we'd beat them nine out of ten times," Carson says next to me scratching the days-old scruff on his face.

"I didn't need to beat him nine times. I needed to beat him *this* time. We may have had a small bet," I admit. I'm sure the look on my face isn't very sportsmanlike. I hate losing, and with the bet, this was the last one I wanted to lose.

Carson's eyebrows raise. "Care to share what that was?"

"It's not a big deal. I just have to answer three questions honestly."

His look of surprise turns to concern. "I've seen you two together . . . you sure you know what you're doing there?"

"Nope, not at all." I say honestly, right as Dad and Knox ride back up to us.

"Well Bug, looks like the old man and a bull rider just showed you two how it's done." He lets out a gruff chuckle, clearly proud of himself.

"Not to toot my own horn but, *toot toot!*" Knox says, with a smile on his face as he makes a fist pumping action like he's an actual train conductor.

I roll my eyes, fighting my own grin. Bull riders and the one thing they never lack: confidence. That, or they're just plain cocky.

"That was the luckiest loop I've ever seen."

"Nah, sweetheart, I'm just that good."

We watch the rest of the roping before heading back to the trailer to tie the horses up. We ended up third and fourth overall, so at least Knox can't brag about winning the whole thing.

After we get the horses unsaddled, and tack put away, we make our way back to the arena to watch Chet calf rope. Carson splits off to see if he needs help at the roping chute. Right before Dad, Knox, and I reach the grandstands, a man and three little boys approach us.

"Are you Knox Ward, the bull rider?" one of the little boys asks. None of them can be older than ten. All three are wearing long-sleeved pearl snap shirts, with jeans, boots and spurs. It's adorable.

Knox puts his hands on his knees to bend down and look him in the eye. "Yeah, little man. That's me."

"Can we get an autograph and a picture?" another boy asks, holding up a permanent marker and grinning ear to ear, one front tooth missing.

"You bet." Knox chats with them, answering their questions, asking what their names are while he signs their t-shirts and one of their straw cowboy hats. "Are you boys going to be bull riders?" he asks them.

"Yes sir, I'm going to be a world champ."

"No way, I am."

"Nuh-uh, I'll beat both of you."

The three start squabbling and Knox chuckles. "Hey boys, you're not in competition with each other, you're in competition with the bull and that eight-second clock. Stay focused on how you're going to get that bull rode. Don't worry about trying to beat anyone, because you won't win anything if you don't ride your bulls."

The three boys look up at him, nodding their heads and replying with *"Yes sir."* Then he gets on one knee and the dad takes a picture of them.

"Thank you for doing that. You just made their day." The dad shakes Knox's hand.

"No problem," Knox says, smiling at the little cowboys.

He's good with kids. *Of course* he's good with kids. I know he has a nephew, but that doesn't mean he's good with kids or even likes them. But clearly he does. He isn't faking interest in his conversation or trying to sign autographs quickly and leave.

"How do we get as good as you, Mr. Ward?" the one with the missing tooth asks.

"You practice every day, even when you don't want to, and you make it your number one priority. Hard work always trumps talent that doesn't work hard."

The boy looks up at the dad. "Can we practice when we get home?"

"Of course, son." He turns to Knox. "It's been a pleasure meeting you, Knox. Good luck this season—we'll be watching."

"Thank you. Good luck, boys. Keep practicing. I look forward to seeing you on TV one day."

I'm getting butterflies watching him. I blame hormones; I must be ovulating. It's definitely not the fact that the sexiest man alive is currently ruffling the hair on the little blonde's head. Or that I can't get that kiss out of my head.

We haven't kissed again, and I haven't said anything about it, or us. I've been trying to sort through my thoughts, but I just don't see a future for us. He's leaving for rodeos soon, and he doesn't even live here. He has a whole other life in Oklahoma to go back home to. I can tell he's waiting for me to say or do something, being patient with me. And I almost asked him what his thoughts were on it all the other day, but I chickened out.

Over the past few weeks, I've spent enough time with him to learn what type of man he is. He's patient, kind, and selfless, always thinking of others before himself. It's rare to find a man who possesses just one of those qualities, let alone all of them.

And it's getting harder to pretend there is nothing between us.

I know he feels it, too, the undeniable spark—of course, I'm attracted and drawn to him in ways I can't ignore. That kiss proved that. But it's become more than that for me, and it scares me. The more I've gotten to know him, the more I could see myself truly falling for him.

I just don't know if he'll catch me.

Just thinking about him leaving makes my stomach churn. He's become a constant in my life over the last six weeks and as hard as I've tried to keep him at arm's length, we've grown closer than I expected. The other night, I texted him about a funny scene in a book I was reading because it made me think of him. I've been finding myself thinking about him a lot lately.

"You get that a lot, superstar?" I ask once we're out of earshot.

In a rare turn of events, it's his cheeks that turn pink, not mine. "Oh, I wouldn't say a lot, but it's not uncommon either."

So that's a yes—he gets it a lot.

Dad heads off to chat with some old friends while Knox and I find Jessie in the grandstands. We haven't been sitting for two minutes when another little boy comes up asking for Knox's autograph and a photo. He's just as genuine as before, asking him questions and smiling for a photo.

After the boy leaves, Jessie pipes up. "Hey, Mr. Hotshot, Kacey has something she wants you to sign."

"Oh yeah? What's that?" He gives her a sarcastic side eye.

"It's not appropriate for a public place, but it rhymes with noobs. And if you're lucky, she might ask for a picture, too."

Knox laughs. I put my face in my hands and groan. Sometimes I wonder why I'm friends with her. But Knox pulls his phone out. "Smile girls, I want proof of how red Kacey's face is right now."

All three of us lean in close and take a selfie, then Jessie snags his phone out of his hand.

"Okay, now just you two. Smile and say *boobs*."

We both laugh and then turn to look at each other, making eye contact. I can hear Jessie snapping away at the camera before she hands him his phone back. He reaches out and takes the phone without breaking eye contact with me. We slid close together for the photo, so now our faces are only inches apart. I can feel the heat radiating off him and when I feel his hand slide up my lower back.

I lean into him.

Is he going to kiss me?

It feels like my heart is about to pound out of my chest when I hear Jessie say, "Oh, he's up! Chet is riding into the box."

I look away first. Then slide back into my seat and try to calm my breathing. I can still feel Knox looking at me before he finally looks away at the sound of the roping chute cracking open.

Chet is actually a way better calf roper than I expected. He was 9.8 for third place.

By the time the calf roping is over, we're all ready for a snack and a drink, so we head to the concessions and run into Carson. Once we've all grabbed something to eat, we make our way to the coffee stand.

Lainey is out front, chatting with a couple of girls while her baristas manage the trailer. She's dressed in a cute sundress with her brunette hair cascading in waves down her back.

"Hey, Lainey, how's business been today?" I ask as we walk up and the other girls wave goodbye.

A smile breaks over her face as she turns toward us. "Hey, gang! It's been great. This is the first break I've gotten all day. I was about to head over to the mini doughnut stand. How did the roping go?"

I see her glance at Knox. Every woman looks at him, and I can't say that I blame them, but an irrational territorial feeling rises up in me. "It was good, we all placed. Knox, this is Lainey, Lainey, this is Knox. He's been shoeing horses for Jack and breaking a colt for us the last few weeks."

Knox takes off his hat and reaches out to shake her hand. "Nice to meet you. I've heard great things about your coffee shop. I keep meaning to stop in one morning."

"Nice to meet you, too. Stop by anytime—the first one is on the house."

Carson stiffens next to me as Lainey shakes Knox's hand, smiling at him.

"Well, I'm off to get some doughnuts. I'll see y'all around. Carson, see you tomorrow."

She heads toward the doughnuts as I turn to Carson. "What's tomorrow? Are you guys friends?"

"No, I just get coffee there a couple of times a week," he clips out, but his eyes follow Lainey as she disappears into the crowd.

Okay, weird. I figured he only got coffee there when I made him stop before ropings.

We all head back to the stands to watch the bull riding. I ask Knox if he wishes he was getting on and he said a little bit, and that he's getting the itch to get back on the road and ride some bulls.

It's clear he loves it. I just wish I had a little bit more time with him before he goes.

Chapter 21

Knox

I almost kissed her. I wanted to kiss her. I think she wanted me to kiss her. But I'm trying to be patient—to let her decide what she's ready for.

I couldn't focus on the rest of the rodeo. I need to know what she's thinking. I'm slowly learning her tells but she's still hard to read sometimes. One minute it feels like she's letting me in, but then two minutes later she's back behind her walls. I could see it in her eyes though, she knows there is more between us. She just needs to be brave enough to give me a chance. I'm supposed to leave tomorrow, and I *need* to know if she feels the same way.

We're walking next to each other, heading back to our trucks, when she stops dead in her tracks. I turn to look at her and she's gone white as a sheet. She looks like she's seen a ghost.

"Well, would you look at that? The Diamond Hart crew," a guy I don't recognize says, walking up to our group. "I don't see y'all around town very often." He's talking to everyone, but he's only looking at Kacey.

She's now looking down at the ground.

"Kacey, good to see you again," he continues, and she doesn't reply.

Carson steps between Kacey and whoever the hell is making her uncomfortable.

I sidestep to angle toward Carson. I can tell by everyone's unfriendly welcome he isn't someone they like.

"Get out of the fucking way, Garrett," Carson snaps at him.

Yep, we definitely don't like this guy.

He's a couple inches taller than me with blonde hair and he's wearing cuffed 13MWZs and a cowboy hat that looks like someone slammed it in a door. I'm going to go out on a limb and guess he's a super puncher and a total douche.

"Aw, come on, Carson. We're all friends, aren't we? I just wanted to see how Kacey is," Garrett replies.

Jessie grabs Kacey by the wrist and starts dragging her around the group of us toward the truck. Even she doesn't pass him without getting a few words of her own in. "Have you ever thought of using glue instead of Chapstick? I know we'd all appreciate it." She smiles sweetly as she passes him.

Have I ever questioned if I like her? Because I'm her biggest fan now.

Once Kacey and Jessie are out of earshot, Carson practically growls at Garrett. "I thought I told you to never fucking talk to her again." He takes a step in his direction and super douche at least has the brains to back up a step. From the set of his shoulders and the way he's balled his hands into fists, Carson looks like he's about ready to throw a punch.

"Come on, Carson. It was two years ago, and I told you it was a misunderstanding."

"Misunderstanding my ass." Carson shoves him out of his way as he heads for the truck. Garrett doesn't retaliate. Probably smart, considering Carson stands over six feet tall and is built like Henry Cavill. I wouldn't mess with him either.

I jog to catch up with him. "Who the hell was that?"

"No one," he bites out.

"It was clearly someone. Kacey's ex?" I guess. He glances at me, then nods once.

"What's the story there?"

He lets out a breath and sounds defeated when he replies. "It's not my story to tell. And douche isn't a strong enough word."

We're back at the truck waiting for Chet and Cody. I can't stop thinking about the look on Kacey's face when she saw Garrett. It was pure hurt and regret. I've never seen her look like that. Looking down at the ground, arms crossed holding her middle, not speaking or standing up for herself. That's not the girl I've gotten to know over the last six weeks.

Sure, she might be quiet sometimes, but it's not because she feels less than or hurt. She speaks when she has something to say, and she keeps her circle small. But the Kacey I know smiles, laughs at my dumb jokes and rolls her eyes at Carson. She's alive.

That girl back there was a shell.

She's sitting on the running board next to Jessie. I can tell Jessie is trying to distract her. She's showing her some video on her phone.

Neither Carson nor I have spoken since we got back to the truck. I don't know what to say. I want to ask her if she's okay and what I can do to fix this. I hate seeing her like this.

Finally, I decide I'm done waiting. I walk over to her. "Come on," I say, holding my hand out to her. "Let's go, I'll drive you home."

She looks at me for the first time since we ran into Garrett. "You don't have to do that, and I don't want to leave Jessie and Carson alone. You know how they are—we'd have to hide a body later." She only half-heartedly delivered that joke, and none of us are buying it.

"Don't worry about us, there's beer in the cooler. Who knows how long your dad and Chet will stand about gabbing? Go home, get some rest." Jessie smiles at her, but it's a sad smile.

Kacey looks over at Carson. He just nods once then looks back toward the arena like he's keeping guard. He probably is.

"Okay." She grabs my hand. "Let's go."

We're a couple miles down the road and she's looking out the passenger window. She hasn't said a word since we left.

I want to reach across the truck and hold her hand. I've never been big on hand holding or other displays of affection, but apparently, I'm a completely different person around this girl.

When we reach the edge of town, I work up the nerve to ask, "Are you okay?" It sounds lame when I hear it out loud, but I don't know what to do. I'm not good at things like this. Shockingly, Trey is actually the one who always has all the right words when people are upset.

She doesn't reply for a long time, and I'm beginning to think she won't when she says, "I'm guessing Carson told you who that was."

"No, but I guessed."

She sighs and turns from the window. "He's my ex. We dated for two years and it ended badly."

"I'm sorry. He seemed like a real douche," I say with more bite than intended.

She huffs out a laugh. "Yeah, you could say that."

I take my eye off the road to glance at her. "I know you have Jessie and Carson, but if you ever want to talk about it, I'm a great listener."

She's looking down, picking at her nails. I barely hear her quiet response. "Thanks."

I pull up to her house and put the truck in park. When I look over, she has her hand on the handle but isn't opening the door. I've learned over the past few weeks while working with her and Buck that she likes to process thoughts internally. Once she has it figured out, she'll share it with me or act on it, but she'll sit and think something through first. I admire her for it. Most people act on impulse or rash snap judgements, but not Kacey. She thinks things through.

When she lets go of the handle, and looks down at her hands in her lap, her voice sounds numb. "He was Mr. Perfect for the longest time. He'd write cute notes, buy me gifts, and work around the ranch. He always knew exactly what to say at the right moment. I thought we'd get married, have kids and build a life together."

I turn in my seat to face her. "What happened?"

She looks out the windshield at the old pine tree, swaying in the wind next to her house, and clears her throat. "He didn't know I was there, the day I overheard him on the phone and found out it was all a lie." Her eyes dart back and forth, like she's reliving it all over again in her head. "I'm still not sure who he was talking to. I walked in to hear him telling someone how I'm nice enough and a good lay, that he can put up with me if it means he gets the ranch someday."

I ball my hands into fists; I can feel my anger at this piece of shit rising. She sucks in a breath before continuing. "He told them he was going to try and get me pregnant. He went as far to say how he had a plan for getting me off birth control so he could try knocking me up. Then he had the audacity to laugh about it to whoever it was he was talking to."

Now I have to reach out and grip the steering wheel to try and stay calm. Carson was right. Douche isn't a strong enough word.

What kind of person does that to someone? Now I wish Carson would've hit him. Hell, I'll hit him, given the opportunity.

"I'd always been pretty good at telling who was interested in me solely because I'm Cody Hart's only child. There aren't many ranches like this—it's extremely financially successful, and someday, it will all be mine—but Garrett was the one I didn't see past. I fell so hard for him. If he would've proposed, I know I would've said yes. I should've known better."

I take a deep breath, letting my anger simmer. "Kacey, look at me, please."

She swallows before slowly turning to face me, finally looking up to meet my eyes.

"I'm so sorry that happened to you. No one deserves that. You are more than this ranch, you understand that, right?"

"Yes. I do now," she whispers. "He didn't care about me at all. He never did. After I overheard him, we had a huge argument. He tried to gaslight me and turn it all around on me, but I knew then all he cared about was trying to be next in line to the ranch." Her voice changes altogether when she says, "It taught me a valuable lesson though." I can tell she's not angry or even sad, she's resigned.

It all makes sense now. This is why she won't let me in, she doesn't trust anyone. And I can't say that I blame her.

"I'm guessing that lesson has something to do with the reason you've kept me at arm's length." I have to say it. I've seen the way she looks at me, she feels it, too. She just won't let herself take the chance.

Her eyes snap to mine before she quickly looks away. "Yes. I haven't dated since. I can't bring myself to trust anyone's intentions." She pauses and looks back to me. "But if I could, I'd want it to be you."

It's on the tip of my tongue to tell her about Megan. About how I don't date either, how her betrayal changed me—broke something inside of me. I wasn't sure I'd ever want to share my life with another woman again, but I realize now I want that with Kacey. I'm not sure when it happened but I do. But now isn't the time to dump all my baggage on her, so I push the thoughts out of my mind.

"You told me once I'm the most patient man you've ever known. I'm patient enough to wait until I've earned your trust, Kace. Thank you for telling me." I open my truck door. "Come on, I'll walk you up." I climb out of the truck and go around to open her door.

She turns to face me when we reach her doorstep. I hold both her hands in mine and look into her eyes. "If you ever need anything, anyone, or even just a chauffeur who will walk you to your door—" This earns me a small smile. "—you can always count on me. I care about *you*, Kacey."

"Thanks, that means a lot. You're leaving soon, aren't you?"

"Yeah, I have rodeos I've entered, and Trey has been waiting for me." I rub the back of her hand with my thumb, dreading telling her goodbye.

She looks down at our hands. "What are you doing tomorrow?"

I was planning to leave tomorrow. It would give me an extra day at home before I leave for the summer. But if she wants to hang out, I can leave the next day. "Not much. I don't have any clients scheduled. I just need to pack and load the truck."

"Would you want to go for a ride? If you have time."

I can see her cheeks turning red and I smile before answering, "Yeah, sweetheart, I've got time." I let go of her hand to cup the back of her head. Pulling her in, I give her a kiss on the forehead. Unlike before, she feels relaxed and comfortable in my arms. Holding her feels right.

"Night, Kace."

"Night, Knox."

I head down the steps and get halfway to my truck before I turn around. "Plus, I have to come back—I have three questions I'm dying to ask you." I give her a wink and hear her grumble something under her breath that sounded a lot like "left late" before turning to head inside.

Chapter 22

Kacey

I give up at 5 a.m. I haven't been able to sleep all night, so I might as well get up and have some coffee. It's either lie in bed and think about Knox or drink coffee and think about Knox.

I choose coffee.

After I make my way to the kitchen and grab a cup along with some fruit, I settle on the couch with my favorite blanket. I've gone over and over my conversation with Knox last night. I can't believe I told him about Garrett. I've only ever told Jessie and Carson, no one else. That alone shows how much of my trust he's already earned in just a few short weeks.

Riding home from the rodeo with him, after spending the day having fun, laughing with him and seeing a glimpse of how things could be if we were together, I felt like he needed to know. It isn't him that's stopping me from giving him a chance, it's me.

Over the last few weeks, he has shown me time and time again that he wants to get to know the real me. Not rancher Kacey, or roper Kacey—just me, Kacey. No matter how many times I tried to create distance, he just showed up again the next day, being the same sweet, kind, and patient man.

I'm still scared to let him in, but I can't completely keep him out any longer, either. I know he's leaving, and I have the world's worst timing, but maybe my dad is right. He could always come back.

Half an hour later I can't sit and think about this anymore. I need to get up and do something productive. I start cleaning my house and doing some meal prep for the next few days before heading to the barn around 7 o'clock for chores. My phone vibrates while I'm prepping grain buckets.

Knox

What time should I come over? I should be done packing by 11. I can grab lunch in town for us if you want.

Kacey

Whenever you're done works. Lunch would be great, thanks.

Knox

Sushi or burgers?

Kacey

Sushi!

Knox

That was a test. You failed

Knox

But I'll get you raw fish so you can risk food poisoning if that's what you want

Knox pulls in shortly before noon and parks in what's become his spot outside the barn.

Sitting on the tailgate of his truck eating, I ask, "How do you not like sushi? It's so good."

I have sushi and he ordered beef pad thai.

He raises an eyebrow at me. "I prefer to eat cooked meat, preferably beef. Not to mention Trey got food poisoning from sushi once. It was gas station sushi though, so that was on him. I had to get him barf bags for the truck; it was gross."

I laugh. "Oh yeah, never trust gas station sushi. *Everyone* knows that."

"If you knew Trey, you would know there isn't much that scares him. It's either because of a lack of brain power or he's extremely brave. I haven't decided which." Knox smiles as he pops the last piece of his beef in his mouth.

We finish eating and grab the horses I had saddled before he got here. We start riding out through the pasture to one of my favorite mountain trails, and it's a beautiful day for a ride. The sun shines over the crest of the mountains as the spring breeze blows past us.

It doesn't get any better than this.

The leather of my saddle creaks as I turn to look at him. "Alright, I know you're dying to ask, so let's have it. What are your questions?"

"Right, I won. I beat you. So, I get three questions. Because I won," he says with the biggest grin on his face.

I roll my eyes. So humble, this one. "Yeah, yeah, live it up, bull rider. It won't happen again."

He thinks about his first question, but it doesn't take him long. "What is your most treasured memory?"

I pause. That wasn't what I was expecting him to ask. Most guys would've asked some dumb, inappropriate question. Leave it to Knox to ask something deeper. I don't need to think about my answer, it's a memory I treasure, and replay in my mind every summer.

"I was six, and Mom and Dad took me to the fair. Back then, we didn't get off the ranch much. Dad was still working long days to keep the ranch afloat, so it was a big deal. I remember sitting in the back seat of the truck and I was so excited. I'd never been to the fair, but Mom told me all about it. She said I could get cotton candy, see all the animals, and ride the rides.

We spent all day there; they walked every barn with me, got me cotton candy, and bought me ride tickets. Dad won me a stuffed animal from one of those rigged carney games and he was my hero for the rest of the day." I look forward, turning Hooch toward the trail, but I can feel Knox watching me. Listening to every word.

"We ended the day by going on the Ferris wheel and I can still remember the way my parents looked at each other and held hands. I didn't know it then, but looking back, they were so in love. I think that's why I love that memory so much."

I often wondered if I'd ever find a love like that, but after Garrett, I gave up on that dream, and some days I wish I hadn't.

There is a soft smile on Knox's face when he replies. "That sounds like the perfect day. You miss your mom a lot, don't you?"

"Every day. I wish she could see the ranch now. She'd be so proud of my dad." Talking about her hurts, but it's good. I wish dad and I talked about her more. I was so little when she died, now I feel like I couldn't really know or remember all of her since I was just a child.

"I bet she'd be proud of you, too." He reaches over and gives my hand a squeeze. "You're an amazing woman, Kacey Hart."

I have to swallow the lump in my throat. Having Knox truly listen and say those words means more to me than he knows. I can tell he's trying to get to know me on a deeper level. I don't think I've ever had a man care enough to even ask about my mom.

"I can't relate with the pleasant Ferris wheel memory, I must admit. My sister and I got stuck on one when we were little. She cried, which made me laugh, but my dad whooped my butt when we got down for laughing at her instead of comforting her."

I try to smother my laugh but fail miserably. "Your poor sister. She's probably scarred for life."

"Oh, for sure. She hasn't been on a Ferris wheel since," he confirms as he shifts in his saddle and looks up at the sky. "It's clouding over fast, and the wind feels like it's picking up, too. Think we should turn back?"

I glance up and sure enough, it's going to rain. Our perfect spring day is gone in minutes—typical mountain weather. "Yeah, we better. You never know how bad it will rain up here."

As we turn our horses around to head back to the barn, I ask, "Alright, so what's question number two?"

His eyes study me for a heartbeat, like he's second-guessing the question on the tip of his tongue. "What's your biggest fear?"

Damn, he isn't holding back on these questions.

"Losing someone else I love. No one is guaranteed tomorrow. We never know how much time we get with someone. I think everyone has a little bit of that fear in them."

"I've never lost someone in the same sense you have, but I agree. Before my dad left, we used to be close. He taught me to shoe horses and even built my first practice barrel. I was seventeen when he left—or maybe 'disappeared' is a better word—and it left a hole for a long time. Our relationship has never been the same."

"I'm sorry. No parent should disappear on their child. No matter how old they are."

It's lightly raining on us now, and we pick up our pace. We kick the horses into a trot, and the closer we get, the harder it starts to rain. Half a mile from the barn, Knox looks over at me, grinning before kicking his horse into a dead run.

Always up for a race, Hooch follows his lead. I ride up next to him and he's laughing as he drops his reins to hold his arms out, looking up into the rain. I can't help but laugh at him.

What does he think this is? The *Titanic*?

We slow as we approach the barn, ride inside, and untack the horses. It's not cold, but when you're soaked to the bone, it gets a little chilly. I throw my saddle on the rack.

"Come on, let's put the horses away and go to my house to dry off. I'm freezing."

As soon as the horses are put away, Knox grabs my hand, and we sprint through the pouring rain to my house. I realize as I open the door that he's never been inside my house. I'm immediately glad I cleaned this morning.

The old ranch house has a surprisingly open floor plan. When you walk in the front door, you're just to the left of the living room and you can see the kitchen behind it. There is a stone fireplace my great grandpa built by hand with stones off the ranch, and my couch sits in front of it. I rarely use the upstairs loft, and my bedroom is down the hall.

"Come on in, I'll grab some towels." I toe off my boots and head for the bathroom, leaving a trail of water the whole way.

When I get back to the living room, he's right where I left him on the entryway tile. I hand Knox a towel and he starts to dry his hair. His jeans are soaked and water drips from the hem of his t-shirt that clings to his chest, showing every cut of muscle underneath.

"I'm going to go change really quick. Do you want to dry your clothes? I think I have some sweats that will fit you while they dry." I don't think I have a shirt that will fit, but that's okay. I have no issues with him going shirtless for the afternoon.

"Yeah, that would be great." He strips off his shirt.

Yep, I have no issues with this at all.

I head into my bedroom and throw on some joggers and a sweatshirt. After digging around for a minute, I find the sweatpants I think will fit him. They're old gray joggers from my trips to Estes with Jessie, oversized on me, but they should fit him.

I head out to the living room and give him the sweats. "The bathroom is down the hall on the right. I'm going to make some coffee to warm up. Do you want any?"

"Sure, that sounds good. Do you want me to start a fire after I get changed?"

I glance over at the fireplace to make sure I have dry wood inside. "That would be great."

After the fire is started, we both settle on the couch as we sip on our coffees. I grab my blanket and cover up while saying, "You have one more. What's your third question?"

He yanks the blanket mostly off my lap to cover up with it. I gasp.

Who does this guy think he is? This is my favorite blanket.

With a huff, I yank it back, then he laughs as he yanks it back to his side. This is a war he won't win. I pull it back and try to tuck it under my feet. He scootches down the couch so he's right next to me before pulling it out from under my feet and covering us both with it.

"What question have you always wanted to ask me?" he asks, like the great blanket battle didn't just happen.

"Ooo, it's like a reverse in UNO," I say, making him chuckle. The question I have is one I've wondered for a while now. "I guess I'm curious what you want your future to look like."

He grabs my feet and pulls them across his lap before answering, "I want to win a gold buckle. Being a world champion has always been my career goal. Outside of that, I don't want anything fancy. I'd like to find some property to build a home on, find the right woman, and settle down, maybe have a couple of kids. And never trim another broodmare again." He winks at me.

I roll my eyes. "Oh please, they aren't *that* bad."

He gives me a look that tells me he thinks otherwise.

"As for your other plans," I continue, "you say it like it's not a big deal, but I think it sounds pretty great. How long do you want to ride bulls for?"

"People ask me that all the time and the truth is, I don't know. I'm thirty now, so I'm getting older for a bull rider, but I still feel like I'm at the top of my game. I figure my body will tell me or I'll wake up one morning and just not want to do it anymore. All the traveling and time on the road gets old. It's hard to maintain relationships and do other things in your life when you're gone so much."

"Is that why you don't date?" I might have done some internet stalking and noticed he hasn't had a girlfriend in years. I watch him closely to see if I've gone too far with my questioning, but he doesn't seem bothered. He's looking straight ahead, watching the flames flick in the fire.

"I used to date, but after my last girlfriend, Megan, and I broke up, I made a rule for myself: No dating until I retire from riding bulls."

"What did she do to make you come up with such a rule?"

"It's complicated. When I was home, we had so much fun, but when I was on the road, she would get upset that I wasn't there for her. It was like she expected me to be in two places at once. She wanted to be with a rodeo cowboy but got upset when I wasn't home. We worked through it, and I was riding so well I went into the finals as number one in the standings." He runs a hand through his damp hair.

"So why did you break up?"

"She came with me to Vegas for the finals and turned into a nightmare. She wasn't even the same person. She insisted on going to every red-carpet event or PR party, even when I was tired and just wanted to go back to the room and rest. She took any chance to be in the limelight, loving the fact that she was with the number one bull rider. But by the end of the finals, I wasn't number one, I was fourth. I only rode two bulls, but I should've easily ridden six. I choked. And she left me—publicly—for another cowboy who rode better than I did."

"I'm so sorry, Knox. That's terrible. You didn't deserve that."

"I know that now, but it took me a while to get my head back on straight. Thankfully, Trey gave me the kick in the ass I needed, but I haven't dated since. I'm not saying I haven't had a few flings, I'm no monk, but I figured I would find someone after I retired from riding bulls. This lifestyle is hard on relationships and it's such a short career. So, I made the no girlfriend rule and decided to keep my sole focus on riding bulls. I've stuck to that rule for years. Until I met you, and now I'm about one kiss away from scrapping it all together."

"But why me? I don't date; I told you that."

He tucks one leg up onto the couch under mine so he can turn and face me. "I know. I heard you, but that hasn't stopped me from thinking about you all hours of the day, from rushing to the ranch to see you and spend time with you. I understand your hesitation—hell, I have my own reservations. You know that now, but I can't stop myself when it comes to you."

His blue eyes are sincere, and I want nothing more than to crawl into his arms and admit I feel the same. I can't stop thinking about him, and I count the hours in the day until I see his truck pull in.

He brings one hand up to cup my face. "I know what I say next is going to scare you because it scares the shit out of me, but I have to say it. I know I'm leaving, but Kace . . . I've never felt so drawn to someone and you might not feel the same way but—"

"I feel it," I blurt out, interrupting him. "But what does it mean for us? You said it, you're leaving, and you don't even live here. Your home is in Oklahoma."

He runs his hand through his hair again, I've learned he does that when he's nervous or frustrated. "I know . . . I don't know what it means. All I know is I want you. Whatever little bit of time we get. And I know that's not fair, but it's all I have to offer."

When our eyes meet, I can see it. The burning desire, the need to touch me and show me how much he wants me. I hope he can see it reflected back in my eyes. I decide at this moment that I don't care how much time we have. We have this moment, and I can live with that. I don't care if he can't commit to a relationship. Hell, I'm terrified of a relationship, anyway.

I climb into his lap and straddle him, putting both my hands on his shoulders. I feel him tense beneath me for half a second, then his mouth collides with mine. It's not a sweet kiss, nor gentle. It's something that has been building since the day we met, and I don't think either of us could stop it if we wanted to. It's all-consuming.

He grips the back of my head with one hand while the other explores every curve. He gets to my hips, and I rock into him, moaning his name.

"Knox."

He breaks the kiss and starts trailing light kisses down my neck. "Say it again."

I know what he wants, and I gladly give it to him when he kisses the spot right above my collarbone. "Knox," I moan and circle my hips, grinding into him again.

His lips meet mine again, and I can feel him through the sweatpants, hard and aching for me.

I run my hands up his chest and fist one hand into his hair. "I need more," I say between kisses.

He grabs the bottom of my sweatshirt and pulls it over my head. I'm not wearing a bra—it didn't seem necessary; the sweatshirt is oversized. I hear him suck in a breath before he flips me onto my back so quickly I don't see it coming.

He looks me in the eyes as he says, "You are the most beautiful woman I have ever seen, Kacey Hart." He runs both of his thumbs lightly along the underside of my breasts. The fire inside of me—the one I've been trying to keep at bay since the first day I saw him—is stoking to life. And I'm ready to let it burn.

I grab him and pull him in for a searing kiss. This man kisses with his whole body. I've never felt more exposed and cherished at the same time. His tongue runs along mine while one of his hands finds the waistband of my sweatpants. "If you want me to stop, tell me. This only goes as far as you want it to."

"Don't stop," is all I say before I kiss him harder.

He slides his hand into my sweatpants and runs a single finger down my center. My hips jerk, and he breaks our kiss. His head falls to my shoulder as he groans. "Sweetheart, you're soaked." He circles my clit with his finger, being careful not to apply pressure where he knows I'm dying to have it. "Did you get wet for me in the barn that day, too?"

"Yes," I pant. "Knox, please." I beg, digging my nails into his back and shifting my hips, looking for the pressure I so desperately need.

"Mm-hmm, I love it when you say please." He finally glides two fingers right where I need them, then moves down, circling one of my nipples with his tongue. "Do you want me to make you come, sweetheart?" he asks, his voice a deep rasp.

"Y-y-yes."

His mouth moves to my other nipple, and I can already tell, this man is going to ruin me for any other.

Chapter 23

Knox

I hadn't planned to spend the afternoon with Kacey naked beneath me, but I'm not about to take it for granted.

After everything she told me on our ride, I finally feel like we're making progress. She's starting to trust me, and I wasn't going to ruin it by seducing her. But she started this, and now I'm determined to see her finish.

When she asked why I didn't date, it was a relief to finally tell her. There was a moment where I was remembering that summer, and I can't think of a single good memory, even when I was number one. Megan always made me feel bad that I wasn't there for her, but in the next breath was so proud and bragged about me to her friends. I was a headcase all summer.

Kacey moans beneath me as thoughts of leaving for the summer and our future—or lack thereof—try to creep into my mind, but I push them out.

I move over to her other breast and lick a slow circle around it. She's breathing quicker and I can feel how wet she is for me. My cock aches, but this isn't about me. I want to see her come apart for me.

She arches her back when I suck it into my mouth. I don't warn her before I slide two fingers inside of her and she clenches tight around me.

"Oh my god, yes," she gasps.

I pump my fingers in and out, but I don't touch her clit. "You're so tight around my fingers . . . and I can't take my eyes off these perfect tits."

I can feel her get wetter at my words.

Good, my girl likes it when I talk dirty to her.

I kiss my way down her body, yanking her sweatpants as I go. She spreads her thighs for me, unashamed of her need, and I love it.

"I can't get enough of you, Kace. Do you taste as good as you feel?" Once I get to her clit, I don't hesitate to find out.

I lick her slowly at first, teasing her before I suck her clit, hard. She bucks her hips into me as I use my other arm to grab her waist and hold her so she doesn't fall off the damn couch. I keep going, working her closer to the edge. "You taste fucking amazing."

"Knox I—" She can't finish her sentence, but I know what she's saying.

I lift my head to look her in the eyes. I can see the protest on her lips before I put pressure on her clit with my thumb and she throws her head back.

"I want to watch you. I need to see you come apart for me."

She moans and rides my hand. It's the sexiest thing I've ever seen.

"Be a good girl and come for me." I grab one of her nipples and roll it between my fingers.

She gets so tight on my fingers it makes my dick twitch. I can feel her start to pulse and she's dripping wet.

"That's it, sweetheart. You're so beautiful."

She grabs my arm that's playing with her tits and digs her nails in. She moans my name and rides my hand as her orgasm rips through her. I keep pumping my fingers and lean down for a kiss while she rides it out. I could watch her come all day.

Once she's finished, I flip us on the couch so she's laying half on top of me tucked under my arm.

She kisses my chest and looks up at me. "That was . . . amazing. I've never . . . ."

I chuckle and kiss the top of her head. She runs her hand down my stomach and pulls on the strings of my sweatpants. I grab her hand, pull it up to my lips and kiss it.

"Relax, we don't have to do anything else. This isn't why I came here today; I hope you know that."

"I do. I just . . . want to return the favor," she says with a small smile.

"Trust me, that was just as fun for me as it was for you. I'm a grown man, I—"

My phone starts to ring on the coffee table. I grab it to see that it's Trey and send him to voicemail.

"Sorry, it was Trey. I don't need you to do anything, Kace, I'm here because I want to spend time with you and if we have sex right before I leave for the summer it will feel like a one-night stand and that's not what I want—"

My phone rings again.

I'm going to murder him.

She reaches to grab it off the coffee table. "Okay, I can understand that. You should answer it, he might need something," she says softly, handing my phone to me.

She lays her head down on my chest, snuggling into me as I answer.

"What, Trey?" I answer, exasperated.

"Where ya at, buddy? I figured if you got home in time, we could throw some steaks on the grill before we clean the camper."

"I haven't left yet. I don't think I'll be back until tomorrow." I start lazily rubbing Kacey's back with my other hand.

"*What?* You said you were leaving today." I can feel Kacey tense. "You better not bail on these rodeos or so help me—"

"I'm not bailing," I snap, cutting him off. "When have I ever bailed on you? I'm just leaving a day later than planned. I'll be home by noon tomorrow and we'll load the camper."

"And I guess I'll be cleaning it by myself tonight. What is your deal? I've hardly heard from you since you got there and now, you're not even going to get a full day at home before we leave. You'll have to find a twenty-four hour dry cleaner in Texas."

"It's fine, just clean the camper, please. I'll see you tomorrow."

"I better see you tomorrow or I'll come find you. I don't even know what rodeos I'm supposed to be at this weekend. You're my secretary; I need you."

"Ha. Yeah, yeah, I'll be there." I hang up the phone, tossing it back onto the coffee table.

Kacey immediately sits up and grabs her sweatshirt. "You were supposed to leave today? Why didn't you tell me? We didn't have to go riding; you could've left. I'm sure you want time at home before—"

I can tell she's spiraling, so I cut her off, grabbing her fore-arms, pulling her back to me. "Kace, I chose to stay an extra day. I wanted to go riding with you. After I leave, I don't know when I'll get to see you again. I wanted as much time with you as you'd give me."

I feel her release a breath and some of the tension leaves her body with it.

"I don't know if you've noticed or not," I say as I run my nose up her neck, tickling her with the week-old scruff on my face, "but I'm obsessed with you." She giggles and tries to climb away, but I wrap my arms around her. "Wait a minute, are you ticklish?"

"No, not at all," she clearly lies, while actively trying to get away from my hands that are now walking up her rib cage . . . tickling the "not at all" ticklish woman. She's laughing and smiling—my two favorite things.

I finally relent, and we snuggle back into the couch.

"Where do you go first?" she quietly asks while she watches the fire.

"Mount Pleasant, Texas. Then Hugo and Durant, Oklahoma this weekend. After that, we'll head down to Weatherford, Texas, for their Extreme Bulls and Rodeo."

I can tell she's getting sleepy. Her breathing has slowed, and she's fully relaxed into me. Judging by the dark circles under her eyes, I doubt she slept much last night.

She yawns and says, "My dad gave me his Rodeo Network login so I can watch. He said not all rodeos are on there, but a lot are."

"Yeah, I tend to stick to the bigger, higher paying rodeos and they're aired regularly. I'd love it if you watched. I really want to keep getting to know you. I know it won't be easy, but you can always call me."

She nods as she dozes off, resting on my chest.

We both sleep on the couch for a couple of hours before getting up and making dinner. She lets me help, and we move around the kitchen like we've been doing this for years. That's how it's been with us since day one. She might not have always been open with me, but we fit together seamlessly.

Once my clothes are dry, we both shower.

"Did you leave anything at Jack's or is it all in your truck?" she asks.

"It's in my truck," I answer.

She doesn't reply, just grabs my hand and tugs me to bed with her.

I pull her to my chest and breathe in the scent of her shampoo.

"Do you think Buck is going to miss me?" I ask.

She chuckles. "I'm sure he will. He might need to buck Chet off just to make himself feel better. Might make me feel better, too."

"What's your deal with Chet? I can tell you two don't get along. It seems he has a little bit of a chip on his shoulder, but overall, he doesn't seem so bad to me."

She yawns and nuzzles softly into me. "That's a story for a different day."

I'm still awake long after she's fallen asleep, memorizing the planes of her face, and how her soft strands of hair feel between my fingers. I want to soak up every moment, because in the morning, I'll leave, and I don't know if she'll want me to come back by the end of the summer.

Chapter 24

Knox

Texas

T he first few days on the road have been a complete shit show. It rained in Mount Pleasant and Durant. Thankfully, we had Hugo between the two, which is a covered arena so we could get our gear dried before the rodeo. We also had a flat tire headed to Durant we changed in the rain.

That was fun.

I haven't talked to Kacey much because of all the chaos, just a few texts here and there. Not to mention I don't want Trey knowing about her yet. He'll get too excited and ask a million questions I'm not in the mood to deal with right now.

On the plus side, even with all the bad luck, rain, and mud, we've both pulled a couple of checks this week. Now we're headed to Weatherford, Texas for the Extreme Bulls and Rodeo. It's one of my favorites. Great bulls, some of the best bull riders in the world, a nice arena, and a huge crowd that loves bull riding.

Now that I think of it, the draw should be posted by now. "Hey, can you see what bulls we drew?" I ask Trey. I'm driving and don't want to be on my phone.

"Yeah, as soon as I snap this girl back." He raises his phone to take a selfie, flipping his ball cap around backwards, repositioning his sunglasses.

"Of course, don't rush. She's higher on the priority list," I drawl sarcastically.

"She's going to be there tonight. I'm giving her my companion pass. She might have a friend. Want me to ask for you?" He grins. All Professional Rodeo members have a companion pass for one friend or family member to get into every rodeo and watch. Trey tends to use his to pick up chicks.

"I'm good, there's a gym close to the arena I'll probably go workout afterwards. Can you please check the draw?"

"Well, since you said please." He taps away on his phone, logging into the online portal all Professional Rodeo athletes have. "You got -48 Buck Nasty. Didn't they win a round on him at the finals last year?"

"Yeah, in the rank pen, he won't be a day off, but I like him. Should be in the gate to the right and bucky about it." I check my maps to make sure I don't need to turn soon. I'm pretty familiar with the route to Weatherford, but I'd rather not be late.

"Aw, hell yeah!" He slaps the center console. "I got Matchbox 19. Didn't you win Lovington on him last year?"

"Yeah, he's a black and white spotted bull. He's a fun one."

"You got the video?"

"Yep, on my phone." I take it off the holder on the dash and hand it to him. "It would've been last August," I tell him.

A few taps later, Trey gasps excitedly. "*Who* is this?" He whips my phone around to face me.

It's the photos of Kacey and me at the open rodeo. I've looked at them at least once a day, and I updated her contact photo to one just zoomed in on her. How could I forget and hand him my phone? Now we're going to play twenty questions.

I reach to grab my phone back, but he pulls it out of my reach. "Dude, give me my phone back."

"You look awfully friendly. And who's the redhead? You know I have a thing for redheads." Now he holds up the photo of the three of us.

"Don't worry about it. Did you find the video?" I try to change the subject.

"She's the reason you stayed another day, isn't she? She's cute, Knox. I'm pumped for you, man. Are you two dating? Does she rodeo? She looks like she rodeos. When do I get to meet her? Is the redhead single? I'd love to meet the redhead. She has that look about her, you know?" He sees the look on my face and back peddles. "Oh shit, is it the redhead you were hanging out with? Because if so, I also dig blondes—"

Is it illegal to push someone out of a moving vehicle?

"Will you shut up?" I snap in an annoyed tone. I accent the sentiment with the dad look. He would go on all day long if I let him. "The blonde is Kacey. She's the daughter of a rancher in Colorado where I was shoeing horses. We've become friends, but I'm not sure if it will become more than that or not. Okay?"

He looks at me with his brows drawn together and asks, "But you want it to? To be more, I mean. Look at your face in this picture, dude. You like her."

"Yes, I want it to be more but . . . ." I suck in a deep breath and roll my hand on the steering wheel. "She's guarded and you know how things are for me. We take off for months at a time and they go find someone who is actually there, that they actually get to spend time with. Hell, I haven't even had time to call her since I left."

He holds my phone to me. "Call her now."

That's just like Trey. He sees life as simple and straightforward. Ride bulls, chase women; do what he wants, when he wants. He doesn't care about other people's opinions or expectations. Very few things get under his skin or bother him. He lives life carefree, day by day, and it works for him.

"I can't. She's working cattle today and by the time she gets done, we'll be at the rodeo grounds getting ready to ride." I sigh and toss my head back into the headrest. "With her long workdays and my schedule, this will never work."

"So what? Call her and leave a message if you have to. Don't be a pussy and let this fall apart before you even give it a shot. If I can talk to seven girls at once, you can handle one. Buck up, cowboy." He slaps the phone to the front of my chest.

I laugh at him. "Seven girls, huh? Quantity over quality the theme this year?"

That earns me a rare glare. "No, asshole. I'm just bored." He sighs. "Once I find the right one, I won't even look at another woman, mark my words. But until then, I will enjoy all the fish in the sea or whatever it is they say." He goes back to typing on his phone.

"That is definitely not how that saying goes."

"Don't think I didn't notice you dodging my question. You going to call her or not?"

"I don't want to bother her while she's working. I'll try after the rodeo. She's an hour behind us so it shouldn't be too late."

Trey's right. I need to fight for this. I've never felt this deeply for anyone before her, and no amount of time or miles will keep me from fighting for what we could have.

We pull into the rodeo grounds forty minutes later and get checked in. The Rodeo Network reporter asks if I can do a pre-show interview in an hour. I say yes and head back to the truck to grab my gear bag and start getting ready, already anxious for the event to be over and my chance to call Kace.

Chapter 25

Kacey

I'll be done working cattle in about an hour. Want to come over? I'll cook.

Deal. I'll bring dessert and wine.

He call yet?

No. I'm sure he's just busy.

I'm sitting on the tailgate, holding a bloody towel to my forehead. Carson is digging around in the first aid kit while Chet talks on the phone.

"I'm fine, guys. It's a minor cut; head wounds just bleed more," I say to calm them down. Rein jumps up on the tailgate and lays down next to me.

Carson looks up and glares at me. "You were thrown a good eight feet and smacked your head on the panel. You could have a concussion."

"I do not have a concussion." I roll my eyes at him. "I wasn't knocked out, and I feel fine." Well, mostly fine. I have a slight headache but who wouldn't with Carson and Chet mother-henning them?

Chet walks over, his spurs clinking, and holds the phone out to me. "He wants to talk to you."

He called my dad. Tattle tail.

I take the phone. "Hi, Dad."

"Here, swap the towel for these," Carson says and hands me some gauze pads.

"Hey, Bug, I'm about to leave the locker. I'll be there in twenty minutes. Chet said you got thrown, hit your head, and cut it?" I can hear the concern in his voice.

"No, stay; you don't need to come all the way over here." We're clear on the other side of the ranch. "He makes it sound worse than it is. It's not that bad, it's not even an inch. It doesn't even need stitches. We can butterfly strip it," I reassure him.

"You need to go to the hospital and get checked out—"

"No," I snap, harsher than I mean to. "I am not going to the hospital." I *hate* hospitals. I've only been to the hospital once since the day my mom died. Carson needed stitches and there was no one else to drive him. I ended up waiting in the truck after nearly having a panic attack.

He sighs, knowing my aversion to hospitals. "Chet said you could have a concussion."

"I'm going to give Chet a concussion in a minute," I say, annoyed. Carson snorts next to me, and I hear Dad sigh over the line. "I'm fine. I can finish working these cows. And Jessie is coming over tonight; I promise I'll let her look at me. Okay?"

I hear Carson say under his breath, "Like hell you'll finish working these cows."

I glare at him.

"You're sure you don't have a concussion? I'm serious, Kacey." He's worried, I don't blame him. I get a little overbearing when he gets hurt or sick, too. After losing Mom, we're both protective when it comes to each other's safety.

I try to keep that in mind and use the most confident but reassuring tone that I can. "I'm good; I promise. I'll meet you at the ranch when we're done with these pairs."

"Alright. Hand the phone to Carson, please."

Great. I'd bet all the money in my wallet Carson is going to get assigned babysitting duty. This is part of being a woman working in a "man's field." I get babied or not taken seriously often. Carson and my dad are pretty good about understanding that I can handle myself. It's mostly the cowboys who think women shouldn't be here or the feed salesmen who refuse to talk to me, only wanting to talk to "the man in charge." Every woman in agriculture experiences it but that doesn't make it sting any less.

I hand him the phone and start digging around the first aid kit for butterfly strips.

I try to listen but can't hear anything Dad is saying. I hear Carson's replies though.

"Probably twenty-five to thirty is all."

I bet he asked how many head of cattle we have left to work.

"I wasn't planning on it," he says and turns to Chet, motioning for him to get the other cowboy with us to get back to work. "Will do." He hangs up the phone, handing it back to him.

I find some butterfly strips and jump off the tailgate.

"Oh no you don't," I hear Carson say as I head for the mirror on the truck.

"Relax, I'm just going to put these on." *And then go back to work.*

He reaches over my shoulder and plucks the strips out of my hand. "Hey!"

He crosses his arms, his worn denim shirt pulled taut as he looks down at me. "You're done for the day. Go sit down and keep pressure on that. It's still bleeding. You shouldn't put those on until it's been cleaned, anyway. We'll finish these cows, then head back to the house."

I take the gauze off my head and immediately feel blood run down my face.

Shit.

"I was planning to clean it, I'm not an idiot," I mumble as I head back to the tailgate.

It took them longer to finish working the cows since they were down a person. This set of cows was also extra spicy today, which never helps. They've been on this pasture with little human interaction for a while now and it shows. We always try to work cows slow and quiet, but this group has required a lot of yelling and slamming of gates.

Before it was said and done, Carson had a hand slammed between two gates and Chet had to bail over a gate, almost landing on his head. I might have laughed at him.

They finally get done and Carson drives me home. We walk in my front door to find Jessie on my couch eating chips while she reads and my dad in the kitchen drinking a beer, talking on the phone.

He hangs up when he sees me. "Hey, Bug, let me see." He wastes no time looking at my head. "It's just under an inch and not too deep. I bet we can clean and strip it. Jessie, what do you think?"

That's literally what I said. Why does no one listen to me?

Jessie gets up and examines my wound. "I agree. How do you feel? Any headache, dizziness, blurred vision, or nausea?"

"A little headache after it happened, but it's gone now," I tell her.

"How did this happen?" she asks.

I grab a bottle of water from the fridge and fill her in. "We were working some particularly spicy pairs today. Carson was running the sorting gate with Rein, and I pushed them into the tub, heading to the chute. One got turned around, and I thought I'd get the gate shut in time, but I didn't. She hit the tub gate—hard—and threw me back a few feet into a panel. I hit my head on the lower rung but was able to get up and over the panel before she could turn around and eat me."

Carson snorts—his version of a laugh—at my description. "I ditched my gate and ran down to her, but Rein beat me there, nearly taking that cow's nose off. Kacey had blood all over her face, she looked like an axe murderer."

"I bet. Head wounds always bleed terribly. Well, let's get it cleaned up," Jessie says and grabs a bag of things she brought with her.

Of course, my dad texted her beforehand.

Since it's been decided that I am fine, Dad and Carson take off as Jessie and I head for the bathroom. She cleans my cut then sits on the bathroom counter filling me in on all the hospital drama while I shower.

I make us tacos and tell Jessie how annoying Carson and Chet were today after I hit my head. She laughs when I tell her about Chet going headfirst over the fence.

We're eating when she finally asks, "Still no call?"

I shake my head.

"Have you tried calling him?"

I set my taco down and sigh. "No . . . I've thought about it, but he's been texting me and I know they've been busy and had a few rough days. Plus, it's only been a week since he left, and we aren't officially dating or anything. I don't want to come across as clingy."

She rolls her eyes at me. "You're one of the most independent women I know. You're not clingy. It's okay to want to hear his voice and see how he's doing. Maybe he's nervous to call you—ever think of that?"

"Maybe, but he isn't really the nervous type. I'm guessing he's just been busy. I could try to call him when we're done eating, he shouldn't be riding yet." I take a bite of my taco and set it back on my plate.

"Where is he at tonight?"

"Weatherford, Texas, for an Extreme bull riding."

We finish eating and I tell Jessie I'm going to go call him from the bedroom as I head down the hall.

"Okay, good luck. I'm going to turn the TV on."

I sit down on my bed cross-legged and bring up his contact. From his texts, I know the first few days on the road haven't been going very smoothly for him and Trey, so I hope today has been better. I was so busy I haven't texted him all day, but I know he made it to Weatherford. He sent me a Snapchat when he got there.

I press his number and wait. It rings three times before he answers.

"Hey, sweetheart." I can hear the smile on his face and now I'm smiling, too.

"Hey, just wanted to call and see how it's going and wish you good luck tonight."

"KACEY!" I hear Jessie yell from the living room like the house is on fire.

What the hell? She knows I'm on the phone.

"Thanks, today's been good. How was your day?" Knox says. I hear background noise—he must already be up at the arena.

"Kacey, come here! NOW!" she yells again. I climb off the bed and jog down the hallway, worried.

Maybe something really is wrong.

"It was good, we worked some pairs—" I start to tell Knox, but now I'm at the end of the hallway and see Jessie standing up pointing at the TV, at Knox, who's apparently doing an interview, but he's standing there on the phone with me, *on live TV*.

I make some nonverbal yelping sound. "Knox! What are you doing? Hang up!"

He laughs. He literally laughs at me and I'm watching it on TV. "Turned your TV on, did ya?" He winks at the camera.

"I'm hanging up. You're crazy." I hear Jessie next to me, jumping up and down, making weird squeaking noises, but I can't look away from the TV. I've really missed that smile.

"Alright, alright, I'll call you back later." He grins through the TV, and I hang up the phone.

He puts his phone back in his pocket and immediately begins telling the interviewer—who is very confused about what just happened—about the bull he has drawn tonight. Completely unfazed by the fact that he just blew off a live TV interview to answer my phone call.

"That was the sweetest thing *ever*. You have to marry him," Jessie says while still jumping up and down. "I'm going to rewind it and record it. This will go viral."

"You are not posting that on the internet." I plop down on the couch. I think I'm in shock over the fact that the man just answered my phone call on live TV.

Has he never heard of just calling someone back?

She grabs the remote and starts rewinding it. "I'm at least recording it so you have it. You can show it to your kids someday."

I burst out laughing. Big, uncontrollable belly laughs.

Jessie throws herself down on the couch next to me and joins me.

I put my face in my hands and try to catch my breath.

"That was crazy, wasn't it? He answered my call on live TV."

"That he did. I do believe that man has it bad for you, my friend."

I take my head out of my hands and look at her. "I think I might have it bad for him, too. And it terrifies me."

Chapter 26

Knox

I can't explain it, but I knew it was Kacey calling me when my phone started buzzing during that interview and I had to hear her voice. The bull I have tonight is a bucker; he's only been ridden once. That was at the finals last year. Hearing her voice, wishing me luck, letting me know she'll be watching was exactly what I needed after this shit week.

I won't lie. Before that call, I was nervous. Not nervous something bad would happen, but nervous because I don't want to buck off, and I know I can win on him. Since hearing her voice, knowing she's watching, I feel like I can take on the world now. I'm excited, and I know I'll ride him.

The bull riding has started, and Trey and I are both in the last section. He's third out and I'm last. The producer has made me and Buck Nasty the matchup of the night. The top bull here, against the four-time national finals qualifier and veteran bull rider. Everyone wants to see who will come out on top.

I have my rope, chaps, vest, and helmet all ready to go, waiting for my bull to be loaded. My boots and spurs are already tied, so as I wait around, I lend a hand to guys who need it.

Some need a spot so a bull doesn't slam him into the slide gate. A contractor has me hold a neck rope to keep a bull from trying to flip over, and a few guys have me pull their ropes. I like to keep busy; it keeps my mind from overthinking.

The last section finally rolls around. I put on my chaps as they load Buck Nasty into the alley, then head over to him to put my rope on. Trey is already loaded into the chutes on the left-hand delivery side, and I'll be out on the right-hand deliveries.

"Shit, looks like you drew deep tonight, Knox."

I look up to see Wade Taylor from the Burning T standing across the load alley from me.

"Gotta ride the buckers to win a world title," I confidently reply. "Can you hook my rope from that side?"

Wade chuckles, reaches under the bull with a wire hook and grabs my rope, then hands it up to me. "If anyone can, it's you. You're the toughest S.O.B. I've ever known."

"I appreciate that. Your bulls looked good in the first section. The bull I rode in Lawton, 025, is going to be in the rank pen one day." I get my rope set where I like it and climb down.

Looking through the panels, he replies, "Thanks, we have a bunch of young bulls right now that show a lot of promise."

"That's a good problem to have," I say with a smile. "If you're not busy, think you can pull my rope for me?"

"Oh yeah, I'm just hanging around until I can load out. I'll come give ya a hand." He climbs over the alley and follows me up to the chutes.

I climb back behind the chutes and put my vest on as Trey nods his head. Matchbox 19 has the same trip he always does. Rears and kicks out two big jumps and turns back to the left. He feels like a dream. He has even timing and feels like he does all the hard work for you. Trey sits up and rides him like he was born there. At six and a half seconds, he lifts his outside foot and starts to spur him, showing the judges he has total control. When the whistle blows, he pulls his tail and sticks the landing. Matchbox 19 makes another round as the bull fighters step in, then he runs out the center gate.

Trey is excited—as he should be, that was a beautiful ride. He stands on the top rung of the fence, waving his arms in an upward motion, hyping up the crowd. They love it. The judges love it, too, marking him 89 points.

Great—he was two more points than I was on Matchbox 19, and now I'll never hear the end of it.

Trey runs up to the chutes and yells, "See, that's how you're supposed to ride him, old man!"

I shake my head. *He's so predictable.* "Yeah, yeah, I'll admit, it was a pretty ride."

"Aww, you think I'm pretty." He smiles up at me, fluttering his eyes like an idiot.

Wade chuckles next to me.

"Shut up, you know that's not what I said. Now leave me alone, I need to focus."

The last guy out the lefts nods his head and Trey steps up on top of the chute he's standing at.

"Alright, Mr. Serious, go ride this fucker. Good luck, man." He slaps the top rung on the chute, then heads for the walk-through gate.

There are two more guys before me. I grab the top rung of the chutes on my side and jump up and down to get the blood flowing. I say my usual affirmations in my head.

Whatever it takes. Keep moving. I came to win. I deserve to win.

I catch my breaths getting shallow, so I start taking deep breaths while closing my eyes, visualizing myself on a bull making the correct moves. Noting the feel of the loose hide and how it moves under me as I pull with my right leg and raise my left knee, throwing my free arm over my head as the imaginary bull kicks.

My eyes open as they pull the slide gate to my left and in steps Buck Nasty. He's a big mouse-colored bull weighing around 1,900 pounds, with a white stripe running between his horns down to his nose.

"You're mine, motherfucker," I say under my breath. *This is my time.*

I wipe the sweat from my brow, pull my helmet on, then have Wade pull my glove back so I can tape it on. I jump up and down again and slap the inside of my thighs as Wade unties the tail of my rope. When I stand, I climb above my bull, resting my feet on the top rung on the other side of the chute as I fold my chaps back over my knees so they're out of the way when I get on the bull.

The guy before me nods and the gate swings open. I don't watch to see how things go for him. I set both feet on Buck Nasty's back and slowly slide onto him.

Man, he's a big bastard.

My mouth is dry, I'm nervous but still confident. In this moment, I can't think about anything. If I start thinking about the end result, good or bad, it only distracts me from being in this moment right here. If I want to ride this bull, I have to have a clear mind and a will to win.

"Pull it up," I say to Wade.

I warm up the rosin on the tail of my rope, I can smell it burn as it starts to get sticky. The last bull leaves and the arena crew all get set at my chute. I vaguely hear the announcer say my name and start hyping up the crowd. I put my hand in my rope, and knowing he goes right, I set my hand a little further to the right of his backbone. Just in case I get a little behind, it will give me a second chance to catch back up.

Today, I know I'm in my zone, I'll be where I need to be. My mind is calm, and I can't even hear the noise around me. Not the other bull riders offering last words of encouragement, not the roar of the crowd or even the announcer talking about me over the loudspeakers.

Wade pulls my rope tight and hands my tail to me as I pull it over the palm, then wrap it back around my hand, and back over the palm. Then I run the tail between my pinky and my ring finger. The suicide wrap. I normally wouldn't do it, but I'm not going to buck off the bull to win it on because my hand pops out.

After I finish my wrap, I take two deep breaths, slide up over my hand, and push up on my legs. Once I feel ready, I nod my head, and I hear the clang of the latch.

My world explodes, and there's no time to think, only react. Buck Nasty has a ton of power as I set my hips to my rope for the first kick. When he extends his hind legs to their full length, above his head, it feels like an invisible force is pulling at my vest, trying to get my face to meet the back of his head. I flex my lower back muscles and use my feet to keep myself from bowing out over him.

He slings his head, and I can feel that he's in the right lead. He rears and kicks again, this time he's moving right and fast.

I set my hips and hold them just like I did before, only now I throw my free arm over my head.

The bull in my visualization didn't move this fast with this much power. Probably should've added that. Noted for next time.

The next round goes by in a flash. I get shaken to the outside, but when he kicks, I lift my outside knee and foot to kick my hips back into the middle of him. I immediately drive forward on my legs to meet his rear. I can hear myself grunt between my gritted teeth every time I pump my free arm over my head.

Every jump, he yanks on my arm, trying to break my grip from the handle of my rope, but I refuse to let go. Round after round, I give it everything I have to stay on Buck Nasty's back. Then, the buzzer finally sounds.

I grab my tail as fast as I can without getting myself jerked down and I let Buck Nasty sling me off his back. I land ten feet away in a ball, shoulder first. At least the arena dirt is softer out here. I get to my feet and run to the fence where it's safe.

"He did it, ladies and gentlemen! The man from Oklahoma just conquered one of the rankest bulls in the business!" the announcer bellows over the microphone as the crowd loses their minds. "How about this, a new arena record to win this year's Extreme Bulls title. 92 points!" the announcer says, as the crowd lets out another roar.

The bull leaves the arena, and I thank my bull fighters. One of them hands me my rope and slaps me on the shoulder.

I walk out of the arena, and Trey is waiting.

"When are you going to let me win one for once?" He smiles as he lifts his hand for a high five.

"Not today, apparently." I laugh as I slap his hand.

"That was probably the rankest bull ride I've ever seen, you deserve it." He holds my hat out to me so I can put it on for the interview.

"Thanks, man. Hey, can you take my gear to my bag?" I hand him my helmet, put my hat on, and unzip my vest.

He nods and I hand over my gear. As he walks away, I go back into the arena for the buckle presentation and interview.

Afterward, I head straight to my bag and grab my phone. I don't waste a second.

"Congratulations!" Kacey answers, and my heart swells.

Chapter 27

Knox

After that night, Kacey and I talked every day, sometimes twice a day. And starting off my summer run strong with a win in Weatherford was great. Trey and I had a few more rodeos in the south after that, but tonight was our last. Now we're headed west for the summer. Vernal, Utah, is our first stop and I'm driving north on I-27 when it dawns on me—it wouldn't be very far out of our way to stop at the ranch. We have an extra day before we need to be in Vernal.

Trey is asleep, so I make the executive decision to change course. I grab my phone off the dash and update my maps for the Diamond Hart Ranch. If I drive until 3 a.m., then have Trey trade me, we could be there by midmorning. This will give me one night with Kacey, one night to convince her we should give this a real shot.

It's 3:15 a.m. when I finally reach across the truck and shake Trey awake. "Hey, wake up. We need to trade, I'm getting tired."

He groans at me, rolling away. "Just pull over. I'm tired, we'll drive it tomorrow."

I see an off ramp and hit my exhaust brake to slow and exit. "No, we're driving all night. We're stopping at the ranch."

Without moving his body, he slowly turns his head like an owl. "We're—what? What ranch? We don't ranch."

"Kacey's ranch. It's not very far out of our way. I can spend tomorrow with Kacey, then we'll go to Vernal."

This wakes him up and he turns to face me fully, setting his elbow on the center console, resting his face on his palm. "There are girls all over the rodeo. Why'd we have to detour 500 hundred miles just for this one?" The shithead is quoting the movie *8 Seconds*.

I reach across the truck and smack him. "Love knows no bounds."

He finishes laughing, completely unfazed by my death glare.

"Stop being dramatic. It's not 500 miles; it's like an hour and a half." I pull over on the shoulder of the off ramp and unbuckle.

"No, it's a twenty-four-hour detour, is what it is. But it's okay, I love love. Speaking of love, will the redhead be there?" He smirks at me and opens his door.

I make a mental note to tell Kacey not to invite Jessie around. I want quality time with Kacey—I don't want to waste my time keeping Trey from humping Jessie's leg.

"Just drive, I need some sleep. Wake me up at seven and I'll trade you back."

"Yeah, you better rest up. Don't want to be tired for all the *quality time* you're going to spend with Kacey." He raises his hands, making air quotations with his fingers before taking off his hoodie and putting the truck in drive.

I roll my eyes and lean the seat back, quickly passing out.

Trey wakes me up at seven and we trade.

I shoot a quick text to Kacey, asking her to call me when she can. I want to give her a heads up that we're coming and make sure it's okay. Someday I'll be able to surprise her, I'm just not sure we're at that point yet.

"Ugh, that graveyard shift will get a guy," Trey says as he cracks his neck side to side. "But anything for you, buddy. Can we stop for breakfast? I'm starving."

The truck screen lights up with Kace's call. I shush Trey and answer over the truck speakers, "Morning, beautiful."

"Hey, you. You're up early," she says with the sound of feed buckets being filled in the background.

"I haven't exactly gone to bed. What're you doing today?"

"Oh my word, get some sleep. I'll ride out and check the mares and foals soon, then I told Chet I'd help him and a few of the cowboys move some yearlings to the feedyard. You guys driving all day?"

I check the maps and see we're two hours from the ranch. "That's up to you," I tell her.

"Huh?"

"I'm about two hours from the ranch."

I hear her stop filling buckets, and there is a long pause before she squeaks out, "This ranch?"

I can't help but chuckle at her, and Trey covers his mouth, trying not to laugh next to me. "Yes, your ranch. Is that okay?

We have tonight off, then we can drive the rest of the way to Vernal tomorrow."

"Yeah—*yes*, of course," she says quickly. "Let me talk to Chet, I'm sure one of the other cowboys can move yearlings—"

"No, I don't want to affect your work. I can come help if you want. I could take Buck out."

Trey is waving his hand around, trying to get my attention.

"Ask about the redhead," he whisper shouts.

"What?" Kacey asks.

I smack him in the stomach, making him grunt. "Nothing, that was just Trey saying something. So Buck?" I ask again to distract her.

"It would be great for Buck to get out and work for a day."

"Alright, it's settled then. I'll see you in two hours."

I can't help but smile. I get to see my girl in two hours.

Chapter 28

Kacey

I complete the rest of my chores at lightning speed. He's coming back, already. He's only been gone a couple of weeks. I don't let myself think about what this might mean. I don't want to read too much into it.

After chores, I head back to the house and do a quick check in the mirror. I swap my old beat-up jeans for a pair of Kimes—I know they're his favorite. Then I go to the kitchen and make breakfast burritos. I haven't eaten and I'm betting they haven't either.

By the time I've finished, I'm walking down my porch steps as they pull in the driveway. Knox has his rodeo truck and camper. It's newer than his other truck, but it's still black, and it's partially wrapped with a sponsor. It's a fourth gen Ram dually with a matching black Capri camper and toolboxes with a generator mounted to the back.

I have to take a couple deep breaths and calm my heart rate. I'm so excited to see him. After he answered during that interview, things have changed between us. Yes, we talked more, but it's more than that. Something feels different now, I just can't put my finger on what. I think him showing up here after only being gone for a couple weeks also shows that.

I meet them at the drive and Knox jumps out of the truck and picks me up, wrapping me in a big hug.

"Hi, sweetheart," he whispers with his head tucked into the hair at my neck.

"Hi," I reply as he sets me down and our eyes meet. I hear the other truck door shut and gravel crunching, but I can't look away yet.

"Where's my hug?" I hear the man who must be Trey ask.

I can't help but laugh. After everything Knox has told me about him, this tracks.

"Shut up," Knox tells him.

I turn to face Trey while Knox introduces us. He takes off his hat and shakes my hand like every good cowboy does. Once introductions are complete, I go into the house and grab the burritos while they move the truck and camper down by the bunkhouse where they can plug into electricity.

I walk to the bunkhouse and hand them their burritos. I look over the truck and camper as we eat standing next to it.

"Have you ever seen such a beautiful rig before?" Trey asks with a mouthful of food.

"You could try talking after you swallow your food, or at the very least, cover your mouth," Knox scolds him.

"Okay, *Dad*, I'll be more polite." He swallows and clears his throat. "Kacey, have you ever seen such a beautiful rig?"

"I can't say I have. Everyone I know has a horse trailer."

"Come on, I'll give you a tour," Trey says and heads for the door.

I look at Knox.

He just smiles and nods toward the camper, telling me to go ahead.

I step up onto the toolbox as Trey opens the door. It has a six-foot counter on the left side with cabinets underneath and wall-mounted ones above. Between the counter and the upper cabinets is a TV on a swivel mount that pulls out. On the righthand side is a shower, then a twin-sized bed. Up in the nose, over the truck cab, is another bed that looks queen size.

"The twin is my bed, Knox is up top. When another bull rider hops in, there's another twin that folds down from the wall." Trey pulls a latch, and another bed drops down.

"Well, this is a cozy set up y'all have here. It's surprisingly clean for a couple of bull riders," I say, walking out of the camper.

"I'll give it to Trey, his life may be a mess but, I never have to clean up after him," Knox says, crumpling his aluminum foil into a ball.

"Hey, my life is organized chaos—exactly how I want it," Trey retorts.

"Oh yeah? Where are we entered after Vernal?" Knox raises a single brow.

"You see, I don't need to know, because you know. It's all part of my strategy." He shrugs.

Knox rolls his eyes, then points to the box I'm standing on. "In the lower toolbox is extra equipment and tools. In the upper is our gear bags and hanging clothes."

I step down from the toolbox.

"Sooo, I've gotta ask about your red-headed friend," Trey says. "Knox refuses to tell me her name."

Ha, of course he wants to know about Jessie.

"I was trying to keep the peace as long as I could," Knox explains.

I nod. "It's true, they'll meet eventually, but I agree—it's best to keep the peace."

"The two of them together is a liability; we may need a lawyer on standby."

"You do realize I'm standing *right* here. I can hear you," Trey interjects.

We both turn to him and say at the exact same time, "Yeah, we know." Turning back to each other, Knox gives me a wink, and we laugh.

"You ready to head out? I have the horses saddled. We need to meet Chet and the guys in ten minutes."

"Yep, let's go." Knox grabs his cowboy hat out of the camper and my stomach does a little flip. I love him in a cowboy hat.

"Okay, well, I guess I'll just hang out here. All by myself," I hear Trey whine as we walk away. "No redhead or nothin'."

"You'll be fine. Go take a nap. You bitched all morning about how tired you are," Knox hollers back.

We get the cattle moved and put the horses away before heading back to my house. Knox grabbed a change of clothes out of the camper and said Trey is happily playing Xbox.

Once we get to my house, we both take a shower. I take my time and do an everything shower. I need a few minutes alone to calm my raging hormones. Spending all day with him, watching him handle a horse, the lingering feeling of his arms wrapped around me . . . I wanted to grab the man by the belt and yank him to me more than a few times today.

Once I'm showered and dressed, I feel more in control. He said he didn't want to sleep with me and leave for the summer, and I need to respect that. Even if I don't necessarily agree with his logic, I can respect it.

I walk out of my room and down the hallway. Right before I get to the guest bathroom door, Knox walks out in nothing but a towel.

Fuck. Me.

So much for having my hormones under control. He still has water running down his chiseled chest. He turns his shoulders slightly, making his abs flex, and I can see the tattoos on one rib cage clearly.

This is so not fair.

I know I'm staring, but I can't stop myself. I'm also pretty sure Knox just said something to me, but all I can hear is the pounding of my heart. I'm running my eyes over his torso when he moves his arm, reaching up to run his fingers through his damp curls. My eyes snap to his and I see him watching me with a shit-eating grin on his face.

"Like what you see?"

I shake my head. "Sorry, you just caught me off guard, is all. Not used to having someone else in the house." I hurry past him and into the kitchen as he chuckles behind me.

Knox follows me into the main living area, grabs his bag, and heads back to the bathroom. I start prepping dinner and it's not long before he's moving around the kitchen helping. I finish seasoning the burgers and he offers to grill them. When he reaches around me to pick up the plate they're on, I can feel his body heat and smell him. That bergamot and sandalwood with a touch of leather.

He grabs the plate with one hand and places the other on my hip, sliding in next to me.

I have to stop myself from leaning into him.

We make small talk while we eat, and I catch him up on what's been going on at the ranch since he left.

He tells me about his upcoming rodeos and asks about Estes Park. Jessie and I booked our rental cabin the day after Knox answered during his interview. She said there was no way we weren't going to see him after that. So at least I know I'll see him again in a few weeks, even if it's just for one night.

My kitchen isn't overly small, but as we clean up dinner, it seems like we can't go a full minute without brushing up against one another or touching in some way. By the time Knox finishes washing dishes, my skin is on fire, and I need to touch him. I need to feel his hands on me, my lips on his. I know he can sense it; I've felt the tension coming off him all night. This attraction between us has never been one-sided.

I put the last plate away and shut the cupboard. When I turn around, he's leaning against the counter, his hands propped on the edge. His blue eyes search mine. What he's looking for, I don't know. I walk over to him and start to lightly run my fingers up his arms.

He flexes beneath my touch. "What are you thinking?" he asks.

I look up and meet his eyes. "That you're a lot more patient than I am."

"What do you mean by that?" He takes his hands off the counter, and they find my hips to pull me closer.

"Are you going to see anyone else this summer? Or is it just me?" I watch his face change from shock to curiosity.

"Sweetheart, I think you know the answer to that."

"Still, I want to hear you say it. You know I'm not seeing anyone else and have no plans to."

"Alright," he says as he pulls me even closer. He looks me straight in the eye. "It's just you." He dips his head and runs his nose up the side of my neck to my ear. "I don't want anyone else. I've never wanted anyone else as much as I want you." His husky voice skates over my skin, causing goosebumps to run down my arms.

I run one hand up his arm and gently tangle my fingers in his hair. I pull him to me for a kiss, and he meets me halfway. The kiss is long and deep—neither of us can get enough. He nips my lower lip while gripping my hips hard, like he's trying to hold himself back.

Screw that, I don't want him to hold back. I want him to lose control.

I rock into him just like he depicted that night on my porch. He hums into my mouth, and I can feel him already getting hard for me. But the next second, I break the kiss and step back, creating some distance between us.

"Would it still feel like a one-night stand?" I meet his eyes and see them flare. Then I finally do what I've been dying to do all day. I reach out, grab him by the belt, and yank him to me. "Because it wouldn't to me."

"*Fuck no*," Knox practically growls, before crashing his mouth to mine. He kisses me, spinning me around, grabbing me by the ass and lifting me onto the counter in one fluid motion. He breaks the kiss and starts trailing kisses down my neck. "You're so much more. It terrifies me."

"Me too," I whisper, "but I'm brave enough to try if you are."

He presses his brow to mine, swallows hard, and nods once. "Anything for you, sweetheart."

Then we're moving. I grab the hem of his shirt and pull it over his head; he does the same to me before kissing me senseless again. He picks me up and starts walking toward my bedroom. "I'll fuck you on that counter someday, but tonight I plan to take my time, and we need a bed for that."

I'm planting kisses down his shoulder when we reach the bed.

He gently lays me down and starts kissing his way down my body, removing clothing as he goes. First my bra, then he peels my jeans down at a torturously slow pace. My socks are next, and finally my thong finds the floor. He fully stands up and gazes down at me.

"You're so beautiful, Kace."

I sit on the edge of the bed and spread my legs apart. He steps between them so I can undo his belt. His jeans fall to the floor, leaving him only in his black boxers. I grip the waistband, pulling them down. He's fully erect and precum is gathering at the tip. I lick my lips, wanting him in my mouth, but he runs his fingers into my hair and tilts my head up to look at him.

"If you keep looking at me like that, I'm going to come before we even get started."

I laugh, and he picks me up and throws me back onto the pillows.

"Think that's funny, huh?" he asks as he climbs on the bed and grabs my ankle, pulling until I'm fully laying down and he's hovering over top of me. Knox walks his fingers up my ribs, tickling me, before he leans down and lightly bites the side of my neck. His hand stops and he whispers in my ear, "How many times should I make you come tonight?"

I suck in a breath. "I— I—" His fingers are tracing the underside of my breast, and I can't focus. I've never been this turned on or been with someone so vocal in the bedroom.

"How about you just keep count, and we'll tally it up in the morning?"

All I can do is nod my head. My thighs try to pull together but Knox is between them, so I just end up tightening my legs around his hips. I know I'm soaking wet.

He starts at my jaw, trailing kisses down to my taut nipples. "Where should I start? I'm thinking here." He slowly licks a circle. "I love your tits," he says before he sucks one into his mouth.

I gasp at the sensation and arch off the bed into him.

He hums, only making the sensation better.

I can feel my pussy pulsing. I need him inside me. Now.

"Knox," I breathe.

He lifts his head and moves to my other nipple. "Yes, sweetheart?"

"I need you. Inside of me. *Now*." I pant as his tongue licks a circle around the peak.

I feel his muscles go taut, and he pulls back and smirks at me. "Alright, but I get to play later. We're still counting." Then he's off me, grabbing a condom from his jeans and rolling it on.

He lifts my leg, planting kisses down the inside of it, working his way to my center. "I can't wait to feel how tight you are around me."

This man's dirty mouth might be the death of me. I'm desperate for friction, so turned on I can hardly breathe. I reach down and wrap my hand around his cock. Giving it two pumps that have him grunting and leaning into me. When I reach up, pulling him down over me, he tsks.

"So demanding. Tell me how you like it."

"I want to see you lose control," I say, before I can stop myself. But it's the truth.

Heat flickers in his gaze, and I swear they turn a darker shade of blue before he's pushing into me. He doesn't wait for me to adjust, he fully thrusts into me, stretching me almost to the point of pain. But we fit together perfectly.

I rock my hips, and he kisses me while he starts to move. He sets the perfect rhythm, bringing me right to the edge. "You feel amazing. I've wanted this pussy since the first day I saw you." He picks up his pace and I arch into him. Again, and again, he thrusts into me.

"Oh god, Knox—"

He palms my breast and rolls my nipple between two fingers. It's too much, I can feel the orgasm building. I'm going to come.

"That's it, sweetheart. I want to feel you come on my cock." He moves his hand from my nipple to my hip and pumps into me faster, deeper.

My nails dig into his back. And when I can't hold on any longer, I shatter around him, coming harder than I ever have.

"Oh, fuck," he pants as he loses all control, thrusting into me, coming with my name on his lips.

He pulls out of me and collapses next to me, pulling me to him so my head is resting on his chest. He kisses the top of my head.

"One," I say.

And he laughs, holding me tighter.

Chapter 29

Knox

It's 3 a.m. and I almost have her to number five.

I have both hands kneading her ass as she's on her knees, holding the headboard, riding my face. She tastes so damn good. I can't get enough of her. The moment I sank into her tight, wet heat, I knew I was done for. I've already fallen for her kind heart, quick wit, and brilliant mind. I see now this was inevitable.

There isn't a force on earth that could keep me from this woman. We were made for each other. I just have to get her to see it, too. I know she has feelings for me and is clearly attracted to me. But I also know she doesn't fully trust me. Not yet. I'll do anything I can to earn that trust, I just hope we can survive the rodeo season. Then we'll have several months to spend time together and make this a real relationship.

She starts to rock quicker, and I slide one hand up to her bouncing tits. I know she's close, and she confirms it by letting out a whimper when I roll a taut nipple between my fingers. I hum, increasing the sensation on her clit and it sends her over the edge.

"Fuck—*Knox!*" she screams my name.

I get off on her getting off. I love feeling her come apart for me. I've taken my time tonight, learning every curve and desire of her body. Like the way I can make her drip down her legs with my words alone, or how she tightens around me when I fist her hair and lick the sensitive nape of her neck. She isn't shy about her desires, and I love it.

I continue to lick and suck, letting her fully ride out her orgasm. Once she flips over and lays next to me panting, I roll over and smirk at her. "That's five."

She laughs with the biggest smile on her face. The way she isn't afraid to laugh with me, tucked away in her bedroom brings a full smile to my face. "I don't know about you, but that's a personal record for me," she says.

"Same," I say as I grab her, pulling her to me. I can't go more than a few seconds without touching her. We took a break after round three and she slept, but I couldn't. I just listened to her breathing. I don't know when we'll get this again. I want to soak in her scent, the softness of her hair and the little noises she makes in her sleep. At one point, she took my hand, intertwining our fingers together like she did in the barn. Just like the first time, she was asleep, completely unaware she was doing it.

I only made it two hours before I was waking her again—my craving for her too strong.

I kiss the top of her head. "Tell me you're mine."

"I'm yours," she whispers. "When do you have to leave?" she hesitantly asks.

"Early. We have a decent drive to get there."

She rolls over and props her chin up on her hands. "Promise me you'll be safe. Don't take any unnecessary risks."

I can see concern and a little bit of fear in her eyes. I need to tread lightly. With losing her mom, I know she'll be extra sensitive about the danger I'm in every time I ride.

I nod my head. "I promise." And I mean it.

I've always tried to turn out the eliminator bulls that are dirty hard to ride and try to kill you. It's hard enough not to get run over by the mean ones. When you make a living with your body, getting hurt can cost you your income for months. Or end your career. Those types of bulls just aren't worth it to me. I also try to get off away from the bulls and land on my feet. That's the key to staying healthy in this game.

I smile and look into her green eyes and give her a little wink. I can see the worry start to leave her face.

She nods, satisfied at my answer, and lays her head back on my chest. I run my hand through her hair as she wraps her arms around me and falls asleep.

Two hours later, I slide out of her hold as gently as I can, trying not to wake her. She has to work today and has maybe gotten three hours of sleep. I stand next to the bed, watching her sleep for another minute before leaning down and planting one last kiss on her forehead.

"Bye, sweetheart. I'll see you in Estes."

It takes every ounce of my love for bull riding to get me out that door. I know I'd be miserable if I wasn't riding, but it's crushing me to leave her behind. I've heard some of the married riders talk about how hard it is to leave home and even known them to turn out of a rodeo and fly home for a few days. I never understood it, until now.

I've never struggled with addiction—never needed a vice to get by. But now, I finally understand what it means to crave something, because Kacey has become my greatest obsession. The thought of losing her is unbearable.

I quietly get dressed and gather my things, trying to control the negative thoughts running through my head. The thoughts telling me she'll get scared, she'll be lonely, and she'll end things before I even really get a chance with her. I have to trust she knows her own mind and she can do this.

When I get into the living area, I dig around until I find a pen and paper. This summer will be hard, but I refuse to let the past dictate the present—I'm not going down without a fight.

Chapter 30

Kacey

The space on the bed next to me is cold when I wake up. I knew he didn't want to wake me, and we'll FaceTime tonight, but I hate that I didn't get to tell him goodbye.

We talked about the summer last night, made plans to Face-Time every other day and, at the very least, text every night after he rides. He explained how busy the summer gets, the amount of driving they have to do. I didn't realize the number of miles and how many rodeos the top athletes compete in. He averages 50,000 miles a year and 150 rodeo performances. It's no wonder it takes a toll on not just their bodies, but their relationships.

Knowing this, I love how passionate he is about his dream. Just listening to him talk about bull riding, you can hear how much he loves it. I want to be there for him and support him however I can. My fear last night stopped me from telling him that, so I'll find ways to show him.

I'll be counting down the days until Estes Park when I can see him again. I could see the fear in his eyes—fear that we won't make it through the summer. And I know he could see the fear in mine for his safety. But I meant what I said last night—I'm his.

There is no one else.

Rolling out of bed, I can feel how sore I am. It's a good sore though, it reminds me this is real. I've never been with someone who made me feel so alive. It was the best sex I've ever had.

I head for the bathroom to start going through my morning routine.

Seeing the passion and love on Knox's face last night reminded me that's how I used to feel about ranching. Ever since Chet was hired, and I wasn't offered the foreman job, I've felt like I'm not good enough. I don't take enough responsibility or help grow the ranch. It's been weighing on my shoulders so much I think I've lost a little bit of my love for the ranch, but I want to get it back. I just don't know how.

I head for the kitchen to start my coffee. When I round the island, I see a piece of folded paper leaning against my coffee maker with my name across the front. I smile. He knew I wouldn't miss the note if he left it here. I never go without my morning coffee.

I unfold it and start to read.

> *Kacey,*
> *I didn't want to wake you, but we had to leave, or we wouldn't make it to Vernal in time.*
> *When I came to Colorado this spring, you were the last thing I thought I'd find. As soon as we met, I felt a connection like I have never felt before. And it only gets stronger and stronger every minute I spend with you. Not seeing you the last few weeks was tough,*

and now we're going into a longer run of rodeos. But I now know if there's a relationship that stands a chance of surviving a rodeo season, it's ours. I can't promise this summer will be easy, but I can promise I will do everything in my power to make this work and give us a real shot.

I'll see you in Estes, sweetheart.

- Knox

I feel tears welling up, but I take a deep breath, holding them back. I feel like an idiot. Why did I wait so long to give him a chance? We could've had weeks together, but I was too afraid to open myself up. I won't make that mistake again, *we will* make it through the summer and get our chance to be together.

I press the start button on my coffee maker, then pull out my phone and send him a text.

Kacey

Go kick their asses out there. I'll be here waiting for you and cheering you on.

Chapter 31

Kacey

"Yep, he's definitely unconscious," Chet says from the chair across the room.

We're all at my dad's for family dinner, but instead of eating at the table, we're in the living room watching the Livingston, Montana rodeo on TV. I haven't missed a single rodeo that was aired. Knox has been gone for a couple weeks, but we've been able to keep in touch pretty well until the last few days. He's in the middle of the Fourth of July run now, which I learned they call Cowboy Christmas because there are so many rodeos with a ton of money to win.

When he told me about their schedule, my jaw dropped. They started in Saint Paul, Oregon, then went to Basin City, Washington. After tonight they'll go to Red Lodge, Montana and Cody, Wyoming on the same day. Then drive all the way to West Jordan and Oakley, Utah. They're not getting much sleep and riding a bull or two a day for eight days straight. Sounds more like hell week than Christmas, if you ask me.

"I don't think it stepped on his head. I think he got kicked on the way down," Carson analyzes the replay from his seat on the couch next to me. I look away, not wanting to watch it again.

"I agree. He's waking up, though," Jessie says as the man in the arena gets to his feet with the help of the sports medicine team. He makes his way out of the gate as the next bull rider climbs in the chute.

Jessie and I leave for Estes Park in five days. Saying I'm excited to see him is an understatement. Knox tried to enter the rodeos so they would have one night off in Estes, but the association put them out differently, so he has to leave shortly after the rodeo is over. I tried to hide how disappointed I was. I'll only get a few hours with him, but he warned me about this, and I can handle it. A few hours are better than nothing, and I'll get to watch him ride in person for the first time.

"Looks like Knox is next," Dad says, as he slides up in his chair, propping his elbows on his knees. He was a rodeo fan before Knox, but now he's obsessed. He's even been keeping up on the standings.

I take a sip of my drink and try to breathe normally. I get nervous when Knox rides. I know he takes all the precautions he can, but it's still so dangerous. Look at the dude who was just unconscious—he'll probably get on another bull tomorrow like it never happened.

They're crazy.

The rider gets bucked off and they move the camera to Knox. He's already in the chute warming his rope up. Now I'm sliding to the edge of my seat, wringing my hands together.

Carson pats me on the back. "He's got this."

Carson has come around more to the idea of Knox and me. I think Knox showing up on his way to Vernal spoke volumes to him and my dad. Now Carson ends up at my dad's most nights watching the rodeos.

The announcer's booming voice comes over the TV. "Y'all are going to like this match up. We have four-time national finals qualifier Knox Ward on 608 Prime Time. This bull has only been ridden a handful of times, but they've never been under 88 on him. Knox has been riding phenomenally this year. The man is thirty years old, but like fine wine, he just gets better with age."

Knox takes his wrap and slides up.

"Come on, Knox. Show 'em how it's done," the announcer calls over the mic.

He nods and the gate flies open. Until Knox, I didn't really know much about bull riding, and I still don't, but I can see this bull *bucks*. He is jumping higher than any bull I've seen, with his back feet kicking all the way out. He throws his head back and makes another round, but Knox is matching him jump for jump.

"He's got him," I hear Dad yell.

At 6.5 seconds, we all suck in a breath as we see Knox come too far off his rope. He gets back into position enough to make it to the whistle, but it's not enough to let him pull the tail of his bull rope and make a good get off.

I see him reach down for his rope right as the bull makes another big move, yanking the rope out of his hand. He ends up flying backwards, almost onto the bull's ass. When the bull kicks, Knox goes flying right into the bucking chutes. He slams into the chutes completely sideways, you can hear the gates rattle, even on TV. He falls to the ground like a sack of bricks and the camera pans away to show the bullfighters going to work, getting the bull away from him and out the gate. I clasp my hands together as they start to shake.

"Ouch. He rode him, though," Chet says.

Jessie angrily yells at the TV, "What the hell? Put the camera back on Knox!"

It seems even camera crews in Montana are terrified of her, because they pan back over to Knox and he's already up on his feet and inside the chute. Someone swung the gate around to protect him in case the bull came back. He's got his hands on his knees; it looks like he's trying to catch his breath.

"Talk about selling tickets, he's the wreck and rank ride all in one night. That had to hurt, but you know what will make him feel better? A score like this: 88.5 points!" the announcer says, as Knox takes off his helmet, grits his teeth and climbs out of the chute.

I let out a breath I didn't realize I was holding.

"I think he's okay. He looked okay, right?" I say to no one in particular. I just need someone to tell me he's okay, even if it's only to make me feel better. It's not like any of us really knows if he's okay.

"Yeah, Bug. He got up quickly and climbed out on his own. I'm sure he'll be sore, but he can't be too hurt if he's climbing out of there on his own two feet," Dad reassures me.

Carson points up at the TV. "Look, he's there helping Trey."

My eyes snap back to the screen. He's right, you can see Knox is back up on the chutes by Trey on the side of the camera frame. He took his chaps and vest off and put his cowboy hat back on. He's talking to Trey who already has all of his gear on and Knox seems fine.

"See? He's alright. Bull riders are tough."

"This is his traveling partner, right?" Jessie asks.

She wasn't at the ranch the day they stopped, and she has only seen him with his helmet on. I never bothered to look him up online, so when they got to the ranch and I saw his shaggy blonde hair, blue eyes, and smile that could drop a nun's panties, I knew he and Jessie would be fire and gasoline. He's *exactly* her type.

"Yeah, he fell in the well and 'got ran the fuck over' last night. He's gotta be sore," I tell her.

"Language," my dad scolds.

"It's a loophole." I smirk at him. "I was quoting Knox, I don't want to misquote him."

Carson scoffs next to me as my dad glares at me. Outside working, he's worse than a sailor, but he's always had a rule about cursing in the house.

"What's the well?" Jessie asks.

"Knox explained it to me last night. When a bull starts to spin, they refer to the inside of the spin as 'the well' because once you fall in, there's almost no chance of climbing back out. He said some bulls are naturally welly because of how they buck, and they get a reputation for dropping guys in."

We watch Trey buck off at 6 seconds, then all of us move to the kitchen to clean up dinner. Pretty soon, my phone is ringing. I pull it out of my pocket to check the caller ID.

"Go," my dad says, "talk to him. We've got this covered."

"Thanks, I'll text and let you know how he is." I wave goodbye as I walk out the back door and answer Knox's call.

"Hey, we're packing up to head out. Wanted to call you quick."

"Are you okay? Looked like that dismount hurt." I catch the tremble in my voice and take a deep breath. I trot down the back steps of Dad's house and start walking home with Rein on my heels.

I can hear Knox moving around packing up. "Yeah, I'm all good, just knocked the air out of me a little."

"Good to hear. It was a great ride. Think you'll win it?"

"Thanks, probably not. There're some good matchups tomorrow night, but I should get a good check."

"As long as you're pulling checks, you'll keep climbing in the standings," I say encouragingly.

"Exactly," I can hear the smile on his face. "Hang on one sec, I'm going to start the truck, and you'll connect to the speakers." I hear doors shutting and the dinging of the key in the ignition.

The phone connects to the truck speakers right as Trey asks, "What was your bull's name?"

"Prime Time," Knox answers.

"Yeah, Prime Time to get your shit wrecked." Trey laughs and I hear shuffling like Knox hit him.

"Oh, fuck off. You're the one who got thirsty last night and dove into the well."

"I wasn't thirsty, I thought I saw a penny," Trey jokes back.

"It's not a wishing well, you idiot. Unless you were wishing to get your ass ran over, then wish granted." Knox laughs at whatever look I'm sure Trey just gave him. "Face it, you got excited, made too big of a move and end up diving in the well."

"Hey, I wasn't excited. I never get excited. I'm as calm and collected as a monk."

Knox busts out laughing. "Monks shave their heads. Can I shave your head?"

"Touch my hair and we are no longer friends. The ladies love my blond locks."

"You're telling me I could've gotten rid of you at any point over the last few years if I just shaved your head?"

I watch Rein run up ahead of me, sniffing around. The guys keep going on the other end of the line. I like it. It makes me feel like I'm there, even if I'm states away.

"Psh—you know I'm great. You'd get bored without me," Trey says confidently.

I clear my throat, and the line goes quiet for a second, like they forgot I was there. I've noticed this before when I'm on the truck speaker, they get bickering like siblings and forget I'm listening. It's really entertaining. If anyone ever followed these two with a camera, they would have a new hit reality TV show.

"No, I'd get some peace and quiet, that's what I'd get," Knox states, before addressing me. "How was your day, Kace?"

I fill him in on my day and tell him, "Jack came by to shoe a couple of horses. I think he misses your company."

"Oh yeah? Did you tell him I do a better job than he does?" I know he has a cocky grin on his face.

I laugh. "Well, if I did that, you'd have to come back to shoe horses after he quits. Matter of fact, that doesn't sound like a bad idea."

"Wait a minute now. Tell him in September; I can be back to shoe in October."

I hear his maps telling him to turn up ahead.

I walk up the front steps to my house, and Rein curls up in her dog bed. "Alright, I suppose I can wait to tell him. I just got home. I still need to shower and do a load of laundry. Talk tomorrow?"

"Of course, we're about to stop and get some food. Night, Kace."

"Night, Knox."

I hear Trey singsong, "Goodnight, Mrs. Ward!" as I hang up the phone.

Click.

I can't help but shake my head at the nickname he's taken to calling me.

Five more days until I can see Knox, feel his arms around me, and kiss him. I can do five days.

Chapter 32

Knox

Estes Park, Colorado

Trey and I have done well since Livingston. I've bucked off once, and Trey twice, but the bulls we rode paid well. We're both sore, but we're used to it. I hardly notice anymore, it's just part of the game.

"Man, my calf hurts where that bull stepped on me," Trey whines in the passenger seat.

He really is tough. Sometimes I think he just likes to complain to break the silence in the truck.

"Eat a spoonful of concrete and harden the fuck up." I glance at him with a grin.

"Okay, Mr. Hardass. Do you have a spoon? I know where I'm going to shove it." He narrows his eyes at me in challenge.

"We're almost there, then I'll get you one right after I kick that calf."

His eyes go wide. "Oh, you wanna go there? I know your ribs are still sore, old man."

He isn't wrong. That hit in Livingston did more than knock the air out of me, like I told Kacey. It bruised them pretty bad. My whole side is purple.

"Yeah, but I'm a real man, so I don't complain about it."

Trey mumbles something under his breath as we pull into the back gate in Estes Park. It's about three hours until the rodeo starts. I flash our credentials and drive in to find a place to park.

"What time are they coming?" Trey asks as I back into a parking spot. "I want to grab a shower before your future wife and her smoking hot friend get here."

"I think 'future wife' is a bit of a stretch," I say, narrowing my eyes at him. "And for the love of god, please leave Jessie alone. She's Kacey's best friend—I don't need you making things awkward."

He's dead serious when he looks at me with a straight face and says, "Tell her to get ugly friends then," and hops out of the truck.

I lean my head against the seat and sigh. This could be an interesting night. Part of me wishes Kacey had come alone, but I also wouldn't want her driving all the way here by herself. I'll just have to hope Trey doesn't end up with his balls in a vice by the end of the night.

I climb out of the truck and text Kacey to let her know we're here.

Knox

Hey, just got parked. What time are you two thinking of coming to the grounds?

Kacey

We're downtown shopping right now, but we'll head up soon. I can't wait to see you.

Knox

Same, sweetheart. I'll meet you at the gate. I have my companion pass for you and I'll get Trey's for Jessie.

Kacey

Perfect, I'll text you when we get there.

Two hours later, we're both showered and I'm pacing behind the camper while Trey sits on the boxes.

"Dude, you need to chill. I'm sure she'll be here soon." He doesn't even look up from scrolling on his phone.

I stop pacing and turn to face him, crossing my arms. "I know. Now can I please have your companion pass? I need it for Jessie."

He glances up with a smirk on his face and says, "I know. But I think I'll hand-deliver it to her myself," before going back to scrolling.

"You're such a pain in the ass," I say as my phone vibrates. It's a text from Kace—they're here.

I smack Trey's foot off the knee he has it propped up on. "They're here. Get up and button your shirt. And please try not to come off as a cocky bull rider."

He stands and starts tucking in his pearl snap shirt. "Noted, cocky calf roper it is," he says as he finishes tucking in his shirt. "You never get this worked up before you ride. I think someone is in *love*." He draws out the word "love."

I reach in the camper door and grab both our cowboy hats while Trey does something weird to fix his hair. He's a pretty boy through and through.

"I'm not worked up. Now let's go." I set his hat on his head and walk off, not waiting to see if he's following.

I hear gravel crunching as he hurries to catch up to me. "I noticed you didn't disagree on the love part, but I'm going to let it go." I give him my sternest dad look. "Okay, okay, I'll stop." He holds both hands up in surrender.

I see Kacey before she sees me—she's smiling and laughing at something Jessie said. She looks happy, carefree. Her long blonde hair flows down her back in loose waves. She's wearing a blue sundress with cowboy boots. My ribs feel tight, like I can't take a full breath. She's the most beautiful woman I've ever seen.

We show our credentials to get through the gate, then weave through the crowd to them. Thankfully, they're standing off to the side of the gate and the crushing crowd of people.

As we approach, I take a quiet breath to calm myself.

When she sees me, her face lights up, greeting me with a smile, making that tight feeling in my chest return.

I greet her with my own smile before wrapping her in my arms.

She holds me tight as she buries her face between my shoulder and neck.

My ribs are sore, but I hold back my wince. Having my arms around her feels right. Sure, I've had girlfriends come watch me ride before, but Kacey isn't like any other girl.

When she finally pulls back, I run my hand behind her neck and pull her back in, giving her a kiss on the forehead.

"Hey, sweetheart."

"Hi," she squeaks excitedly.

I let her go and hold out the pass I had in my other hand. "What do you say, be my companion for the night?" I give her a wink.

"Aw, that is so sweet. Does it come with a diamond ring?" Jessie interjects.

"No, he left that in the truck. Hi, I'm Trey." He smiles, taking off his hat and sticking out his hand to shake Jessie's. She shakes his hand while looking him up and down, assessing him. Then she narrows her eyes and smirks.

Shit.

I sigh deeply and pinch the bridge of my nose. "We knew this would happen. You just have to let them fight for dominance. It'll be fine."

Kacey snickers beside me.

"I'd be happy to let you use my companion pass on one condition," Trey informs her.

Jessie crosses her arms, causing her corset-style top to push up her cleavage. "What's that?"

To Trey's credit, he doesn't glance down. Their eyes are locked on each other in some form of battle. "You just have to answer one question. I promise it's nothing too personal."

"Fine, shoot," she says, rising to his challenge.

Trey gets that look in his eye and gives her his signature player grin. "Are you a fan of Big and Rich?" he asks and I immediately know where this is going.

I take a step toward him as Jessie tilts her head in confusion, replying, "Yes, why?"

"So, you'd be open to saving a horse and riding—"

I hit Trey in the stomach, hard.

He lets out a grunt and doubles over. "That fuck'n hurt," he wheezes.

I rip the pass out of his hand and hold it out to Jessie. "Sorry, he's like a puppy, still in training." I look at Kacey and she's covering her mouth to suppress a laugh.

Jessie takes the pass, gives Trey one last glance, and says, "Have you tried a shock collar? I hear they're great training tools." Then she turns and links her arm with Kacey's. "Let's go. The birthday girl needs a drink. I could also use a drink."

My jaw drops. "Wait, it's your birthday? Why didn't you say anything?" I feel horrible. This is something I should know. I want to get her a present and—shit. I don't even get one night with her. This is the type of thing Megan would use against me and get resentful, saying I wasn't there for her birthday or other events. I don't want Kacey to feel like I don't pay attention to her or that I don't care.

She groans, throwing her head back. "It's not my birthday."

"She's right. It's in two days, but we're celebrating all week," Jessie informs me.

"Well, happy early birthday. First round is on me—*after* the rodeo," Trey chimes in, still holding his stomach.

I pull myself out of my spiral. "I wish you would've told me." I hate how I sound slightly hurt. Trey might buy a round, but we can't stay long. We *have* to head to another rodeo.

She lets go of Jessie's arm and steps closer to me. "It's really not a big deal, and I'm sure you need to go get ready. We'll meet up after for a drink. We can celebrate then." She gives me a reassuring smile.

"Alright. I'll try to get a birthday win for you." I tip my hat back, wrap my hand around her waist, and lean in toward her.

She meets me halfway for a kiss. "Good luck, you got this." She pulls away, winks, and heads for the grandstands with Jessie.

Trey slaps me on the shoulder. "Come on, Romeo. Let's go spur a couple bulls."

Chapter 33

Kacey

There are people everywhere as we make our way to the closest drink stand and get in line. I heard someone say it's sold out all four nights.

"I can't believe you didn't tell him this is your birthday trip. We do this every year. He looked so hurt," Jessie chastises me.

I sigh, looking down at my boots on the blacktop. "I thought about it. I just didn't want to put any extra pressure on him. I know Knox, he'd want to do something special, but he doesn't have time right now. I don't want him to lose sleep just so he can get a little more time with me or make a big deal of it." I look up and find Jessie watching me. "This is his busiest time of year, he's tired and sore. I don't want anything to get in the way of his goals."

"I can understand that. From what you've told me, he hasn't had supportive partners in the past. He's lucky to have you." Jessie loops her arm through mine and leans her head on my shoulder. "Ya know, he looks at you like you're a Disney Princess." She sighs dramatically. "I want a man to look at me like that someday."

"You'll find that. I'm sure of it." I give her arm a squeeze.

We had just grabbed our drinks—Jessie ordered two for each of us so we don't have to go back for a while—when my phone vibrates.

Knox

> It looks pretty packed out there. Those passes don't have assigned seats, but there are bleachers back here you can sit in. Go to the walk-through gate on the east side and you'll see them.

Kacey

> Okay, thanks.

I turn to Jessie. "Looks like we're rolling VIP tonight. We can use these passes to get to a set of bleachers in the back."

She holds both drinks up in the air and hoots. "Fuck yeah. Let's get out of this crowd. I hate people."

We find the gate easily, show the security guard our passes and he lets us right through. We are seated in the small bleachers; they're front row seats right next to the roping boxes. We have a good view of the bucking chutes as well.

"These are awesome seats," Jessie comments before taking a drink of her beer. Her hands—always covered in rings—catch on the arena lights.

I watch her look around like she's looking for someone. "Yeah, they are. So, you want to tell me what that silent thing between you and Trey was about?"

Her head whips back around to face me. "I have no idea what you're talking about," she huffs.

I scoff. "Yeah, sure. Your stare down with serious eye contact was *nothing*."

She shifts in her seat and takes another drink before fessing up. "Okay, fine. He's extremely attractive. One hundred percent my type. Happy?"

I nod. "And?" I draw out the word.

"You could've warned me. Don't think I didn't hear your comment about dominance, asshole." She squints her eyes at me. "He might be pretty, but he's a player. I could tell just by watching him walk up. Besides, I'm not interested in dating a bull rider. I'm a nurse, I see enough torn-up bodies at work. I don't need one at home."

I don't need her to remind me of the dangers of this sport. It's all I can think about every time Knox climbs into the chute. I have to remind myself to breathe, release the white-knuckle grip I have my fists in, and trust that he's a professional, takes every precaution he can, and he knows what he's doing.

He's going to be fine. Or at least that's what I keep telling myself, and hopefully someday I can believe it.

I glance at the chutes, then look down. My stomach turns. "Right."

She immediately turns and grabs my arm. "I'm sorry, you know I didn't mean Knox. I don't even mean it like that at all," she rushes to say. "I just don't need more to worry about in my life. I can barely take care of myself and Gran."

I squeeze her knee. "It's okay, I know what you mean. And you're right, they get hurt. It's more of a question of how bad, not when."

She tsks. "Nah, not Knox. Have you seen that man? He's jacked. You could throw him in a hurricane, and he'd walk out without a scratch." She bumps my shoulder, trying to lighten the mood.

I chuckle and shoulder bump her back, but the conversation has sobered my mood. "Yeah, yeah. I've seen him shirtless. You're not wrong."

We make a drinking game of anyone who bucks off or misses their calf. Pretty soon, our cups are empty and they're rolling the barrel out to start the bull riding. While the alcohol has relaxed me some, I'm still a ball of nerves. How do the other girlfriends and wives handle this? Knowing each night someone you love risks their life for a paycheck and sport they love? I don't know if I can do this. But I'm not sure what scares me more, the danger of the sport or the thought of not being with Knox anymore. I feel stuck between a rock and a hard place.

"Looks like Trey will be before Knox tonight. He has his helmet on and looks ready to go." I'm already sitting on the edge of my seat, bouncing my knee. If I thought I got nervous at home, this is ten times worse.

Jessie, however, is not nervous at all. She's braiding a small lock of her hair, humming along to the music they're playing over the loudspeakers. Now that I think about it, she might be the perfect bull rider's girlfriend if she'd let herself. Her exposure to injuries, stressful childhood, and penchant for living a little on the wild side would have her fitting right in.

The first bull rider makes it to the corner when the bull starts to spin, but his inside foot comes up and he nearly hits the back of the bull's head with his facemask. He's able to block the hit with his free hand, but the bull's momentum sends the guy's body twirling in a helicopter motion, while his hand is still caught in his rope.

I hold my breath, watching the bullfighters move in to help him.

Once there is enough G-force put on his arm, his hand pops out and he goes flying, landing in a heap on the dirt. He scurries to his feet and tries to limp back to the chutes as fast as he can, clearly in pain. The bull leaves the arena, then the bullfighters help him the rest of the way to safety.

All of a sudden, it sinks in. Knox could die. It doesn't happen often, but bull riders *can* die. His words play back in my head.

Danger is very real, but fear is a choice.

Knox knows how dangerous it is and chooses to do it, anyway. I don't know if I can handle this, but I know I can't lose what we have, so for now, I will shove my fear into a box and pray this gets easier with time.

Jessie taps me on the knee. "Here's Trey."

She sits up and leans forward so she can see through the fence better.

I can see Knox pulling Trey's bull rope and saying something to him as he wraps his rope around his hand.

The announcer lists Trey's wins and career highlights. "This man is on track for his second trip to the national finals rodeo in December. He's proven time and time again he can ride the buckers. Show'em tonight, Trey." They start playing a Score song and he nods his head.

The chute gate flies open and his bull kicks hard and stutter steps out two jumps. He turns back to the left, away from Trey's hand, but it doesn't affect him. He looks completely in control. The crowd grows louder and louder each round Trey makes on the bull. Knox is hollering from the back of the bucking chutes.

At seven seconds, he gets yanked to the outside but doesn't let go. He has one foot under the bull and the other one coming across his back, but he hasn't hit the ground yet. The whistle blows and he opens his hand right as the bull jumps forward, throwing Trey through the air. He tucks into a ball, doing a couple of somersaults before he pops up onto his feet like nothing happened. He throws his arms in the air, hyping up the crowd.

I can't help but laugh. "Well, he clearly lives for the crowd's attention." I turn to Jessie.

She has her eyes locked on Trey, following him across the arena as he picks up his bull rope. "I have a feeling Trey lives for attention, period," she replies.

Chapter 34

Knox

I hear the eight-second whistle for Trey before I jump down off the chutes to go grab my gear. I've seen Trey's legendary crowd hype performance before, and I have a feeling he'll go all out with Jessie here tonight. I don't know what was decided during their weird stare-down, but he was hyper-focused behind the chutes tonight.

The crowd roars as the announcer gets them to stomp their feet in the grandstands. I buckle my chaps, throw on my vest, and head for the alley. My bull is at the back, so I start getting my rope on him. I take extra time making sure I like how it's set. The bull I have is one I can win on, but he's also known to be mean. I refuse to ruin Kacey's birthday by getting wrecked out. I'll ride him, then make a good dismount, and hightail it to the barrel or nearest gate.

I'm trying not to read too much into the fact that Kacey didn't tell me this was her birthday trip. Jessie clearly didn't know it was a secret, so maybe Kacey just forgot to tell me. I plan to rope Jessie into helping me get her flowers and a gift, even if I can't be there in person.

The longer this goes between us, the more I'm realizing just how much I've fallen for her. And I'm slowly trusting that she's in this for the long haul. All the late-night phone calls after rodeos, and encouraging text messages, I'm pretty sure she hasn't missed a single ride that's been on TV. She might not be ready to verbalize her feelings for me, but she's showing me every day.

I finish setting my rope and grab my helmet. Trey is back at his gear bag, stripping out of his vest and blue chaps. "I'll be up to pull your rope. You have a birthday girl to impress." He smirks at me. For all his joking around, I know he's happy for me. Driving overnight to the ranch, offering to drive after rodeos just so I can put all my focus on her when we talk. He might be a shithead sometimes, but he's a good friend.

I climb down in the chute, and Trey pulls my rope up so I can warm the rosin. I hear the announcer going over the bull's stats and mine. The clown stands on his barrel, hyping up the crowd as I take my wrap. They play "Gladiator" by Zayde Wolf as I call for the black muley and the gate flies open.

He turns back into the gate to the right. I angle my hips and shoulders, then throw my free arm over my head as he kicks. He steps ahead and throws his head to the outside. I know if I make too big of a move, he's going to well me. This bull might not have horns, but I know he has a reputation for clearing an arena.

I square up when I climb over his shoulders on the next rear, but he beats me around his next corner. I manage to catch up at the last second using core strength alone. One reason I workout so much isn't just to keep from getting injured, it's to buy myself a second chance to get back in the middle of a bull's back when most guys would have gotten bucked off.

He makes two more rounds before he gets smart. He gives a big jump forward and I'm nearly too late setting my hips to my rope, then he turns back to the left. He thinks he's smart, anyway. Joke's on him—I love bulls that turn away from my hand. I keep my free arm low; he doesn't feel welly this direction and I'm feeling confident in my seat. I pick up my outside foot and raise it as high as I can, then drop it back down at the exact moment his front feet hit the ground. This is known as spurring. It's not meant to hurt the animal, piss him off, or to break his spirit. It's to show the judges that I am in complete control.

This bull is good, but it doesn't matter what he does, he can't throw me. The whistle blows and I grab my tail, breaking the bind and I step off on my feet. Lucky enough, I'm only four feet from the fence so I can make a quick getaway while the muley bull tries to run down the bullfighters. I step up on the panels and sit on the top rung, letting the twinge in my ribs fade.

I take my helmet off and watch the bullfighters do their thing. They're letting the bull get inches from them and stepping around them like *"Psych! Not going to get me today,"* they're having fun with him. These guys are some of the best in the world.

After the bull leaves the arena, I climb down and pick up my rope, which got thrown right in front of the bleachers where Kacey is sitting. I grab the rope and look up to find her in the crowd. Our eyes meet and I mouth the words "Happy Birthday" and give her a wink.

Her face turns red as Jessie smacks her knee, saying something to her, and it makes me smile.

"We saved the best for last and he's going to be this year's champion bull rider with 87 points," the announcer bellows.

I head back behind the chutes, do my interview, and quickly pack my bag so I can meet up with Kacey. I've never seen Trey pack so fast. Normally, he has to clean all his gear and pack it perfectly, but today, he just tossed everything in his bag.

"That interaction with Jessie must have you all sorts of worked up. You never pack this fast," I tell him as I fold my chaps up and toss them in my bag.

He's shoving the last of his gear in his bag and zipping it up. "I am not worked up. I figured we were in a hurry, it being Kacey's birthday and all."

"True. Would you mind hanging with Jessie for a bit so I can get some time with Kacey?" I tuck the corner of my vest in and finish zipping up my bag.

"Oh, you're going to owe me big for this one." He raises a brow, trying to conceal his shit-eating grin.

We both throw our bags over our shoulders and walk out the gate. "Yeah right, pretty sure you don't see spending time with Jessie as a burden."

We make our way over to the small set of bleachers the girls were sitting on.

"You did great," Kacey says. I drop my bag as Kacey runs up and wraps her arms around me. "Best birthday present ever."

I look into her sea green eyes. "Thanks, sweetheart. I'm glad you think so, since I don't have anything else for you. A warning might have been nice." I grin at her as I hear Jessie try to smother a laugh.

"What about the diamond ring in the truck?" Trey chimes in.

He's such an idiot.

Thankfully, Kacey ignores him. "Getting to see you so close to my birthday is all I want." She runs her fingers through my hair at the base of my neck. I give her a quick kiss and she releases me.

We head back to the truck and load our gear bags.

Trey grabs three beers out of the cooler and hands one to Jessie.

"Birthday girl?" he asks, holding up the last beer.

She glances at me.

"We all know Knox isn't drinking," Trey reads her mind.

"No thanks, one of us has to drive and Jessie has taken full advantage of her day off," Kacey tells him while still looking at me like I might disappear.

I hold out my hand to her. "Take a walk with me?"

Kacey takes my hand and looks over at Jessie. "You good here?"

"Yeah, yeah, I promise I'll be *nice*," Jessie assures her in a tone that doesn't sound assuring at all.

Trey pulls out two lawn chairs for them. "You don't have to be nice; I like feisty women."

"Let's go before the fight starts." I pull Kacey toward the horse barns right as I hear what sounds like a lawn chair getting shoved over and Trey laughing.

We hold hands and walk until we round the end of the third barn in the row. Kacey pulls back on my arm and gently pushes my back up against the barn wall. "How long until you need to leave for Calgary?"

"I have a little while and I want to spend it with my girl-friend," I tell her as I run my hand up to the nape of her neck, threading my fingers in her hair.

She loops her arms behind my lower back. "Girlfriend, huh?"

"I mean, I thought that's what this was. You gonna tell me I'm wrong?" I challenge as I start planting kisses all over her face and neck, causing her to giggle and squirm.

"Yeah, yeah, that's what this is, *boyfriend*. But seriously, how long, Knox?"

I lean my head back and sigh. "Thirty minutes. It's a long drive and we never know how long it will take to get through border security." When I look back down at her, she's watching my jaw. I didn't even realize I was flexing it. I want more time with her, and it's frustrating I can't have it. "If it wasn't the Calgary Stampede, I'd turn out and spend the day with you."

"Absolutely not. That's not the mindset I want you to have. You need to go, and you need to win." Her tone is firm, she means business.

"I know. I just miss you and it's your birthday." I lean my forehead against hers. "I don't want the fact that I miss your birthday, or you have a big roping and I'm not there to support you, to affect our relationship. We don't even know when we'll see each other next," I tell her honestly. It's hard not to let my thoughts run right to every reason that would cause her to resent me and eventually end this relationship.

She moves her hands up to my face and forces me to lean back and look at her. "So?"

"So?" I repeat, confused by her response.

"So, we don't know when we'll see each other next. So, you're not visiting on my birthday. I never said I needed you there for my birthday, ropings, or anything else. You're the only one thinking these thoughts. You were honest with me in June. I knew what I was signing up for, and I'm not going anywhere. If I have an issue, I'll tell you." She holds my gaze, making sure I see the honesty in her eyes.

"I don't know what I did right, but getting to call you mine is the best thing that's ever happened to me." I press a soft kiss to her lips. With her reassurance, I can take my first full breath since this night started. She's trying so hard to trust me, I have to do the same for her.

"Now that we have that settled," Kacey says smirking and running her hands down my chest, "how would you like to spend the next twenty-five minutes?"

"It's your birthday—well, almost—what would you like to do?" I ask with a wink.

We spend the next twenty-five minutes making out like high schoolers.

Chapter 35

Knox

Dodge City, Kansas

The last few weeks have been brutal. Calgary is a progressive format, so when Trey didn't make it out of his bracket—and I did—we had to split up. I had a break between my bracket and the semifinals, so we drove overnight to Casper, Wyoming. I rode there, then caught a ride back to Calgary for the semifinals with some bronc riders. I didn't advance out of the semifinals while Trey went to two other rodeos.

At this point, I feel like the living version of the Johnny Cash song "I've Been Everywhere." After Calgary, we had back-to-back rodeos in Salinas, California, Nampa, Idaho, Ogden, Spanish Fork, and Salt Lake City, Utah. We had one day off to drive to the Midwest for a handful of rodeos before heading back to Deadwood South Dakota then Eagle, Colorado.

Kacey was supposed to come to Eagle but got stuck at the ranch when the ranch hands were taken down by a case of bad food poisoning. Now we're back to square one; not knowing when we'll see each other next. Trey and I are in the Midwest again this week, then head straight to the Pacific Northwest where we'll stay for most of August and September.

I'm exhausted, sore, and missing her, but I've climbed to number two in the world standings. When Kacey couldn't make it to Eagle, I was close to turning around and driving to the ranch, but she talked me out of it. Encouraging me to keep going, reminding me I'll be number one soon and that she'll get me all to herself starting October first.

Now we're sitting behind the chutes in Dodge City Kansas, it's 112 degrees outside with no shade or breeze. I don't know who thought a rodeo in the middle of Kansas in July was a good idea, but they thought wrong. Every year I complain about this rodeo, but every damn year I enter it again.

"What are the symptoms of heat stroke?" Trey moans next to me where he's leaning against the fence to the back pens.

"How would I know?" I counter while putting rosin on my rope tied to the fence.

"You're old. Old people have strokes, so I assumed you knew," he mouths off without hesitation.

"It's too hot out to deal with you," I say as I walk away, searching for more bottled water.

An hour later, I'm on the back of the chutes, pulling Trey's rope after I've ridden my bull for 85 points. "Breathe, Trey. Move with him, you got this," I say encouragingly.

"Man, this rosin is like fuck'n butter." He pats the bull's hump with his gloved hand, trying to use the dirt and hair to keep his rosin sticky.

"I tried to tell you to add some dry rosin, too. But no, the old man doesn't know shit," I grunt as I pull with all my strength.

"Yeah, yeah, you were right. That what you want to hear?" He adjusts his hand in the rope before I pull it all the way tight.

"Too late now. Split the pinky and hold on like your life depends on it." I finish pulling his rope and he takes the suicide wrap. He nods and the gate swings open.

The bull blows up in the air, his front feet are three feet off the ground when he reaches the full extent of his kick. Trey is riding him perfectly as the bull turns back to the right. He might win this Extreme Bulls. Then, just like that, it takes a turn for the worst.

That's the thing about bull riding. One minute you're winning—you feel on top of the world and invincible—but the next minute, you're bucking off, beat up and busted, losing your only source of income. It's a never-ending roller coaster.

The bull blows up again and Trey's hand pops out of his handle, but he still has his tail and he's still trying to make it to the whistle. One thing about Trey is he'll never quit until he hits the dirt. He slides down the bull's back as it rears, then when the bull transitions into the kick, Trey is sitting on the bull's ass.

The worst position to be in.

Trey does a complete backflip flying into the air and comes down directly on his head. He's out cold on impact.

Fuck.

I climb over the chute and jump into the arena. The bull fighters step in to try and get the bull's attention so he doesn't come back to maul Trey's lifeless-looking body, but the bull ignores them. He has Trey in his sights and runs at him. Dropping his head, he pushes and stomps all over Trey. The crowd collectively gasps. The pickup men ride in on horseback and get a rope around the bull's horns, dragging him away from Trey and out of the arena.

I'm the first to reach him, but I can see Sports Medicine running over. His vest is held on by one shoulder strap, the rest is all torn up.

I poke him in the side of the face through the cage of his helmet. "Trey. Trey, wake up."

The crowd has gone silent; you could hear a pin drop. Or in my case, I can literally hear Trey snoring.

I poke him again and say, "They're bringing the backboard." If there's one thing a cowboy hates, it's leaving the arena strapped to a backboard. We'll be bleeding everywhere with a broken leg and still crawl out of the arena and drive ourselves to the hospital. Most of us don't have insurance and there are no programs willing to help with medical bills.

Trey's eyes slowly open. "No backboard," he grunts. "I'll take a pillow though, kinda sleepy."

I'm immediately relieved to hear him joke. "You just took a nap, does anything hurt?"

He takes a sharp breath. "More like 'what doesn't hurt?' What happened?"

"You got knocked out, then got camped on before anyone could help."

Sports Med reaches us when Trey answers me. "Yep, should've gone with the dry rosin. Help me up."

Travis, the head of Sports Med, kneels next to Trey and asks, "Was he unconscious?"

Trey tries to get up and an EMT scolds him. "Hold still. We need to assess your neck before you can get up."

"Knox?" Travis turns back to me, waiting for the answer.

I clear my throat. "Yeah, he woke up quick though and cracked a joke."

Travis huffs out a laugh. "Sounds like Trey."

I stand and step back, letting them check his neck and spine for any signs of damage. I can hear the announcer finishing a short prayer before he tells the crowd Trey is awake and moving. You can hear a collective sigh of relief.

After a minute, Trey has caught his breath and gets fed up. He pushes up on his elbows, looking at me.

As rodeo cowboys, we get hurt all the time. We're used to it, and we know when it's serious and when it's not. We also have extremely high pain tolerances. Those who don't, don't make it very long on the rough stock side of the arena.

I bend and grip his elbow, pulling him up, both of us ignoring the EMTs' protests. The Sports Med team knows cowboys better, they don't say a word as I loop one arm around Trey's back, and he throws his arm over my shoulders. The crowd cheers, happy to see him on his feet. He takes a couple breaths that cause him to grit his teeth before Travis grabs onto the back of his chaps, and we help him out of the arena.

———

Kacey

> How's he feeling today? Have you seen the doctor yet? What did they say?

Kacey has been checking in on Trey every hour. She made me give him the phone last night so she could talk to him herself. I like that she cares about my friend enough to check in.

Knox

Just three broken ribs. He'll need to take a few weeks off but he's good.

Kacey

Oh good. I'm glad it's not worse.

"I can go with you just to help drive," Trey says from the exam table he sits on, buttoning his shirt back up. He shifts his weight and the paper crinkles beneath him. We stayed in Dodge City last night and got him X-Rays at a local doctor today. It's cheaper than the ER and he wanted to see how he felt.

He broke three ribs and is extremely sore, but he's lucky. No concussion, organ or spine damage. Thank god for our vests and helmets—they protect us a lot more than most people realize.

"Bumping up and down the road won't help those ribs heal. Not to mention we both know you won't be able to stay off the back of the chutes. You need to go home and heal, then come back out and make the finals," I instruct him without looking up from my phone. I'm going over our rodeo schedule—it's not good. We entered hard, we both want to go into the finals' top five.

"I'll be fine. You can't drive all this by yourself. Just let me—"

The doctor walks back in, cutting him off. "Alright, Mr. Bennett, I sent your script in. Unless there is anything else you need, you're free to go."

We thank him and head for the door.

Once we're in the truck, I turn in my seat to find Trey taking shallow breaths after the walk out of the office. He's climbing so slowly into the truck. Broken ribs suck, and there is nothing you can do for them but give them time. I broke a couple a few years ago, I was back in four weeks. They still hurt like hell, but I could grit my teeth and ride.

"Thirty days," I say to him. Our association allows us to take a thirty-day doctor's release. This takes us out of any rodeos we have entered and we don't have to pay our entry fees—unlike when a rider turns out of a rodeo and still has to pay the fees. It will cost Trey several thousand dollars in fees if he doesn't take a doctor's release.

He leans his head back on the headrest before rolling it sideways and admitting defeat. "Alright. Thirty days, then I'm back, but I'm not taking those pain pills he prescribed."

I chuckle. "I wouldn't either. I'll call my sister, see if she can meet us halfway and pick you up." I've always been leery of taking pain pills—too many professional athletes get hooked on them and ruin their careers.

I guess I've rubbed off on Trey.

I call my sister, Payton, and she immediately jumps into action. She agrees to meet me halfway to pick Trey up and I have no doubt she and my mother will cook a mountain of food for him.

"Is she bringing Wacey?" Trey asks. "That kid cracks me up."

My nephew Wacey is the best—he's seven now and loves hanging out with Trey and me. He always has a smile on his face and tries to play pranks on everyone. He also says he's going to be a bull rider someday, much to my sister's dismay.

"I'm sure. It's summer, so he's not in school." My sister is a photographer, making her schedule flexible and he pretty much goes everywhere with her. Her husband works in the oil fields and is gone *a lot*, so, often, it's just the two of them.

I drop Trey off with my sister three hours later, then turn right back around and drive twenty-one hours to Missoula, Montana. I barely make it in time for the Extreme Bulls, and I don't ride my bull. For the next four days, I bounce between Hermiston, Oregon, back to Missoula for their rodeo, then to Logan, Utah, totaling forty hours of driving.

Kacey has been checking in more frequently, and I can tell she's worried about me.

I'm exhausted. I can't keep going at this pace, but I also don't have a choice. Next week is going to be even worse. When we enter rodeos, we tell them what dates we'd prefer, but we don't always get those dates. Our preferences are put into a computer system that analyzes our credentials and spits out when we are supposed to compete.

I texted her next week's schedule and did something I never thought I'd do. I asked if she would be able to fly out and come with me for a bit. I've never traveled with a girlfriend—maybe for a day or two, but nothing beyond that. Kacey said she can't leave the ranch, and I understand that. Plus, I'm sure she's looking at a map thinking I'm crazy—and she wouldn't be wrong. But if you're going to take up this line of work, you must be a little crazy, right? No sane person would take this kind of mental and physical abuse.

Chapter 36

Kacey

I walk in the backdoor of Dad's house, letting the screen door slam behind me.

"You in here?" I holler. His truck was out front, but the house is quiet.

"Out here," I hear him say from the deck.

I step out onto the deck to find my dog has already found him and is collecting her pet tax via some scratches behind the ear.

"Hey," I say as I plop myself down in the Adirondack chair next to him. I rub my tired eyes with my thumb and forefinger and let out a sigh.

Watching Trey get knocked out and stomped on was horrible. I had to look away. When rides go smoothly, I can pretend it's not as dangerous, but when things like that happen, it's hard not to picture it being Knox. Especially when it happened to his best friend.

"What's wrong?" Dad stops petting Rein and looks my way.

"Nothing. I'm just worried about Knox. Every time I talk to him, he sounds more and more exhausted having to drive without Trey, and his schedule next week is a mess. He asked if I could come out on the road to help him, but I told him I can't."

I wish I could. I miss him so much. I got so used to him being around the ranch every day and I didn't even realize it, and now he's gone. I wanted to say yes, and in a different life, I could've, but I can't leave the ranch.

Dad brushes his hand down his beard thoughtfully. "Why? You could go help him."

I whip my head around to look at him. "What? No, I can't. I have to be here."

"Kacey, you haven't taken time off in . . . well . . . ever. We have ranch hands for a reason. Go with him until Trey's back. I know you miss him, and he needs your help."

I stare at him, trying to process what he's saying. *Is he seriously telling me to take the next three weeks off and go rodeo with Knox? Doesn't he need me here?* I know we're done foaling, but we have colts to start and cattle to work.

"I can't just leave. I have colts I'm working with and—and . . . ." I can't really come up with anything else. The colts are my main job right now. I help with the cattle as needed, but my primary job is managing the horse barn.

"We have other people who can work those colts. What's more important? Knox or the colts?"

His words hit me square in the chest.

"Knox," I answer without hesitation.

This might be a once in a lifetime opportunity for us. I felt horrible missing Eagle and crushed when we realized we might not see each other until the end of the season. My heart rate picks up at the thought of three weeks with Knox. And I've hardly traveled anywhere outside Colorado. It's too hard to leave the ranch for extended periods of time.

Does Knox really want me to travel with him for three weeks?

I know he misses me; he tells me every day. He was so close to turning out of Eagle and coming here just to get a few hours with me. But three weeks of traveling together? It's not exactly a vacation. What if I say or do the wrong thing? I have no idea what to expect or do at these huge rodeos. Regardless, it's time together, and that's what I'm aching for.

I wring my hands in my lap and voice my fear. "What if he gets sick of me? Three weeks is a long time on the road."

My dad chuckles.

Okay, glad my concerns are a joke to him.

"Bug, I've seen the way that boy looks at you. I'm sure there isn't anything he wants more than for you to travel with him. Your mother and I loved every second we spent together. We spent every day working this ranch together, even on our worst days, nothing could separate us. Those were some of the best years of my life."

Okay, not a joke. My eyes burn as I try to fight back tears. "You never talk about her."

He sighs. "I know, and I'm sorry. After she died, it was just too hard. There was so much to do—I had to figure out how to balance the ranch and take care of you. But I should've told you more stories and shared with you how smart she was. How her smile would light up on Sunday morning when she saw you eyeing that stack of chocolate chip pancakes. She loved you so much and she was my entire world. I never dreamed of a day I would spend without her. I miss her every day." His eyes turn glassy, but he blinks it away.

"I miss her, too." I swipe at a tear before it can fall.

"I'll try to be better about talking about her. You remind me so much of her."

Rein makes her way over to me and nudges my hand for pets. I run my hand down the soft fur on the top of her head and it's a comfort. "Thanks, I'd like that. So, you really think I should go?"

"I do. You're young and there's an entire world out there for you to see. And Knox seems like the kind of person you should experience it with. So yes, get out of here." He smiles through his thick beard like I haven't seen in a long time.

"Alright, I'll go call him." We stand and I give Dad a big hug. Rein tries to join, making us both laugh. "Take care of Rein while I'm gone?"

He glances down at her. "You're getting a bath and coming inside."

I shake my head. He spoils her rotten every chance he gets. I'm sure I'll come home to a retired cow dog lounging on the couch.

***

Two days later, I'm waiting on the curb of the Boise, Idaho airport. It worked perfectly for me to fly here, since he rides in Caldwell tonight.

I see his truck and camper round the bend, waiting in the line of cars to pick up passengers. When I called him after I left Dad's, there was no hesitation. He wants me to come help him, but more than that, he's so excited to show me his world. I just hope I fit in, pro rodeo and jackpot ropings—or even ranching—are completely different. I have no idea what to expect.

He had yesterday off, and I was grateful he could rest. He only rode one bull last week and I know it's eating at him. The average bull rider might only cover twenty-five percent of their bulls, but that's not Knox, he's used to covering forty or fifty percent of his—that's why he's one of the best in the world. I know it's just stress and exhaustion; he'll turn it around this week with me helping drive.

He pulls up and jumps out, running round the front of the truck. When he steps up the curb and wraps me in his arms, I realize I was holding my breath. His bergamot and leather scent envelops me, I know I made the right choice in coming here. He's slowly become my home without me even knowing it. He pulls back and gives me a big smile.

I can't help myself; I pull him in for a kiss.

"I missed you," he whispers against my lips.

"I missed you, too."

He grabs my bag and says, "What on earth did you pack? Bricks?"

I chuckle nervously. "Not exactly, but I did throw a few books in. I wasn't sure what I'd do while you got ready and things, so I packed those."

He throws the bag over his shoulder and climbs up to the camper door. "We can stop at bookstores whenever we're near one. You're probably going to go through them quickly."

It's official—he's every woman's dream man.

Jessie

Don't forget to find me a nice cowboy to keep me warm this winter.

Kacey

LOL there is always Trey.

Jessie

I said nice. Not a player.

Kacey

Fair enough.

We get to the rodeo grounds in Caldwell an hour later. After the rodeo tonight, we'll drive six hours to Canby, Oregon, then back down south to Gooding, Idaho. We'll finish the week in Moses Lake, Washington and Kalispell, Montana. Knox got put out wrong this week, which means we'll basically drive back and forth across the northwest.

"Come on, I'll show you around before the perf."

Knox leads me through the parking lot full of horse trailers, Capri campers, and sprinter vans. People are starting to get ready for the performance, horses are being saddled, rough stock riders are getting their gear bags ready. There're a few bareback riders huddled up working on riggins and kids are running wild, roping a dummy steer on hoverboards. Some of the best cowboys and cowgirls in the world are in this parking lot, but to me it just looks like one big family. They help each other, support and cheer for each other. It's unlike any other sport on earth.

Knox shows me the gate I can go through with my pass before we head toward the back pens. He's telling me all about the contractor who brings livestock to this rodeo, the Burning T Rodeo Company, and how all his kids help run the rodeos. They're from Oklahoma and he's known them for a long time. As we walk up to the back pens where the rough stock is kept, Knox tells me he's happy with his bull tonight, but that's not the one he wants to show me.

"I rode this bull at the finals last year for 89 points to win the round. He's a fan favorite," he says as he opens a gate and leads me down the alleyway, separating two different runs of pens. He stops at a pen holding a single brown and white spotted bull with short horns on each side. He's beautiful.

"Hey, big guy. Miss me?" Knox asks through the panel and, to my surprise, the bull walks toward us.

I take a step back and Knox laughs. "It's okay, he's friendly. Watch." As the bull comes up to the fence, he turns sideways, positioning his shoulder next to us. Knox reaches out and starts scratching the hump on his back. "He bucks like hell, but he's a big softy if you scratch him. There are actually quite a few bulls you can pet. It shocks people. They think they're all mean—and don't get me wrong, there are a ton of mean ones—but they don't buck because they're mean or mad. They buck because they love to do it. Someday, ol' Jawbreaker here will decide he's done and stop bucking. Then he'll retire back to the ranch to make baby buckers."

I step forward and reach out to scratch him, putting my hand near Knox's. "There is zero chance you can pet a bull at the ranch, just a warning for you."

He laughs and wraps his arm around my shoulder. "Wasn't planning on it." He's been holding my hand or touching me almost constantly since he picked me up.

I don't mind, I think he needs this as much as I do.

Chapter 37

Knox

I warm the rosin up on my rope. This is the last bull of the week, then I get two days off. Kacey and I are both tired, but it's been amazing having her with me.

I still can't get over the fact that she took three weeks off and flew out here to help me. I thought maybe she'd come for a week, not three. I don't know a single other person on the planet who would do that for me. My mom and sister support me, but it's different. This isn't something either of them could help me with. Kacey had no reason to do this other than the fact that she cares and wants to support me.

It's cooling off in the Northwest and I'm grateful for it. I have a tough bull tonight, but I'm feeling good, really good actually. Something about having Kacey with me just feels right.

I take my wrap, a deep breath, slide up, and nod. The bull rears up like he's trying to jump over the opening gate.

Shit.

I climb out over him as far as I can. Thankfully, we avoid a wreck. He turns back to the left. He has a belly roll at every kick. I drop my free arm and try to touch my left ear to my left shoulder to keep him from shifting me to the outside. And the way his loose hide rolls under me makes it that much tougher. This is going to be a bear fight the entire ride. No wonder this bull doesn't get ridden very often and has never been ridden by a righthander. He isn't what we call rider-friendly.

My internal clock is telling me we have to be getting close to the whistle. He rolls again and almost gets me to the outside when I use every bit of my core strength to shuffle my hips as hard to the left as I possibly can. He rears and I drive over him, but something feels off. His back end drops like he's falling.

The whistle blows, but I've slid too far away from my rope, and he has gathered himself back up. I panic and try to get my tail as the bull lunges forward. Like in slow motion, I see the tail of my rope wave in front of me as my free hand misses it by a half inch.

Well, fuck. This isn't good.

When the bull kicks, he throws my body forward, nearly hitting a horn on the cage of my helmet. I'm hung up, standing on the dirt next to the bull, but my hand is stuck in my rope.

When a bull rider is hung up, his number one goal is to stay on his feet. If you can stay standing, you're far less likely to get stomped all over. His second goal is to grab his tail and yank it out, freeing his hand, which is much easier to do if you're on your feet.

Unfortunately for me, this bull is smart and mean. As soon as he sees me, he turns back into me, slinging his horns, trying to hit me. I catch one to my right thigh as I reach over him with my free hand, trying to grab my tail. A bullfighter is on the other side trying to grab it when the bull throws his head at him and catches under a knee, sending him up into the air.

His focus goes back to me, and he gets his head under my chest and bounces my ribs off the top of his horned head—knocking every bit of air out of my lungs. When I make contact the second time, he hits me harder, and my hand comes out of my rope. I get flung through the air and hit the dirt.

I look up, see the bucking chutes, and begin to crawl toward them. Trying to suck in any air I can, hoping the bull isn't coming back to finish me off. As soon as I reach the chutes, a latch man grabs hold of me and helps me climb the gate.

The bull fighters did well keeping the bull from me while I made an escape. As soon as he's out of the arena, I stand at the gate with my arms raised, trying to catch my breath. Sports Medicine reaches me asking if I'm okay. I just nod and tell them I need air. It's going to hurt way worse tomorrow than it is right now.

———————————

Trey

You're supposed to let go.

Great, this must have been on TV.

Knox

Shut up. You'd be here if you would've held on.

He sends me the middle finger emoji.

Trey

Seriously though, you good?

Knox

It would be nice if my ribs could stop taking a beating this summer, but yes, I'm fine.

Knox

Now we have approximately twelve good ribs between the two of us. Go us

Trey

Hilarious.

Twenty minutes later, I've caught my air and I'm packing my bag when I look over and see Kacey standing on the other side of the panels.

Shit.

She looks worried; I should've texted her and told her I was fine. I'm not used to having anyone but Trey around, so it didn't even cross my mind. I drop my chaps I was folding and head her way.

She has the strap of her purse in a death grip and she's chewing on her lower lip.

"Hey, sweetheart." I walk up and wrap her in a hug.

"Are you okay?" Her voice is shaky, but she's released the death grip on her purse and now has one on me. My ribs are sore—*again*—but I'm not about to complain about being in her arms.

I'm such an ass. She isn't used to this stuff. Most of the time, hang ups look worse than they are. I should've immediately let her know I was okay.

"Yeah, I'm okay. I'm sorry I didn't text you, I'm not used to having someone to text." I really am fine. I'll be sore, but I'm not hurt.

"It's okay, it just freaked me out a little bit. You're really okay? It didn't look okay." She releases me and takes a step back, looking me over like she'll see an injury.

"It knocked the wind out of me for sure and I might have a bruise on my leg, but I'm not hurt. I promise." I look into her eyes so she knows it's nothing to worry about. "I laughed when Trey texted me: *you're supposed to let go.*"

She huffs out a laugh. "That's horrible. If you can avoid wrecks like that, that would be great." She smiles, but it's strained. I can tell she's still shaken.

"I couldn't agree more. Let me grab my bag and we'll go back to the truck."

After I pack up, we grab food from hospitality, then head for the camper and both take showers. I watched the video back while Kacey showered and I'll admit it didn't look good, but it also could've been a lot worse.

Once we're both done showering, she's still quiet. She's been quiet all night. I tried asking her about the book she's reading while we ate earlier, but she was distracted, in her head, giving me short answers. I'm starting to worry she's more affected by the danger of the sport than I initially thought.

We're staying here tonight and have the next two days off. I'm sitting on the lower bunk searching for a movie to watch as Kacey stands at the counter brushing her hair. I can smell her shampoo—the scent fills the small space of the camper. I reach forward, grabbing her hips and gently pull her backward into the bed next to me.

She bends one leg up and turns so she's facing me.

"Talk to me."

"About what?" she asks, but I know she knows.

"You know *what*. You've been off all night. I can tell you're still freaked."

She brings her other leg up onto the bed and crosses them beneath her. "Okay, yeah. I'm freaked. You could have been really hurt tonight. I know it's a dangerous sport, but it was a lot harder to watch in person than I anticipated. I just—I . . ." she trails off, her head down, hand nervously rubbing her forearm.

"Just what, Kace?"

"I don't know if I can do this," she whispers.

My heart stops in my chest.

I didn't hear correctly, did I? One bad dismount and she's threatening to end things?

"I'm sorry—" she starts to say as the first tear rolls down her cheek.

"No." I push off the bed. I have to stand. I need to pace, but this damn camper is too small. I settle for running my hands through my hair, looping them together on the back of my head. "It was one bad night, but I'm fine. *We're* fine. You'll get used to the minor injuries."

"You don't understand." Another tear rolls down her cheek and I want to go to her, but I can't breathe.

"Then help me understand, Kace. Things have been great between us. I know you feel it too, so please help me understand where this is coming from."

"I know and I know Megan messed with your head—"

I cut her off. "She doesn't matter. It's you, Kacey; you are it for me. You're the spark, the flame, the full-blown wildfire I never saw coming. You blazed into my life, lighting my soul on fire. I tried to fight it, I really did. I knew the season would be hard on us both, but we can do it. I know we can. So, please, help me understand." Because I don't give a shit about what Megan did, not anymore. But we can't figure this out if Kacey doesn't help me understand.

If I can't fix this—if we can't fix this—I don't think I'll ever recover.

I don't say the words because I knew in my gut she isn't ready to hear them, but I'm in love with her. Hell, I think I've been in love with her since that first night on her porch.

"Knox—" she chokes out, fighting back more tears. "I promise I'm not trying to mess with your head, it's *my head* that's the issue. Seeing you get tossed around like that . . . it brings up memories . . . and I can't watch that happen to you." She stands in the small space, leaning against the counter and covers her face with both hands.

"What memories, Kace?" I put my hands on her shoulders until she lowers her hands and looks me in the eyes. And when she does, the look of pure anguish on her face almost brings me to my knees.

"I can't just sit there and watch you die; I can't fucking do it again. I just sat there, helpless, as she died." The words tumble out of her mouth between sobs. Big fat tears start streaming down her face now, and I wipe them away as my heart plummets into my guts. "The truck came out of nowhere, crashing into the driver's door. It flipped our truck on its side, and I sat in the backseat, begging her to open her eyes, but she never did. The first responders arrived and did C.P.R., and I stood there, watching. But she never woke up."

Her mom. She watched her mom die.

All I can envision is a little girl inside of a mangled vehicle, watching as her mother dies. She never told me she was also in the vehicle.

"Shit," I rasp, pulling her into my chest. "Sweetheart, I'm so sorry. I didn't know."

"I don't talk about it." She hiccups.

It all starts to click into place in my mind. The tremble and tone of her voice the night I was thrown into the chutes. The panicked texts when Trey got wrecked out. It's not just the danger; it's the helpless feeling of losing those she cares about and not being able to do anything about it. Most people don't think about losing people they love until they're gone, but Kacey walks around every day in fear that I'll die doing my job.

How do I fix this? Can I fix this?

"Do you want to talk about it? Maybe it will help."

She's tense in my arms but nods once.

I move us to the bed, cradling her in my arms. After a few deep breaths, she tells me about that day. Several times she has to stop and collect herself, calming her breathing. I don't ask questions; I just listen and rub her back. I can't imagine a seven-year-old having to go through and witness what she did.

When she finishes, we sit quietly for a long while. I don't want to push her—I know she's emotionally spent after sharing all of that with me. I want to know if we're okay, or what I can do to fix this, but I don't ask.

I just hold her until she says, "I don't know where we go next."

My voice sounds like it's been dragged through glass. "Do you want to break up?" I hate asking that question, but after everything she shared, I can't stop myself from giving her an out. I love her too much to put her through watching me get hurt and banged up on a regular basis.

"No. But what do we do?"

Hearing that releases some of the pressure on my chest. I know she cares about me—she wouldn't be here if she didn't. So, I say the only thing I can think of, the thing my mom always told me when I was little, and my emotions were too much to handle. "We talk about it. I know it's hard, but that doesn't mean we can't talk about it. You're allowed to be scared and anxious."

She looks up at me, and I keep going. "I've been doing this for years, so I can't pretend to know how you're feeling. To me, it's just part of the game. That being said, I want you to know you can still talk to me about it, or anything, for that matter. And if we need to, we can find someone else you can talk to. Have you ever talked to a therapist about this?"

The more she shared with me about the crash, how bad it was, seeing them try to revive her mom, I'm guessing she has some PTSD. Who wouldn't?

"No, but I'm open to it. Because it's not just you, it's everyone I love. And I'm tired of living in fear all the time. So, I'll think about it. In the meantime, just . . . be patient with me."

"I will. Just promise me you'll talk to me. Bottling things up will only make it worse."

"I promise. I know I have a tendency to bottle things up. I just don't want you to think I don't support you, because it terrifies me. I'm scared because I care about you, thinking about something happening to you is my worst fear."

"I would never think that." I kiss the top of her head. "In a way, being scared for me is being supportive. It shows you care. It's a dangerous sport and you acknowledge that but choose to be with me and support me anyway—all because it's what I love to do. But I promise to be careful, listen to all your fears, and reassure you when things get tough. Your support means more to me than you will ever know."

She shifts, tilting her head up, then kisses me. "Scared or not, I'm not going anywhere. You're mine, Knox Ward."

How she knew the exact words I needed to hear, I'll never know. In this moment, nothing could've soothed my worries more than that.

Her sea green eyes are rimmed red, but dry now. "You're really okay? I need to hear it again."

"I'm really okay, but if it would make you feel better, I'm happy to show you just how good I feel."

Now that I think about it, I might not let her leave this bed for the next two days.

Chapter 38

Kacey

I breathe in the comforting scent of Knox as he flips me onto my back and lowers his lips to mine. Standing at the side of that arena, watching him get thrown around like a ragdoll by that bull terrified me. I've been trying to work through my fear and not let him see how scared I am, but it's been hard. The box I keep shoving my fear into is overflowing and seeing him in danger only made me realize my feelings for him are far deeper than I want to admit—even to myself.

I panicked when I said I didn't know if I could do this, but it's also the truth. I can't let Knox go, but staying with him is killing me. I've never talked to anyone about that day, not in detail. Knox is the first, and as painful as it was, I think it helped. Maybe talking to a therapist would help, and I was serious when I told him I would think about it.

Ever since I lost my mom so young, the fear of losing loved ones has been ingrained in me. Whether it's Carson getting kicked in the head by a horse, my dad's health as he gets older, or Jessie getting attacked by a lunatic at the hospital. I know most of it is irrational, but my mind doesn't stop spinning through scenarios where I lose them. And now I can add Knox—who has the most dangerous job out of everyone—to the mix.

I thread my fingers into his hair, using the physical connection to remind me that he's here, safe and holding me. It's when he whispers against my lips that all thoughts and worries leave my mind.

"Kace," he says my name like it's a prayer. He holds me tighter, and I can feel his length harden through his sweatpants. "Would you like me to show you how good I feel?"

"Yes," I say, more of a plea than a request. I run one hand down his bare chest, over his taut ab muscles, and grasp his hard length through his sweats. He moans deep in his throat when I start to kiss my way down his neck. "I need to feel you, taste you," I say as I roll out from under him, switching positions so I'm on top.

His eyes blaze with hunger, only making my need for him greater. I slowly drag his black sweatpants down, his perfect cock springs free. I sit back on my knees, taking all of him in. The changing light of the TV casts shadows on his muscular shoulders, arms, and abs.

My eyes linger on the tattoos decorating his rib cage. "I didn't know I had a thing for tattoos until you, but they are *so sexy*."

He smirks, but before he can reply, I grip him and pump my hand up and down his length. He sucks in a breath as I lick my lips. Bending down, I run my tongue from base to tip, swirling it around. Then I do it again.

"Sweetheart," he hisses, "keep teasing me like that and I'll fist that pretty blonde hair and fuck your mouth."

I tip my head back just enough to look him in the eyes . . . then I do it again. He reacts quickly, burying his fingers into my hair and fisting a handful, tight enough to send goosebumps over my skin but not to be painful. Knox is the perfect mix of rough and soft, dirty but sweet, danger and safety—and I can't get enough.

I circle his tip one more time before sucking it into my mouth, hallowing my cheeks.

His body reacts on instinct, going taut and flexing his hips up slightly. I can feel him holding back, but that's not what I want. I take him deeper, moaning when I reach the back of my throat. This sends him over the edge.

His breaths turn to panting as he pumps his hips, fucking my mouth, just like he promised.

I take him as deep as I can and grasp what I can't take with my hand. I'm stroking and sucking him as he pumps in and out of my mouth.

"Kace, sweetheart, if you don't slow down, I'm going to come, and I really want to feel your tight cunt around me when I do."

The ache between my legs intensifies with his words. I never would've guessed Knox would be so vocal in bed, but I am not complaining. I relish in my ability to make him lose control. His grip in my hair loosens as I pull back, releasing him with a wet popping sound.

Before I can react, he's sitting up, ripping my shirt over my head. His movements are fast and laced with need, but he's firm and in control at the same time. I'm still straddling him as our lips meet and he palms both my breasts, rolling my nipples between his fingers. I moan into his mouth as I feel them peak at his touch, making me grind my hips into him. My sweatpants block me from the contact I desperately need, and I let out a groan of frustration.

"What's the issue, sweetheart? Don't like being teased?" he asks, as he slips one hand into my sweats, running two fingers through my wet center. He hums. "You're soaked. I bet you're aching."

"*Knox*," I grit out, annoyed at the lack of contact and pressure I need. Before I can say anything else, his arm is around my waist, and he's moved us. Now my sweats are off and I'm facing the top bunk of the camper with him behind me.

"Be a good girl and hold on to the top bunk," he whispers in my ear.

I immediately comply, bending over slightly and gripping the edge of the bunk. I can feel his hard length pressing against my ass and I lean into him.

"Good girl," he purrs into my ear as he runs the head of his cock through my entrance and up to my clit.

I whimper, needing more, feeling like I might die if I don't get it. I lean back into him more, begging with my body.

I hear the tear of a condom as he asks, "What do you need?" He pulls back and I whimper at the loss of contact. I press back further, but he pulls away. "Use your words, sweetheart. I want to hear you say it."

Infuriating man.

"You. Inside of me," I demand.

"How do you want it?"

"I want you to fuck me, hard. Right now or I might lose my mind."

He can hear the frustration in my voice, and he chuckles. Finally, he places his hand at the center of my back, guiding me to bend forward even more. Then, he slides through my slickness—that's now dripping down my legs—one more time before thrusting into me. No hesitation, no warning. He fully thrusts into me, filling me completely.

I throw my head back and cry out in pleasure at the stretch.

"Mm-hmm, you feel good. So wet and ready for me," he says as he pulls out and drives back in. "I can't wait, I need to feel you coming around me," he says before he pounds into me, setting a faster pace, causing me to grip the edge of the bunk tighter.

It's not slow lovemaking; it's a primal need to connect, and it's *exactly* what I need right now.

I climb toward my orgasm at a blinding speed. The feeling of his hands gripping my hips, the stretch, it's all too much and I start to fall over the edge.

"Knox—" I pant. "I—I—" I can't form words as I tighten and convulse around him. When he reaches one hand forward and circles my clit, I see stars. I've never come so hard in my life. I'm completely at his mercy as I ride out my orgasm, and he pumps into me.

I fall deeper and deeper into bliss.

Chapter 39

Knox

She's taking deep, gasping breaths, and I can still feel the aftershocks of her orgasm fluttering around me. I slow my pace, and plant kisses up her spine, giving her a moment to catch her breath.

"I love feeling you come on my cock." I pull her back to me so her back is pressed to my chest. "Give me one more," I whisper in her ear as I trail one hand down her side.

She leans into me and breathlessly chuckles. "I don't know if—" I cut her off by pressing a finger to her clit, causing her to gasp and throw her head against my shoulder.

"I think you can," I practically growl into her ear. I don't know what it is about this woman that turns me near feral, but I can't stop it. No woman has ever turned me on, made me want to please them so much.

Kacey is my undoing, and I revel in it.

I feel her tighten around me in response, and I have to focus on not coming *right now*.

I lay her on her back, but I don't waste any time sliding back into her.

Fuck. She feels amazing. I'm never going to get enough of her.

I take full advantage of being able to kiss her in this position. I run my tongue along hers, tasting how sweet she is. When she sucks my tongue into her mouth, I almost blow. She knows it, too, by the way she moans into my mouth and wraps her legs around me.

I learned earlier she likes it when I lose control. The fact that she has the power to turn me on, sucking me better than anyone ever has, turned her on. And next time, I fully intend to lick that arousal off those pretty little thighs it was dripping down, working my way up until she's screaming my name.

I pick up my pace, knowing I won't last much longer. She's too wet, tight, and warm, with her legs wrapped around me and our mouths tangled together. I can feel her getting closer and I pull back, tucking my head to suck one of her nipples into my mouth.

She cries out in pleasure, and I feel her come undone. She tightens around me, causing me to lose control. I release her nipple and thrust into her—hard—over and over again, letting my orgasm rip through me.

"Fuck, Kacey," I say in a shout as I continue to thrust in and out of her, riding out my orgasm.

I collapse next to her and pull her into my chest.

She absentmindedly traces one of my tattoos, and after a minute of holding each other, she lets out a big, dramatic sigh. "Okay, I admit it. You were right. You're perfectly healthy."

I burst out laughing and so does she.

We spend the next two days tangled up in each other. We watch movies, order takeout, and only leave the camper when absolutely necessary. I'm going to owe Trey new sheets for the lower bunk.

Having Kacey on the road with me has been even better than I expected. We've finally gotten the time we needed together, and she's opened up to me. She's told me childhood stories, talked about her teenage years with Jessie, and even brought up stories of her mom a couple times.

I told her about my parents' divorce and been honest about how much my dad leaving and building another life with a new family hurt me. I've worked through it, but there are still moments when I wish he cared and was there to see me accomplish my goals, meet Kacey, and was invested in the life I'm building. But he's not, and I've come to terms with that. I have so many people who love me and care about me—I'm extremely blessed that way.

We talked about this fall and made plans for the months I won't have rodeos. She wants me to come back to the ranch for a while, and while we didn't make any set plans, I want her to come to Oklahoma and meet my family. My mom, sister, nephew, and brother-in-law are dying to meet her. I haven't brought a girl home in years.

This morning, while she was asleep, and I was studying the soft lines of her face, I whispered to her how much I'm in love with her. The more time I spend with her, the deeper I fall in love with her. I haven't told her yet, I'm still not sure she's ready to hear it, but I know what I feel. Now I just have to figure out how to hold on to it. I don't think I could handle losing her, not now. Not after everything we've shared, the way she's supported me and encouraged me. I can't lose that, I refuse.

We're driving into Ellensburg, Washington, for their Extreme Bulls event. It's the largest one of the season and Trey flies in today. Thankfully, I got the rodeo performance the day after the Extreme Bulls, so we can stay here tonight. Kacey will fly out tomorrow, and neither of us is ready for her to leave, but she needs to get back to the ranch and Trey is chomping at the bit to get back on the road.

The closer we get to her leaving, the quieter she gets. I'm not sure if it's just the fact that she's leaving or if there is more to it. I know she bottles things up and I've tried to give her time to open up, but we pick up Trey in an hour and our alone time will become extremely limited.

I need to know how she's feeling.

I reach across the center console and take her hand, giving it a squeeze. "What's going on in that head of yours? You've been quiet."

She turns to face me and says the last thing I expected. "My dad never once asked me if I wanted the foreman job. He offered it to Carson three times, but he continued to refuse. Then one day, Chet showed up out of nowhere. He hadn't even worked for us before taking over most of the day-to-day operations, and he never talks about where he came from or what his experience is. All Dad said when I asked was '*he knows what he's doing*.' Dad focuses more on growth and the overall business now."

She leans her head back against her headrest and sighs. "I don't know why he didn't ask me. Am I not good enough? I grew up there, working alongside him and Carson. I know I'm good with cattle and horses, and sure, I didn't go get an agricultural business degree, but neither did Carson. I know everything about that place, so why doesn't he think I could handle the job?"

Whoa. She's hardly brought up the ranch since she got here. I know she isn't a fan of Chet, but the way she talks about this, I can tell it's been eating at her for a while. "Have you ever asked your dad?" I ask her gently.

"No," she grumbles under her breath.

I fight to keep the smirk off my face; she's cute when she grumbles. "It sounds like this really bothers you. I think you should talk to him. I've seen you on that ranch—you're more than capable and he knows that, too. There has to be another reason he hired Chet."

"When he saw I was worried about you, he practically bought my plane ticket and shoved me out the door. He had no issue with me taking three weeks off. I've never taken a week off, let alone three. No one on the ranch takes that much time off. Chet hasn't so much as taken a long weekend since he started with us."

I glance her way and see she's biting her bottom lip. I've learned she does this when she's upset. "Has Chet mismanaged anything or done something wrong? I picked up quickly this spring that you don't get along."

She crosses her arms and narrows her eyes in annoyance.

Shit, maybe that wasn't the right question to ask.

"Other than being a sarcastic ass, no. He's not very patient with young horses, but great with cattle, the ranch hands all love him. Dad thinks he's great. Heck, my freaking dog likes him. Technically, he's the perfect foreman." She huffs. "I just don't understand. It's been bothering me for two years and now I'm about to go back there, and I don't even know if they really need me. My dad acted like losing me for three weeks wouldn't hurt them at all. They'd be just fine without me."

I give her hand a squeeze and choose my words wisely. "Kace, your dad loves you and wants the best for you. The way he talked to me about you when you weren't around—" Her eyes flick over to meet mine, not full of anger, but hurt. "He's so proud of you. And I believe there is a reason for everything that man does. If he told you to come out here, he had a reason for it. For the record, I think you would be a damn good foreman. If you want the job, you need to talk to him about it. If he doesn't think you're ready for it, then at least you'll know. He'll be wrong, but you'll know." I look over and give her a wink, trying to relax her.

I honestly don't believe Cody has any doubts about his daughter. He has to have a different reason for hiring Chet. But Kacey needs to know I'm one hundred percent on her side. I believe in her; she would do an amazing job as ranch foreman.

She takes a deep breath. "Thanks. I know I need to talk to him, it's just hard. I don't want him to think I'm whining or entitled. I want to earn it."

"He knows you better than that. There's nothing wrong with having an honest conversation with him about how you're feeling. You love that ranch, don't let this take that love away from you."

She gives me a small smile and squeezes my hand back. "You're right. I'll do it when I get home."

We pull into the airport to get Trey thirty minutes later.

Chapter 40

Kacey

Ellensburg, Washington

Trey is standing on the curb at the airport waving both arms in the air, like we might miss him. As if being the only one in a cowboy hat and perfectly starched jeans wasn't enough, he's wearing a hot pink "I Heart Boobies" sweatshirt.

I burst out laughing as Knox sighs and opens his truck door. "I never should have let him get that sweatshirt."

I'm still laughing when I get out of the truck and Trey gives me a side hug.

"Hi, Mrs. Ward."

"Hey, Trey." I hug him back. Trey called us every single day for the last three weeks. If Knox ignored his call—like he did on our two days off—Trey would just call again. I've gotten to know him pretty well from our truck-speaker conversations. He's actually a really great guy. It's evident in the way he helps Knox's mom and sister when Knox and his brother-in-law are out of town, or how much he supports and cares about Knox.

He might not know how to keep his dick in his pants, but he isn't a shitty person by a long shot.

"Throw your bag in the camper and let's get out of here," Knox says.

Trey goes to load his bags as Knox and I both climb back in the truck. As we open our doors, we hear a high-pitched girlish scream come from the camper. We both run to the back of the boxes as Trey sticks his head out of the door.

"It *REEKS* of sex in here! If I was a virgin, I would've just lost my v card by walking into this camper. Agh!" He shakes out his limbs like a dog.

"Shut up, people are staring. And I got you new sheets already," Knox reassures him before turning around—completely unbothered by his outburst—to get back in the truck. I glance around, and *yep*, people are staring at us.

"You had sex in MY BED?!" Trey yells at Knox's back.

I scrunch my nose, realizing he and Jessie are creepily alike.

"I need Lysol wipes and essential oils, stat. Do we have any sage we could burn?" he asks as he follows me around the corner to get in the truck.

I ignore him and climb in, but he keeps going. "What kind of depravity happened while I was gone? Do I need to call a priest?"

"Probably, chances of you going to hell are pretty high right now. I'm sure there were kids out there where you were yelling about losing your virginity," Knox says as he puts the truck in drive.

Trey moves to the middle of the backseat and slides up to rest his chin in his hands on the center console. "Wait, why do you two get to have coitus in my bed, but I can't?"

I snort a laugh. "Coitus?"

He lowers his sunglasses, giving me a judgmental look. "That's what civilized people call sex. Read a book."

"It's because of the coitus partners you choose. And it's my camper, so technically they're both my beds," Knox claps back.

I watch them volley like it's a tennis match, but Knox looks happy. Trey might give him endless shit, but he's his best friend.

I make my way up to the stands to watch the Extreme Bulls. I'm early, but this place is huge, so I wanted to go up with Knox and have plenty of time to walk around and find my seat. When I get to my seat, I look down the row and a few seats down is a girl in ripped up jeans, a ball cap and high-top Vans with her feet propped on the row in front of her. She's reading. She's so engrossed in her book, she doesn't even notice I'm here.

I see the title of the book and immediately grab my phone to text Jessie.

Kacey

Remember that book we read last year where her dog died and we both bawled?

Jessie

Yes, vividly.

Kacey

A girl in the stands next to me is reading it. She's about halfway through, so she hasn't hit that part yet.

Jessie

Ha. Poor thing has no idea what's about to happen to her.

I pick up the book I brought with me and start reading.

Almost two hours later, we're done with the prayer and national anthem. I know Knox and Trey aren't up until the third section, so I pick my book back up.

"What're you reading?" I hear a soft husky voice ask from down the row. The girl in the Vans has turned in her seat and leaned my way, trying to catch a glimpse of the cover.

"*Fall of Ruin and Wrath* by Jennifer Armentrout," I tell her as I hold up my book.

"Well, I'm assuming if you're sitting in the stands reading instead of watching, you're also with a bull rider." She chuckles as she gets up and moves to the seat next to me. "Hi, I'm Juniper Summers, but everyone just calls me June."

"Kacey Hart, nice to meet you. And yeah, I'm with Knox Ward. What about you?"

"Daxton Summers. He's in the second section."

I feel like I need to warn her. "Friendly piece of advice: don't finish that book in public."

June looks down at the cover, then back up at me.

I laugh at the horrified look on her face.

"It's the dog, isn't it? I have a terrible feeling about the dog. Why do authors do this to us?" She huffs.

We start chatting and I learn that June travels with Dax full-time and she gives me some great tips about dating and traveling with a bull rider. We exchange phone numbers and I'm pretty sure I just made my first rodeo friend.

We chat about books and rodeo until Dax—as June calls him—climbs into the chute. She's sitting up in her seat, videoing him on her phone.

Dax nods his head, and the bull leaves the chute spinning to the right, away from his hand. He gets behind after one round and can't catch back up. He slides to the left side of the bull but isn't letting go. When his hand finally pops out of his rope, he hits the ground and the bull keeps spinning, right on top of him.

I gasp when one back foot lands right on the side of Dax's helmet, crushing his head and twisting the metal cage. His body goes limp. Bullfighters step in to draw the bull's attention, as a pickup man rides in and gets a rope on the bull, pulling him away from Dax.

June stops recording but doesn't move. Her eyes never leave Dax as she quietly says, "Wake up," under her breath.

How is she so calm? I'm freaking out. Shaking in the seat next to her I ask, "Should you go down there?"

"I'll wait and see if he wakes up," she replies, still not taking her eyes off him as Sports Medicine doctors surround him.

A few seconds later paramedics bring a backboard in as sports medicine removes his chaps and vest.

Seeing the backboard and paramedics has bile rising in the back of my throat. I can still see the paramedics lifting my mom onto the backboard and starting chest compressions, frantically working to bring air back into her lungs.

I look away, searching for Knox on the chutes, hoping the sight of him will bring me some comfort.

"Okay, I'm going to head down. It was nice to meet you, Kacey," June says. I can see now she's shaken but still handling this so well. I would be an absolute mess. That was his *head*, what if he's seriously hurt or . . . dies? Then again, Knox said I'd get used to it; maybe women who haven't been through a traumatic event like me can get used to it. Maybe this isn't the first time she's seen him carried out of an arena.

"You, too. I hope he's okay. Let me know if you need anything."

She nods, then hurries down the stairs and around the corner.

A few minutes later, I see the ambulance pull out and another one arrives to take its place.

I can hardly watch when Knox rides. My hands are still shaking so badly I don't even attempt to video. He's 84.5 points—it's not a huge score, but it should get him back to the short round. Trey isn't so lucky, it's his first one back and I know his ribs still hurt. He bucks off around four seconds and doesn't look too happy about it.

Knox is 88 in the short round for third place and receives a big check. He told me about how this final month of the season can make or break you. There are a bunch of events with a lot of money, and he can easily move himself into the number one position if he keeps getting his bulls ridden.

I head down to meet him. As soon as I see him, he grabs me by the hand and starts leading me behind the chutes. I grip his hand so tightly I'm sure I'm cutting off circulation, but I don't care. The feel of his calloused hand wrapped around mine slows my still rapid heart and calms me down.

I don't want to tell him how much Dax's wreck has affected me. I know we promised to talk about it, but he had a great night, and I'm about to leave. I don't want to ruin our last night together.

So, I promise myself I'll tell him about meeting June and watching Dax later.

"What's going on? Where are we going?" I never go behind the chutes. No girlfriends or wives do unless it's a medical emergency. That's their space.

He makes a sharp turn before we get to the actual spot where they get ready behind the chutes. "To the front of the chutes—we've hardly taken any pictures, and you're about to leave me out here all by myself."

"Well, that seems a little dramatic. You do have Trey—I thought you liked traveling with him," I joke, laughing as we step in front of chute number five.

"Yeah, but you are way prettier and way more fun to be around . . . he's not you." He gives me a wink as he pulls his phone out of his pocket. He asks a fan who is walking back from the autograph tables in the middle of the arena to take our picture. I wrap my arm around him, and we both smile and pose.

He takes his phone back and says, "Let's get a selfie, too." He tips his hat back, wraps his arm around my lower back, dips me back slightly and kisses me as I hear the shutter from the camera on his phone. "Thank you for coming, Kace. It means more to me than you'll ever know."

I'm still dipped back in his arms, and I have butterflies in my stomach.

I really wish we weren't in public right now.

I thread my fingers through his curls, ready to kiss him when I hear, "new profile pic," and look up to see Trey looking down from the chute he's standing on, ruining the moment. The smirk on his face tells me he did it on purpose.

Probably payback for defiling his bed.

Knox stands me up, leaving one arm wrapped around my back.

Trey jumps down, positioning himself on the other side of me and throws his arm over my shoulder, gripping Knox's on the other side. "I want a selfie, too."

"I swear to god if you try to kiss her—" Knox starts, but Trey barks out a laugh.

"I wouldn't dream of it."

We all smile and take the photo.

Chapter 41

Knox

We're staying here tonight. Kacey flies out in the morning, and Trey and I will both ride in the rodeo tomorrow. As soon as we get back to the camper, Trey declares he's going to the bar for the after party. After flying all day and getting on a bull, I'm guessing this "burning desire to go to the bar" is so Kacey and I can have some alone time before she flies out tomorrow. I'm not about to stop him.

He throws his gear bag in the box and turns to me. "Hey, Knox, you got any cash?"

"Use your own cash."

"I don't keep any on me. If my wallet's too big, it leaves lines in my jeans."

I give him a squint-eyed stare, and he laughs.

"Come on, Dad, think of it like you're giving me my allowance early."

Kacey giggles and I cross my arms, exasperated by him. "Since when do I give you an allowance?"

"Since I quit carrying cash on me, and now I need some." He shrugs his shoulders.

I groan as I pull a twenty-dollar bill from my wallet. "Is that enough?"

"Maybe in the 1940s when you graduated high school, old man, I know you got a hundy in there." He holds out his hand, curling his fingers.

I pull out a hundred and hand it to him. "Whatever it takes to get rid of you for a few hours. Remember, we need to leave at 9 a.m."

"Ugh, that's sooo early." Trey takes the cash, turning on his heel. "Use protection and stay the *fuck* off my new sheets!" he hollers back over his shoulder.

Kacey crawls into bed next to me, I pull her into me, holding her, kissing her, breathing in the scent of her shampoo. I want to memorize the feel of her body against mine.

She snuggles into my chest and sighs. "It's just a month. We can do one month."

"Yeah," I say through the lump in my throat. A lot can happen in a month and if her dad promotes her at the ranch, her time off will become even more limited. "I don't want you to go," I admit in a whisper. Since Kacey has been on the road with me, I've ridden better than I have all year—even as sore and tired as I am. I love having her with me, and I hate that we won't see each other for a month.

"So you aren't sick of me after three weeks on the road?" she tries to joke.

"No," I say seriously. I cradle her face in my hand, tilting her head up so our eyes meet in the dim light of the TV. "Three weeks isn't enough—no amount of time with you will ever be enough." I hear her suck in a breath before I continue. "I want to spend every second with you. It doesn't matter if it's at a rodeo, driving down the road for hours, or at the ranch. When I went to Colorado this spring, my only plan was to help Jack out and pass the time until the summer rodeos, but then I climbed out of my truck that day and you smiled at me . . . I didn't realize it until later, but as of that moment, I was wholeheartedly yours, Kacey Hart."

A single tear runs down her cheek and I wipe it with my thumb. "It took less than two months for me to say, 'screw the no-girlfriend rule.' I wanted you and now I refuse to lose you. So, if you ever start losing faith in us, questioning us, or just need me to come home, tell me. Because nothing in this world will stop me from being with you."

"Home?" she questions.

"Yes. My home is wherever you are." Another tear rolls down her cheek. "Don't cry, sweetheart. I didn't mean to make you cry."

She blinks rapidly, trying to fight back more tears. "They're not sad tears. I just never thought I would trust anyone again, but you showed me every day how much you cared about me. You've never made me wonder or question if I'm worthy. You've put the broken pieces of my heart back together, and I couldn't imagine living without you now. Sometimes I put so much pressure on myself, and my thoughts spiral out of control, making it hard to breathe. But when I'm with you, I feel whole. I can breathe again."

I run my hand through her hair and look into her sea green eyes. "I promise your heart will always be safe with me. It's an honor to be the man who cares for you the way you've always deserved."

She kisses me then, her kiss saying more than words ever could.

After she's fallen asleep, with the TV still playing the fireplace, I whisper over the crackling and popping of the burning wood, "I love you." Then, I finally doze off, my arms wrapped around the woman who has become the center of my universe.

The next morning, I drop Kacey off at the airport. I give her one last kiss.

"See you back in Mountain Time."

She nods, fighting tears, then turns, heading into the airport. I watch her go, swallowing the lump in my throat before getting back in the truck with Trey.

Together, we drive back to the rodeo grounds.

Chapter 42

Kacey

The Ranch

Kacey

Have you heard if Dax is okay?

Knox

Yeah, I talked to him, he's good. It split his ear open and he got stitches but he can ride again once the swelling has gone down enough to get a helmet on haha he might borrow mine since his is totaled.

Kacey

How are you laughing about this?! That was terrifying. He could've been really hurt.

Knox

Sorry, force of habit. He really is okay, thankfully it looked worse than it was.

I run my fingers through my hair, baffled by how nonchalant Knox is about Dax's wreck. I know they see this stuff all the time, and I'm sure he was worried about him until he found out he was okay, but it's still jarring to see him laugh it off. My anxiety has been off the charts since I watched that wreck, but clearly, he's not bothered.

My fear for Knox isn't getting better like I hoped it would. His words the night of his hangup were comforting, but not enough for me to move past this. I realize now it probably has a lot to do with my mom's death. Watching June handle Dax's situation so differently than I would've solidified that for me, but I still don't know what to do about it.

I spent most of the flight planning what to say and how to ask my dad about the foreman job, so I was surprised yesterday when Carson showed up at the airport to pick me up. He told me Dad had a last-minute meeting with a potential meat buyer, so Carson volunteered to come get me. Grumpy Carson might not admit it, but I think he missed me.

We used the ride back to the ranch to catch up. It sounds like everything went smoothly without me and Carson asked me a few questions about life on the road. I was tempted to ask him about the foreman job—I've never understood why he turned it down repeatedly—but in the end I chickened out. This is a conversation I need to have with my dad, anyway.

So, as I make my way up the walk to dad's house, I shove my nerves down and mentally recite what Knox said to me.

'Your dad loves you and wants the best for you. The way he talked to me about you when you weren't around, he's so proud of you. And I believe there is a reason for everything that man does. If he told you to come out here, he had a reason for it.'

When I open the door, Rein goes running in like she owns the place. Dad totally made her a house dog while I was gone. When I walk into the living room, I find her on a dog bed, next to my dad, who's in his recliner. I give them both a judgmental look.

"Don't give me that look; I got her a bed. She could be on the couch right now."

He's still in his work jeans and pearl snap with the DHR brand on it. I shake my head at them both and sit on the end of the couch closest to them. Dad asks me questions about the trip, what Knox's upcoming schedule is, and how he's feeling. After a few minutes, I take a deep breath and, apparently forget everything I rehearsed.

"Why did you hire Chet for the foreman job and not me?"

His eyes snap to mine. He runs his hand down his beard, contemplating his answer. "I wasn't sure if you want it and—"

"Of course I wanted it," I cut him off. "You know how much I love this ranch."

He sits up in his chair and reaches over, resting his hand on top of mine. "I know you love it. It's because of how much you love it that I don't want you to run it. Not completely, and not by yourself."

"Why? Do you not think I'm capable?"

"Bug, you are *more* than capable. You run circles around most of our ranch hands. I don't want you to spend your life shackled to this ranch. When I was your age . . . ." He sighs, shaking his head. "I don't want you to pour so much of yourself into this place that there's nothing left for you. Or someone else who loves you. When was the last time you saw Chet take time off? If you were the foreman, there would be no roping with Carson, trips to Estes with Jessie, horse sales with me, or traveling with Knox. And that's not the life I want for you. I want you to chase your dreams, do the things you love with the people you love. Not wake up every day and live your life on repeat."

"Oh." I swallow, throat suddenly dry.

"One day, you will run things, go to the meetings, decide who to hire, and make the big decisions. And I have no doubt you will do an amazing job when that time comes. But if you want more responsibility now, say the word. It's your choice, I won't stop you, but please think about it. I can see how much you care for Knox, and this ranch isn't worth ruining that. I'd give this entire ranch away tomorrow for one more day with your mother."

I try to swallow the lump in my throat as my eyes water.

He's right. How had I never put this together?

I spent so much time being angry about it, even resenting Chet who probably has no idea I feel this way. I never looked at the big picture.

Wait, did Carson turn down the job so we could still rope together?

"I never thought about it like that. But you're right, it's a huge commitment. Did Carson decline the job because of me? So we could rope?"

He smiles behind his beard. "That boy loves to rope and train horses just as much as you do. It was his choice whether to take the job, just like it's now yours. Take all the time you need to decide—the ranch isn't going anywhere. I'm sorry I didn't offer it to you before; I just want what's best for you. Now I realize this is a conversation we should've had a long time ago."

"It's alright. I should have brought it up before now. I was so afraid you didn't think I was up for the job that I never said anything, but I understand where you're coming from. And I'm glad I have you looking out for me."

He gets up and holds his arms out. I unfold my legs from the couch and stand. We hug for several seconds before he says, "I love you and I'm so proud of you. I know your mom would be proud of you, too. You are smart, capable, and more stubborn than all of us. You can do anything you put your mind to. Always remember that."

"Thanks, Dad. I love you, too."

I head home a few minutes later, Rein by my side. It feels like an enormous weight has been lifted off my shoulders—knowing Dad's decision to hire Chet as foreman has nothing to do with how capable I am, and everything to do with how much my dad loves me and wants to see me happy.

Knox was right.

Dad told me to think about it, but I don't have to. If it's between Knox and the ranch, I choose Knox. Every time.

I pull my phone out of my pocket, making the decision not to wait a full month before I see him again. Three weeks is enough.

Kacey

Want to burn a couple days of PTO?

Jessie

Sure, I have PTO coming out my ass. Where are we going?

Kacey

South Dakota.

Jessie

I'm going to pretend you said a tropical island with hot cabana boys and mojitos.

Kacey

Sorry. You'll have to settle for hot cowboys and beer.

It's been three weeks since I flew home, and each day only gets worse. I miss Knox more than I thought it was possible to miss another person. We talk every day, sometimes multiple times a day, but it's not the same. I miss the feeling of his arms around me, the sound of his laugh, and the way his eyes heat at the sight of me.

I'm in my bedroom, packing my bag for my trip with Jessie to South Dakota to surprise him at the Governor's Cup Rodeo when she comes bursting into the room. She throws herself onto my bed, right on top of the clothes I have laid out.

"Hey! I'm packing those."

She holds up a light blue top and grimaces. "Not this one, you're not." She unceremoniously throws it on the floor.

I cross my arms and glare at her. "Then help me pack. I worked later today than planned and I'm stressed. I haven't seen him in weeks. I want to look nice."

She rolls off the bed and starts digging around in my closet. "Grab the dark wash Lola Kimes jeans, the light brown body-suit, chocolate-colored boots and wear this." She holds out a dark brown vintage style western jacket.

How does she do that? She can make an outfit in five seconds and it's always cute. It takes me twenty minutes, and I always send her pictures.

"Thanks." I take the jacket and put it on the bed with the other potential outfits I know she'll help me sort through.

We fly out for South Dakota tomorrow afternoon. The first round is tomorrow night, followed by another round Friday. Then, hopefully, he makes the finals on Saturday night. Neither of us bought return flights. I talked to Trey, and he said Knox was planning to drive straight to the ranch after anyway so we could just ride with them. Trey has no idea how he's getting back to Oklahoma, but he seemed unbothered. I don't think a whole lot of things bother him.

All day long, I've been so excited about pulling off the surprise that I can't sit still. I pace back and forth across my room while Jessie pieces together the remaining two outfits I need.

When she's done, she turns around, eyeing me warily. "What's going on with you? You've been anxious since I got here."

"Nothing; I'm just ready to see him. I really miss him."

She watches me carefully before a borderline-creepy smile takes over her face. "You're in love with him," she declares.

"What? I didn't say that." I start folding clothes to put in my suitcase.

"You don't have to. It's all over your face," she says, still wearing her creepy-ass smile.

I throw myself back onto my bed. "Ugh. Fine, yes, I'm in love with him. Happy now? And wipe that creepy smile off your face."

"My smile is not creepy. But yes, I am happy." She plops onto the bed next to me. We both turn our heads to face each other. "Have you told him?"

"No."

"Why not? I'm sure he feels the same way. I could see it way back in July."

"I haven't seen him in person. It's not something I want to say for the first time over the phone."

"That's fair. But you could tell him this weekend," she says with a squeal, kicking her feet. "I'm so happy for you."

"Thanks. I'm glad you're coming. I know Trey annoys you, but if you get to know him better, I promise he's really nice."

"Yeah, yeah, so you've said. I'm going because I love you. Now, let's finish packing."

I take a calming breath, get up to start packing.

I'm so fucking excited.

Chapter 43

Kacey

I'm so fucking annoyed.

The airline delayed our flight *again*. The first time it got delayed, we thought we'd still be able to watch the bull riding, we'd just miss most of the rodeo. Now there is no way we'll get there in time for the bull riding. We won't land until thirty minutes after it's over.

I'm so bummed. This is his last rodeo of the season and it's a prestigious rodeo that is very hard to qualify for. Knox was so excited when he found out he and Trey both qualified. There is a lot of money to win, and he said they treat the contestants great. I just wanted to be there to cheer him on at his last rodeo of the season.

"It's okay. He rides again tomorrow, and you can still surprise him. Text Trey and do it at a bar or something," Jessie tries to console me.

"I know. I'll text him now—he needs a heads up. I have a feeling he'll have a hell of a time getting Knox to a bar."

We finally boarded our flight and almost two hours later, landed in Sioux Falls. Just to make a bad day worse, the Wi-Fi on the plane was broken, so we couldn't watch the rodeo.

Trey and I planned to meet at a bar near the arena as soon as Jessie and I could get there. We practically sprint out of the terminal. When I turn airplane mode off, my phone vibrates several times. I check it in case it's Trey with a change of plans.

Dad

> I'm sorry, bug. Let me know how he is when you can.

Carson

> Let me know what the doctors say.

Lainey

> I'm so sorry, Kacey. Let me know if there is anything I can do.

Chet

> I hope he's okay. Everyone in the bunkhouse is praying for him.

One missed call from Trey.

Trey

> Call me when you land.

What is happening? My heart rate picks up, feeling like it's about to burst out of my chest. I vaguely hear Jessie over the blood roaring in my ears.

"I'm booking an Uber now."

I don't respond to any of them. I can't breathe. Something happened to Knox.

I open the phone app and tap his name.

It rings.

And rings.

And rings.

Please, pick up. Please. Please, I silently beg him.

"Kacey."

I suck in a breath, but it's Trey's voice, answering Knox's phone.

My heart plummets.

"Kacey?" he says again when I don't respond.

"Trey?" I exhale, feeling tears well.

This isn't happening. Maybe it's some kind of sick joke.

Jessie turns to look at me. When she sees the tears in my eyes, she knows something is wrong.

"Yeah, I have Knox's phone. We're at the hospital. He got in a wreck." His voice is hoarse; it sounds like he's in shock. I hear him suck in a breath before he continues. "It was bad."

Jessie leads me to a bench before I collapse onto the curb.

"Where?" I rasp.

"Sioux Falls Hospital and Medical Center. I'll text you the address."

"Is he . . . he'll be okay, right?" My voice doesn't sound like my own.

"I don't know. The trauma team is trying to stabilize him. Jessie is with you, right?"

"Yeah." I look over at her. She's watching me, eyes wide.

"Can you pass the phone to her?"

I hand her the phone, and she looks down at the caller ID.

"It's Trey, Knox is hurt," I choke out as she holds the phone up to her ear.

"What happened?" she asks in a far calmer tone than I could right now. The nurse side of Jessie kicking in.

Trey says something and she nods. She taps away on her phone, changing the address for the Uber.

I stare blankly at the sidewalk, hearing Trey's words over and over, "*The trauma team is trying to stabilize him.*"

"We'll be there in ten minutes." Jessie hangs up and grabs my hand.

"Jessie, what if— What if he . . . " I can't finish my sentence. I don't even want to think the thought, it makes my chest tight, and *I can't breathe*. I feel the panic setting in and start panting shallow breaths.

"Hey. Hey, don't think that." She squeezes my hand. "Breathe, Kacey."

I suck in a deeper breath, holding it for three seconds as she keeps talking.

"He's going to be okay. It's Knox. I'm pretty sure he eats nails for breakfast before going to the gym for five hours."

All I can do is nod my head and take another breath so I don't pass out.

"Our Uber is almost here, let's go." She grabs both our bags and leads me down to the Uber pickup.

We walk into the hospital and head straight for the front desk, but Jessie stops me. "They won't tell you anything. You aren't immediate family. Let's find Trey."

Trey jumps to his feet when he sees us enter the waiting room. He's pale and has clearly been running his hand through his now-messy hair. His cowboy hat sits on a chair, his long-sleeve shirt covered in sponsor patches is untucked and wrinkly. And he's still wearing his dirty jeans from riding. You would never guess him to be a pretty boy looking at him right now.

He rushes to me and pulls me into a hug. I've been trying to hold it together, but feeling the fear radiating off him pushes me over the edge. I can't hold it back any longer. Tears start rolling down my face as I sob into his chest.

"Have you heard any news?" Jessie asks what I can't.

"They won't give me any details, but I'm going to call his mom when the doctor comes out," he answers, still holding me upright.

Jessie has us both sit, and I'm able to calm down before we hear, "Ward family?"

A doctor in a white coat is looking around the waiting room. We jump up and Trey dials Knox's mom, Jen.

"Are you immediate family?" he asks.

"No, we're his friends—he doesn't have any family here. We have his mom on the phone," Trey tells him, and Jen acknowledges the doctor over the phone, asking for an update.

"He's stable now, we had to put him in an induced coma because of the cerebral edema—swelling on the brain—caused by the concussion. He also has a lacerated liver, cracked sternum, and we need to do surgery to remove his spleen. Because of the induced coma and the amount of swelling on his brain, we will admit him into the ICU and monitor him closely after surgery."

"Can I see him?" I ask the doctor.

"Not yet. He's being taken into surgery now. Once he's out and settled in the ICU, one of you can go back and sit with him."

"Is there any brain damage?" Jen asks.

"We don't know yet. The next twenty-four hours will tell us more. Hopefully, the swelling goes down, we can wean him off the medications, and he wakes up."

The doctor leaves and Jen hangs up to call Knox's sister.

We sit in the waiting room for what feels like an eternity. Jessie and Trey never leave me alone. Both try to get me to eat or drink something. Jessie texted everyone back on my phone with an update.

All I can do is sit here and replay all the moments he'd smile at me while training Buck. Or how he kissed me and called me sweetheart. I can feel the brush of his hands on my arms as he told me, *Sweetheart, you deserve to be walked to your door. You deserve to be told how breathtaking you are.* I can hear him whisper, *I promise your heart will always be safe with me. It's an honor to be the man who cares for you the way you've always deserved.*

Then it hits me—I may never be able to hear his voice again. I might not get the chance to tell him I love him.

He can't die. He can't.

I need to see his blue eyes when the sunlight hits them. Feel his arms around me as we talk about our dreams for the future. And we *will* have a future.

I look up at Trey, who is stacking our empty coffee cups on the table next to his chair.

"What happened?"

He gets a faraway look in his eyes, a little bit of fear flashing behind them. It's clearly a wreck he doesn't want to relive again. "It happened fast. I had just ridden, but I got to his chute just in time to watch him nod. He had a younger bull that was pretty wild; he blew up one big one before turning back. When he came back around, he blew up into the air with a really nasty belly roll that threw off his balance. There wasn't anything Knox could do.

"The bull flipped sideways, landing right on top of him. Crushing Knox with his entire body weight, plus the force of the fall. It knocked him out on impact, and his hand was still tied to him, but the fall also stunned the bull, so the bullfighters got his hand out quickly before the bull tried to get up. There was no good way to get the bull off of him. Once the bull got up, it stepped all over him. I stayed with him until the ambulance left, then packed our gear and came straight here."

Trey runs a hand through his hair and down his face like he's trying to wipe the memory away. "This sport is dangerous, we all know these things can happen, but we always pray they don't." Trey looks down at his coffee. "I'm sorry I couldn't do more, Kacey."

Chapter 44

Kacey

It's several hours later when a middle-aged, slightly round nurse with a brunette bob comes to find us in the waiting room. "He's out of surgery and it went well. One of you can come back and see him now."

"You go." Trey gives me a small smile. "He'll want to see you way more than me."

"We'll be here, let us know if you need anything," Jessie adds, as I stand to follow the nurse.

She leads me down a long hallway and through another set of locked doors. The smell of antiseptic churns my already unsteady stomach. It's cold, dark, and quiet—no sound but the beeping of monitors coming from the surrounding rooms.

"Be prepared," the nurse gently tells me, "he has a lot of tubes and wires connected to him right now. There is some swelling in his chest cavity as well. We normally don't allow overnight visitors, but since it's the middle of the night, you can stay."

"Okay, thank you."

She opens a sliding glass door and gestures for me to go ahead of her. I enter and see Knox is lying in a hospital bed, tubes, wires, and machines surrounding him. He's so pale, he looks like he hasn't seen the sun in years.

I walk to the side of the bed, fighting tears. "Can I hold his hand?" I ask the nurse, voice cracking.

"Of course, just don't knock the oxygen monitor off. There is a chair you can use. I also set a blanket and pillow out for you. Someone will be in every hour to check on him. The nurses' station is down the hall to the left. Let us know if you need anything."

The sympathetic look in her eyes has me wondering how many people she's done this for. How many people has she walked down that hallway only for them to walk out missing a piece of their heart? Their loved one lost to them.

After she leaves, I sit next to him, grasp his hand in mine, and let the tears fall. He looks fragile, but Knox is anything but fragile. He's full of life, all smiles and winks.

"Hi, I'm here," I whisper, even though I know I won't wake him. "My surprise visit really went off the rails. This is not the way I expected this to go. We were supposed to meet at a bar." I huff out a sad chuckle. "But I'm here Knox. And I'm not going anywhere until you get better. You have to get better."

I jerk awake, my back killing me from the position I had fallen asleep in. I'm still holding Knox's hand, and I don't remember falling asleep. I think I cried myself to sleep.

"I'm sorry, I didn't mean to wake you," says the nurse checking Knox's vitals and machines.

"No, no, it's okay." I look up at Knox. He looks the same, like he's asleep but pale and covered in tubes and wires.

"I'm going to check his incision now. Why don't you step out and get some coffee?" she suggests, probably gathering from the state of my swollen eyes and shaky hands, I won't handle seeing his torn-up body well. She's right.

I stand and find a quiet corner of the hallway. Pulling out my phone, I dial my dad.

"Dad—" Is all I can manage to choke out as another tear rolls down my cheek. Frustrated, I wipe it away.

I have to get it together. Knox needs me and I can't stop crying.

"Kacey, honey, I'm so sorry. What can I do? Do you want me to come there?" He sounds tired but wide awake, I doubt he's slept at all.

"No, don't come. He's in the ICU, no one can come back here. I just— I . . ." He listens as I cry for a few seconds, then collect myself enough to continue. "I don't know how to do this. I can't breathe." My breaths start to get shallow, and I know I'm slipping into a panic attack.

"Kacey, listen to me. Breathe in . . . hold it." He waits seven seconds before having me release the breath. He repeats this with me several times until my breathing levels out. "Is it the hospital? I know you struggle with them."

"It's more than that, Dad. Knox is . . . it's really bad. He's so pale, swollen, and there is a tube down his throat. What if he never wakes up?" I cry into the phone, saying the thought that has haunted me all night out loud. "I want to be here for him, but I don't know if I can do this. Sit by and watch *again*."

"What do you mean again?"

"Like Mom—I saw it all, and I don't think I can do it again. But I love him so much. I need him to wake up so I can tell him, but I don't know if I can do this."

"Your—" Dad sucks in a breath. "Kacey, you watched? Your mom?"

"Yes," I whisper. "I think they kind of forgot I was there. They were trying to help her, and I was okay."

"Oh, god . . . Kacey, I'm so sorry. I didn't know. Why have you never told me?" I hear him sniffle, and I know he's crying.

"You were sad, and I didn't want to make it worse. Then, the years went by, and I just wanted to forget. But I can't and now I'm here and I don't know what to do." I sob into the phone, wishing he was here to hug me and help me through this.

It takes him a minute to respond, the shock of my admission still processing. After a beat, he clears his throat and collects himself. "I'm sorry I never knew. I want to talk to you about this someday, but for right now, let's focus on Knox. The doctors said he's stable, right?" His voice is steady and calm.

"Yes."

"That's good. He's young and healthy, physically fit. His body is going to fight for him. He's as tough as they come. The doctors are doing everything they can and you're there with him. That's what he needs more than anything—you love him, and I know he loves you. We have to believe he'll wake up. He has so much to live for, and he knows that. The little bit I've gotten to know him; he isn't a man who gives up easily. I believe he'll be okay, and more than anything, I believe in you, Kacey. You're the strongest person I know. You can do this."

"Even if he makes it through this, what is going to keep it from happening again?"

"Nothing. You don't know if or how badly he'll get hurt in the future. Do you want him to quit?"

"No, of course not. I can't ask him to quit. Bull riding is part of who he is. I just don't know if I could handle anything like this happening again."

"Bug, that is the question you are going to have to dig deep to answer for yourself. At some point, we are all faced with choices and our decisions will affect the rest of our lives. Choosing to marry your mom ended with the deepest heartbreak of my life. But it also gave me my greatest gift—her love—and my greatest joy, you. Even knowing how it would all end, I would choose the same road again just for the honor of loving her and the joy of being your dad."

Tears pour down my face.

"You need to consider what life will look like with and without Knox in it. Is the risk worth the reward? Does your love outweigh your fear of losing him?"

I close my eyes, letting his words sink in. We've only been together for a few months, but when I see my future, I can't picture it without him. He's brought me back to life. He's my best friend, my safe place, my home, *my choice*. "He said nothing in this world could stop him from being with me, and I believe him. Our love outweighs anything else."

"It sounds like you've found your answer, Bug. It won't be easy but focus on this moment and what you both need to make it to tomorrow. And then the next day. Everything is going to be okay."

Knox is still in danger, but my dad is right. I have to believe he'll be okay, and we will get our future together.

"Thanks, Dad. You're always there for me. You're right: he's strong, he'll get through this. *We'll* get through this."

For the next thirty-six hours, I don't leave Knox's side. Jessie befriends all the nurses, bringing them snacks, and sharing war stories. She is an ER nurse, not ICU, but they all speak the same language. They end up letting me stay the next night as well. He's still in the induced coma but last night's scan showed the swelling has gone down.

Trey has just left the hospital to go ride again. He and Jessie seemed to have come to some kind of truce and put all their focus on being there for Knox and me. His mom is flying in tomorrow morning. I have been keeping her informed with any updates, and she's trying to get here as quickly as she can. This wasn't exactly how I pictured meeting his mother, but she's been kind on the phone. I can tell she loves her son, and she's glad I'm here with him.

They told me he can't hear me, but I've been talking to him anyway. Maybe it's for my own peace of mind. I know he's far from being out of the woods, the doctor said that Knox waking up after lowering the medication is going to be our biggest indicator of his likelihood of recovery. We still don't know if there will be any lasting damage. They did another scan a few minutes ago and, depending on the results, they'd like to wean him off the medication today.

"Hi, sweetie. How's our cowboy today?" The nurse who originally brought me back to Knox's room is back on duty today. I learned her name is Melissa, she has two kids about my age, and you can tell she's a mother through and through. She's taken me under her wing, checking on not only Knox, but me as well. She brought me protein shakes when I couldn't eat and tea to calm my nerves. Even when her shift was over, she came and sat with me, asking about Knox and me. Surprisingly, talking to her about how we met, and his bull riding felt good. Her kindness kept me sane during those first few hours.

"Hi, Melissa. He's still tough as nails." This makes her chuckle as she reviews his chart. "They just did another scan a few minutes ago, and the doctor is supposed to come by soon with the results. The scan last night showed the swelling was down some."

"Good, I expected nothing less. He needs to wake up soon—I have some serious questions about his career choice."

I laugh and she smirks at me. I have no doubt that was her goal.

"I brought some cookies—come to the nurses' station and help yourself," she says before ducking out of the room to check her other patients.

I've been doing better since my phone call with Dad. I still cry and worry, but overall, I've been able to focus on Knox and be here for him without having panic attacks or leaving the hospital.

The doctor comes in and lets me know the swelling has gone down enough that they will begin to wean him off the medication. Now the decision to wake up will be on Knox. Ideally, he wakes up within the next twenty-four hours.

I stay with him as late as I can, but the nurses can't let me stay another night. So, after Trey rode in the short round, he brought the camper to the hospital, and we all slept until I could go back to the ICU in the morning.

"Any change?" I ask as I stand at the nurses' station sipping my coffee. I set the tray of coffee Jessie sent in for them on the counter.

"Hey, Kacey. No change so far," Knox's other nurse, Lindsey, replies. "But now that he's basically off the medication, he might be able to hear you. Talking to them normally helps," she says, giving me a small smile.

"Okay, thanks. His mom should be here this afternoon, too."

I step into his room and slide the chair up to sit next to him. His color looks better today and someone combed his hair. There is also a bag of cookies on the side table. Melissa, no doubt. These nurses are underpaid angels on earth.

I tell him about Trey getting second last night, even playing the video so he can listen. How they're both officially qualified for the national finals in December now, and that he finished the regular season number one in the world. The internet is filled with supportive and encouraging posts from fans wishing him well. His sponsors have reached out to Trey, asking if there is anything they can do. One even offered to fly his family here.

It's touching to see how many people truly care about him. Including my dad, who has been worried sick about us both and is now using spoiling my dog rotten as a coping mechanism.

The doctor comes and goes on his morning rounds. He emphasizes how important it is that he wakes up soon. The sooner he wakes, the less likely brain damage is.

His mom will arrive in two hours, and while I want her here, I can't stand the thought of leaving Knox. And only one of us can sit with him in the ICU. I know it should be her, and I won't fight her for it, but there are moments where holding his warm hand, feeling the calluses scrape my skin, is the only thing keeping *me* breathing.

I'm having one of those moments, holding his hand and reminiscing on this spring, how much he changed my entire world the day he showed up at the ranch. The machines beep their steady rhythm, as the nurses bustle past the glass door, and I finally break down.

"You promised me. *You promised me* nothing in the world could stop you from being with me. So you have to wake up, you have to come home. Mountain Time, remember? We have plans. We have dreams. Please wake up, Knox. I love you." My voice cracks and tears fall, but I keep going. "You told me you can't lose me; well I can't lose you either. You are the air I breathe, and I can't do this without you. In fact, I refuse. So *wake up*, because I love you," I beg. The confession seems to break apart the silent room.

I rest my head on the edge of the bed, still holding his hand, shoulders shaking as I let the tears soak into the bedsheet. I don't know how much time has passed when I feel his hand shift in mine. I jerk my head up so fast I see stars for a second. His eyes aren't open, but his hand moves again.

"Knox—" I choke.

His eyelids flutter, and then I see them, his bright blue eyes. I'm sobbing again, holding his hand tighter. His eyes flare.

Shit, the tube in this throat.

"Hold on, I'll get the nurse. Don't close your eyes," I plead as I press the button for the nurse. "They'll come get it out."

A nurse hustles into the room and calls for the doctor. "Hi, Knox. My name is Lindsey and we're going to get this tube out of your throat soon. Just stay calm and try not to move." Knox seems to ignore her, squeezing my hand and keeping his eyes on me, never closing them. Just like I asked.

As soon as they remove the breathing tube, Knox's first word is "Sweetheart." His voice is raspy from disuse and the tubes, but I've never loved hearing that word on his lips so much.

Chapter 45

Knox

K acey's crying. And I can tell I'm in a hospital.

What the fuck happened?

Why is Kacey here?

Wait, where is here?

A doctor and a nurse hover close by. I think someone asked me a question, but I can't stop staring at Kacey.

Why is she crying? I hate when she cries.

My head is foggy, my legs and arms feel weighed down by lead. I rub the back of her hand with my thumb, but this seems to only make her cry harder.

"Kac—" I want to comfort her, but I can't get words out. My throat feels like someone rubbed sandpaper down it repeatedly.

"I'm so happy you're awake." She puts her other hand on top of my hand she's already holding. Tears are rolling down her face, but now she's smiling.

The nurse gets me water and lets me take a small drink, helping my throat. "I—I don't understand." I can barely get the words out. I remember being at the rodeo and getting ready to ride, but everything after is blank.

"Your bull went down on top of you the other day."

The other day? How long have I been in this hospital?

She must see the confusion in my eyes. "Knox, you've been in a coma for almost three days."

A coma?

Three days?

Before I can ask questions, the doctor makes me do some neuro tests, checking my pupils, nerves, and motor function. He seems satisfied with the results, saying I don't appear to have any brain damage—I could've just told him that—and moves on to telling me they removed my spleen; I also have a lacerated liver, and a cracked sternum.

Shit. That I can feel.

I'm slowly coming back to myself, and it feels like I've been hit by a truck. I try to take a deep breath, and son of a bitch, that hurts.

"What's your pain level?" the nurse asks. She must have seen me grimace.

"My ribs have hurt since July," I grumble at her.

"Knox!" Kacey scolds.

"Joking is a good sign." The doctor chuckles. He asks a few more questions, and checks a couple of monitors before he leaves, saying, "I'll be back in an hour to check on you."

The nurse gives me a dose of pain meds in my IV before she, too, slips out the door. I mess with the bed adjustments, sitting up as far as I can while Kacey's fingers are flying a million miles an hour over her phone screen.

"Your fingers are going to blister."

Her head snaps up. "Sorry, sending out an update to every-one. Your mom will be here in about an hour."

"She's coming here? She doesn't need to come," I complain. I hate when I get hurt and people make a big deal of it. I'm a bull rider—we're always hurt.

Kacey cocks an eyebrow at me. "You were in a coma. You're lucky my dad isn't up here. He texts me every hour and uses spoiling Rein rotten as a coping mechanism—look." She holds her phone out to me, and I see Rein sitting in a chair at the dining room table.

The laugh starts before I can stop it, causing every muscle in my chest to tighten as all the air suddenly leaves my lungs. I try to breathe in, but all I can get is a tiny wisp of air into my lungs. I groan in pain and close my eyes, waiting for it to subside.

Kacey jumps to her feet. "Oh my gosh, I'm so sorry. I didn't think about you laughing."

I can't help but smile. "It's okay, it was worth it. Besides, it'll feel a lot better when it quits hurting."

She looks at me with narrowed eyes. "Okay, tough guy, you can drop the act when it's just me in here. I won't ruin your reputation." She starts to sit in her chair again, but I stop her.

"Come here." I hold out my arm.

She sits on the edge of the bed, and I take hold of her hand. "I heard you."

Her eyes widen. "Like, the whole time?" she squeaks out.

I fight not to laugh, she's so cute. "No, at least I don't think so, but I heard you before I woke up."

She's looking down at our entwined hands.

"Sweetheart, look at me."

She slowly brings her eyes to meet mine.

"I love you, too."

Tears well in her eyes.

"Please don't cry again," I beg her. "Come here." I pull her hand toward me, and she gently leans in.

"I love you. I was so scared," she whispers as a single tear runs down her cheek.

I press our foreheads together. "I'm so sorry. But I'm right here, and I'm not going anywhere. Nothing in the world, remember? We'll be back in Mountain Time soon." I brush my lips over hers, soaking in the words. She loves me. I never imagined I'd find a love like this. The kind that settles deep within you and wraps around your soul, filling it with belonging and an undeniable sense of home. But I did, and Kacey is the beautiful woman who gave it to me.

I'm the luckiest man alive.

They moved me out of the ICU and into a regular room. A regular room where people can visit. Now my mom and Kacey sit in chairs on each side of my bed while Trey and Jessie share the window bench seat. They've both been oddly civil, and it's weird. I'm waiting for them to snap.

Kacey told me Trey has only left the hospital to ride over the weekend. After seeing how bad it scared Kacey, I'm sure it freaked Trey out, too, but I'm glad he didn't let it affect his performance. Taking second place this weekend secured him a spot to the national finals with me.

Kacey is still reluctant to leave my side, but when my mom and Jessie drag her out of the room to get some food, Trey fills me in on the wreck and shows me a video. He hasn't shown it to Kacey, and she hasn't asked to see it. We both agree it's probably for the best; I haven't seen a wreck that bad in a long time. It's amazing I survived. I still don't remember any of it—the doctor said I likely never will.

"Hey, man, thanks for everything. I'm sure this put a cramp on your bar-hopping this weekend," I tease him.

"Nah, you rate higher than bar hopping. Most days." He grins, putting his phone in his pocket. "I know you would do the same for me, you're the only brother I never had. Thanks for not dying."

I try to hold back my laugh, knowing it will make my chest ache. "Thanks, dickhead. You know, I think this is going to affect my driving next season, so you'll have to drive more."

"Guess I'm going to have to start looking for a new traveling partner then. And a new roommate."

"That would mean you'd have to start paying rent, ya leech."

"Well shit. Never mind." He laughs but then he turns serious. "I really am happy you're alright. Don't ever fucking do that again."

"I mean, I didn't plan to do it the first time, but yeah, let's never do this again."

My mom loves Kacey—I knew she would. My sister even visited with her over FaceTime when I talked to her and my nephew. She texted me afterward, sharing how happy she is for me and mentioning how pretty she is.

She's more than pretty. Kacey radiates beauty. Her kindness, empathy, and loyalty make her who she is.

Jessie and my mom fly out two days later, leaving Trey and Kacey to drive me back to Colorado when I'm released from the hospital one week after the wreck.

It's going to be a long recovery, but I should be ready for the National Finals in December.

And I can't wait to be back in Mountain Time.

Chapter 46

Kacey

The Ranch

"Well, they made it longer than I thought they would," Knox says next to me as we walk down the road to my dad's house for family dinner.

Trey and Jessie walk ahead of us, bickering about god knows what. They behaved so well at the hospital, it was almost like they were friends. Now they're back to fighting like cats and dogs. It even seems like they're arguing when they go silent and glare at each other, like right now.

"I've never known people who could argue while saying nothing at all . . . it's unnerving."

It's been two weeks since the wreck when we almost lost him. It's amazing how far he's come in his recovery. His chest is his main source of pain, but the surgery incision, concussion, and liver are healing quickly.

This will be Knox's first time out since getting home, but everyone has been over to our place to see him. That's how I think of it now: *our place*. His accident changed us both. Now we refuse to waste a single moment we have with each other. He plans to recover here this fall, only going back to Oklahoma to see his family and get some things he needs for the finals. When he asked me to go with him to the finals in Las Vegas, it was an immediate yes.

I thought my fear of losing my loved ones might pull us apart, but it's proven to do the opposite. It's made me stronger and brought us closer together. I've been seeing a therapist, and it's helped more than I expected. I wish I would've done it years ago. My dad and I were able to have a conversation about the day of the accident, and while sharing my experience with him was hard, it was also healing for both of us.

I know watching Knox climb on the back of another bull will be scary, but this is what he loves. Riding bulls is a part of who Knox is, and it always will be—even after he's retired someday. I could no sooner ask him to stop riding bulls than he could ask me to sell my horses. It's a part of who we are.

We all cut across my dad's yard and make our way up the porch steps. Dad, Carson, and Chet are on the porch with the grill going.

"Hey, girl. How are you today? Have you been a good girl?" Dad coos at Rein.

I scoff. "Not even a hello for us? You two are ridiculous."

"No, what's ridiculous is the trick he taught her," Chet grumbles from the railing he's leaning against.

"What kind of trick?" Jessie asks as she heads for the Adirondack chairs, flicking Carson on the ear on her way by, just to irritate him.

"Ha, I'm glad you asked. I can't wait to see your faces," Chet says, wearing an ornery smirk.

"Do you want to show them, Rein?" my dad asks. Rein sits in front of him, looking up, waiting for the next command. "Okay, fetch."

Rein takes off like a bullet and runs in the dog door.

Wait—a dog door?

"You installed a dog door? Really?" I roll my eyes.

"No, *I* installed the dog door," Carson corrects me. "He was too busy teaching her useless tricks."

"It is not useless," Dad argues.

"Fetch? That's it? What's she fetching?" Knox asks right as Rein comes blasting back outside, carrying a can of beer in her mouth.

My jaw hits the floor. Knox is trying his best not to laugh and hurt his chest. Trey and Jessie burst out laughing as my dad takes the beer from my dog and feeds her a piece of steak fat. He's grinning ear to ear, way too proud of himself.

"You have got to be kidding me. How did she open the fridge?"

"I tied a towel to it. She just pulls it open and grabs one off the bottom shelf. It's not hard." Dad furrows his brows at me, like I'm the crazy one.

"The other day, we were down at the bunkhouse, and she ran all the way up here, got one and brought it to him." Chet shakes his head.

I look down at Rein. "Are you even my dog anymore?"

"No," everyone says simultaneously.

Rude.

As we all make our way inside, Chet stops me. "Hey, Kacey, can we talk for a sec?" He looks uncomfortable. His brow is furrowed and his hand rubs at the back of his neck.

"Uh, yeah. Sure."

"I wanted to get your opinion on something. You know that sixty acres with the lake on the southwest side of the ranch?" he asks.

"Yeah, I know it."

"What do you think about putting cabins on it? Maybe five or six and a barn with runs for a few horses. That ground isn't used for anything, and renting out those cabins would generate more revenue for the ranch."

He's asking me this? I try to read his expression to see if he's joking. It's not a bad idea; it's actually really good.

"I think that's a great idea. It'd be an extensive project and ongoing work for someone to maintain, but I bet the return on the investment would be good. And we could keep the older, retired horses there. What does my dad think?"

"I don't know, I haven't talked to him about it yet. I wanted to get your opinion first. I'm going to put some numbers together and run it past him."

I don't think I've ever heard Chet sound so excited. And he wanted *my* opinion. I think I've misjudged him and taken out my own insecurities on him this entire time. All he did was accept a position, and he's done a damn good job at it. He clearly only wants to do what's best for the ranch.

"Okay, let me know if I can help with anything. This is a good idea, Chet." I offer him a genuine smile and head inside.

I breathe a little easier, realizing we aren't enemies. Maybe these cabins can be a fresh start for Chet and me.

Later that night, as we sit on the loveseat on my porch, Knox leans in and kisses my temple. "I don't think I ever thanked you."

"Thanked me? For what?"

"For loving me. I didn't know it was possible to feel so loved and supported until you. When I was riding great, horrible, or wrecked out in the hospital, you never wavered. And I know it's hard—the rodeo lifestyle is the highest of highs and the lowest of lows—from the injuries, to months on the road, it never gets easier. But all season long you stuck by my side; I couldn't have done this without you. I love you so much."

I gently wrap my arms around him, careful of his chest. "You're easy to love, Knox Ward. Thank you for never making me question my worth, for loving me for who I am. From the first day you showed up on this ranch, you showed me how much I mean to you. Even when I was stubborn and didn't want to see it, you never gave up on me."

He kisses the top of my head, and we stay like that, holding each other until the stars shine bright in the night sky, and my feet grow cold. And for the next two months, Knox and I start to build a life together, waiting on his chance at a world title.

Chapter 47

Knox

National Finals Rodeo, Las Vegas, Nevada

"One more, Knox. You've got this," Trey encourages from the chutes above me.

I'm taking my wrap on my last bull of the national finals. The crowd is so loud I can barely hear the announcer.

"Forty-six men have tried this next bull, and forty-six have failed to ride him, but tonight Knox Ward is tying his hand to him. He's sitting number one in the world. Ridden six out of nine bulls so far and as of this moment, he's sitting second in the average. Can he ride the unridden to win a gold buckle?"

The crowd inside the Thomas and Mack arena roars even louder.

This is it, this is my chance. It's my time.

I wouldn't be in the situation I've always dreamed about without Kacey. She has been my biggest supporter. I hadn't been on a bull since the last weekend of September, and I've been extremely sore here in Vegas. But Kacey has been my massage therapist every night, she's got ice for ice baths, and she comes early with me every night so I can go to Sports Med.

Not to mention, she took care of me the entire time I was laid up, all while still working at the ranch. I've never known such a driven, genuine person, and I'm so in love with her. She has made me a better man. Even if I don't win a world title, she's far more important to me than a gold buckle.

I exhale, and all I can hear is my own heartbeat thumping in my chest. I slowly slide up to my rope, letting out one more deep breath, and nod my head.

The bull explodes out of the box, and when he hits the ground, he sucks back, and his head disappears from sight. I flex my lower back and lift on my bull rope. Pulling my knees up slightly, I keep myself from teetering forward, keeping my shoulders square. He blows up again, I push on my rope driving up on my legs. He hits the ground kicking so hard I nearly get whiplash, but he's in a left lead, so I pull my chin back down and look at his left shoulder as I lower my free arm, transitioning my weight to my left leg.

We make another round and a half to the left when he explodes back into the air. I make sure I draw my knees up again, because when his front feet hit the ground, I know there's going to be a monster kick to follow.

I will not let him raise my chin again.

As soon as he reaches the full extension of his kick, I feel he's changing direction, but my weight is on my left leg, so I immediately throw my free arm over my head and pick up my left foot to move my weight to my right side.

I'm still a tick behind.

"Keep moving! Keep moving!" I hear Trey yelling from the chutes.

The bull rears, and I try to drive over him, but I'm too late. As he's transitioning from rear to kick, I shove my hips over to the right and throw them to my rope as hard as I can, hoping I don't get jerked down when he kicks. Everything is moving fast, and this damn clock seems to take an eternity. By the time he hits the end of his kick, I'm back in time with him. He makes one more jump and I hear the whistle blow.

It wasn't fucking pretty, but I made it. I grab my tail and yank it free from my hand, kicking my hips to the left, using the bull's momentum to throw me away from him. I stick the landing, planting both heels in the arena dirt, walking backwards, as I watch the bull run out of the arena. I'm sure I could break a record for how big my smile is right now. I pull off my helmet and blow a kiss up to where I know Kacey is sitting in the stands.

"He rides the unrideable and with that, he is your new World Champion!" the announcer bellows.

———————————

"Congratulations, Knox. You are officially a World Champion. Tell us how you're feeling right now," the interviewer prompts me as they hand me my gold buckle. There are thousands of people watching me as the lights focus on me, standing on stage in the center of the Thomas and Mack Arena, but I only feel Kacey's gaze.

"It's a dream come true. This is a goal I set for myself when I was a little kid. I never would've been able to accomplish it without help from all my friends and family, but I want to give a special shout out to an amazing woman. Kacey, you've been my rock all season—through the good times and the bad. You deserve this buckle every bit as much as I do. I love you, sweetheart."

The crowd lets out a collective, "*Aww*," as I raise my buckle in the air and point up to Kacey. She will come down in a few minutes and she's the first person I want to share this moment with. She's the person I want to spend every moment with for the rest of my life.

After the awards ceremony, I hurry back into the tunnel under the arena stands. I make it halfway to the locker room when I see blonde hair and green eyes running my way. I meet her halfway, scooping her up in my arms.

"Congratulations! I'm so proud of you. I love you." She vibrates with excitement in my arms.

I pull back and kiss her—not a quick peck, but a real kiss. I grip both sides of her face, my tongue finding hers, before leaning back to whisper, "I love you, too."

Epilogue

Kacey

Two years later

The bell above the door of the Plot Twist Café jingles. Carson, Trey, and Jessie file in, the latter two animatedly arguing about something, per usual, while Carson just looks annoyed.

"This better be good," he grumbles as he claims a seat at our table.

I keep my hands laced together in my lap under the table as everyone sits and Lainey heads our way from behind the counter. I instantly see Carson relax, like her presence brings him a sense of calm—Lainey's smile has that effect on people. She pulls up a chair next to him and they all look at Knox and me expectantly.

We texted everyone early this morning, asking to meet us here.

"We have something we wanted to tell you all—" Knox starts.

"You're pregnant," Jessie blurts before he can finish.

Carson's eyes go wide, and Trey looks at Jessie like she's somehow betrayed him by keeping pertinent information from him. Lainey rolls her eyes at the lot of them.

Knox lets out an exasperated sigh, but he's used to Jessie by now. "No. Just let me finish." Everyone at the table relaxes at his words as he continues. "Trey and I leave for the summer run in two days, so Kacey and I wanted to tell you all in person."

I slowly unclasp my hands and lay the left one on the table. Letting the sun glint on the oval cut diamond ring. Jessie and Lainey's eyes instantly snap to my ring finger, both letting out little squeals, making Trey and Carson jump. They aren't nearly as quick to catch on and exchange a glance, confused.

"Look down, *dumbasses*," Knox deadpans.

When their eyes find the ring, Carson smiles up at me—the big brother, I'm-proud-of-you-smile.

Trey, however, isn't so subtle. He jumps up, sending his chair crashing backwards, throwing his arms in the air, whooping. "Finally!"

Knox laughs, then the group collectively stands to embrace us both. After the congratulations, hugs, and *ooohs* and *awwws* from the girls admiring the ring, both Lainey and Carson head back to work.

We have one more thing to tell Trey, and Knox isn't sure how he'll take it. He has thought about it for months, discussed it with me, and even talked it over with my dad. But ultimately, it was his decision.

"Trey, I—" Knox has to clear his throat. I know this is hard for him, but he knows it's time. "I'm not going to publicly announce it yet, but I wanted to tell you now, before the summer run. This is going to be my last year riding, I'm going to retire at the end of the season."

Trey blinks.

Jessie looks from Knox to Trey and back again.

I grasp Knox's hand under the table. His body is tired, and he's ready to come home. He won a world title, qualified for the finals six times, and won countless rodeos. He's had a career most can only dream of, and I'm so proud of him.

"Okay. Congrats, man, we'll be sure to make it one hell of a summer."

I feel the relief roll off the man next to me. I tried to reassure him Trey loves him and wouldn't be mad, but he couldn't let go of the feeling that he's abandoning him. They have been best friends and traveled together for years. When Knox moved here to be with me, Trey never hesitated, he just packed up and followed. Knox likes to joke, saying it's because he owned the house in Oklahoma, but it's more than that. They're brothers—there isn't anything they wouldn't do for each other.

It's safe to say our family dinners have grown in size since that first night Knox came over, but my dad loves it. And now, with Knox's sister and nephew visiting for the spring, the ranch has never felt more like a family.

I see Knox swallow hard, clearing the lump from his throat. "Thanks, man. One hell of a summer and one last trip to the finals, just for old time's sake."

"Yeah, for sure. It's not like qualifying is hard or anything." They both laugh, because we all know it's, in fact, extremely difficult to qualify for. "So once you're done, I get the truck and camper, right? Because I think I—"

"I think you mean you get the first option to purchase it. Ya know, since you've traveled rent-free in it for years."

And just like that, they're off—bantering back and forth like always.

Jessie reaches across the table to squeeze my hand. Her eyes water as she says, "I'm so happy for you. I know there was a time you never thought this day would come, but I always knew. Because you, Kacey Hart, deserve to be loved. And I couldn't have imagined a better man than Knox. I love you both."

"Thank you for never giving up on me. I love you, too."

Truth be told, if it wasn't for my best friend, I might never have given Knox the time of day. She pushed me to take a chance, and that chance led me to the love of my life.

Since then, Knox and I have built a life together. We travel, rodeo, train horses, spend time with family and friends, dream of our future, and most of all, love each other unconditionally. I never knew it was possible to love someone more every day, or to spend every second together and never get sick of them, but that's exactly the kind of love we've found in each other.

"I hope you're ready to help me plan a wedding, maid of honor?" I say as a question. She mockingly gasps, like I would choose anyone else to stand by my side. "I would be honored. Do I get to pick the bridesmaid dresses? Please say yes."

I roll my eyes. "Of course. I would never dream of making a fashion decision without you."

As we walk out of the café, I reach out and lace my fingers with Knox's and I see my own thoughts mirrored in his eyes.

He's my home, my heart, best friend, and other half of my soul. And even though Trey has been calling me it for years, I can't wait to officially be Mrs. Ward.

One moment of your time can make a big impact.

Reviews mean the world to authors and encourage other readers to take a chance on a book. If you would be so kind to leave a review on the platform of your choosing, we would be forever grateful.

Keep up with all things Diamond Hart Ranch

Sign up for our email newsletter and be the first to receive updates and sneak peeks on the next great love stories of the Diamond Hart Ranch series!

https://www.thereistes.com/

Acknowledgments

We can't believe we're finally here and writing this. *Mountain Time* was started on November 5th, 2024 and written in places like the Wrangler National Finals Rodeo, San Antonio Stock Show and Rodeo, Rodeo Houston, and all over the western states. We've laughed, struggled, and found a new passion while writing this book and we couldn't be more grateful to our friends and family for your support along the way.

To our editor, Allison, we are so grateful we found each other. Your knowledge and feedback was invaluable to us. As first-time authors, your willingness to answer our millions of questions and learn about our lifestyle made this book more than we ever hoped it would be. You gave us the confidence to write boldly and share more stories.

To India's Bookwrecked girls: It's wild how strangers on the internet can be some of your biggest cheerleaders and supporters. You knew about this book before anyone else and there was never a day that passed when you didn't cheer us on and share our story with your friends. Your countless hours spent reading and providing feedback helped this book rise to the next level. We can't thank you all enough. (Maybe someday we'll convince Trevor to join our chaotic group chat!)

The memories of our girls (dogs), Rein and Katie Butts who have passed, was something we knew we wanted in this book. Kacey's dog Rein has the name of Trevor's late dog and the look of India's late dog, Katie Butts. They were our best friends and since all dogs go to heaven, we can't wait to be greeted with wagging tails and big brown eyes someday.

And finally, thank you, Reader. Picking up a debut novel is risky. We can't thank you enough for giving us and this series a chance. We hope you enjoyed Kacey and Knox's story, and we can't wait to share more from the Diamond Hart Ranch with you.

About the Authors

Trevor and India Reiste are a husband-and-wife duo who turned their love for rodeo and the cowboy lifestyle into their greatest adventure. Trevor, a professional bull rider for over fourteen years, has spent his life traveling across the country, competing in the world's biggest rodeos. India, his biggest supporter and an avid reader, joined him in bringing their passion for storytelling to life with her knowledge of cattle and agriculture.

Their journey as authors began with a shared dream and a relentless determination to bring authentic cowboy romance to life. Whether on the road in their Capri camper with their twelve-pound wiener dog or back home in southeastern Oklahoma, they embrace adventure, hard work, and the simple joys of life.

Their books invite readers into the world of rodeo, ranch life, and love—where romance, like the West and its cowboys, is wild, real, and free.

Free Fall

A sneak peek at the second book of
the Diamond Hart Ranch series.

Chapter 1

Trey

Fort Worth, Texas
January

I'm running down the sidewalk of a suburban neighborhood barefoot, in nothing but my boxers and cowboy hat.

Knox is going to kill me.

I sent him my location as soon as I woke up this morning. Turns out what woke me up was a boyfriend—one I didn't know existed—coming home to Lacey.

Or was it Macey?

My phone rings. "Where. The fuck. Are. You?" I wheeze between panting breaths. Unless I'm being chased by a bull, running isn't really my thing.

"I'm looking at your location, but you're moving. Are you running?" he asks.

"Yes, I'm running! Turns out she has a boyfriend, and he is not a small man."

Knox bursts into laughter. "Oh, this is too good. Maybe I'll drive a little slower, see if he catches your home-wrecking ass."

Ass. I'm in a life-or-death situation here and he's cracking jokes.

"Don't you dare! I didn't know! Where the hell are you?"

He's laughing so hard I can barely understand him. "Turn around, dumbass."

I look behind me and sure enough, there he is, creeping down the street at a snail's pace.

Wait—is he taking a video?!

Oh, I'll make him regret this.

I hang up. Moments later, I throw the truck door open, and toss my boots, jeans, and shirt into the cab before climbing in. "You'll pay for that." I shoot him a glare.

He stops laughing long enough to fire back, "Tough talk coming from a man in nothing but his underwear. Plus, you're thirty minutes late, so you'll be paying for the next two tanks of fuel."

"Whatever. I've been kicking your ass, anyway, old man. Just drive before he sees us."

Knox is my traveling partner. We've both ridden bulls professionally since we were eighteen and have traveled together for years. I glance around, looking for the mammoth of a man. Our black truck and Capri truck camper stand out in the quiet neighborhood.

We're west of Fort Worth where I won their Extreme Bulls last night. I just wanted to celebrate.

Sue me.

I don't make a habit of sleeping with other men's women; on the contrary, I try to avoid it at all costs. I had no idea she had a boyfriend. She never mentioned it and there weren't any photos in the house during the brief moment I looked around the place.

"Better get your britches on," Knox teases. "Only one hour to Dallas."

I scowled at him but guided my left foot into my pants leg all the same.

Knox is anxious about being late because we're picking up his girlfriend, Kacey, and her best friend at the airport. Her best friend Jessie—the same Jessie I have shamefully flirted with since I met last year, even though she won't give me the time of day. I see the way she looks at me though; she, like most women, isn't immune to my charm and boyish good looks. No matter what I try, she won't give in. Which is unlike most women.

Maybe this will be the weekend she finally caves.

I knew I'd like Jessie before I ever met her. I saw a photo of her with Knox and Kacey on Knox's phone and I just *knew*. That woman is different, a challenge. I've never met a challenge I didn't like. When my parents told me I shouldn't ride bulls, I only got on more bulls. When everyone said I'd never make a living rodeoing, I only rode more bulls and made more money.

So, when we finally met in Estes Park last year, and I saw the fire in Jessie's eyes, it was game on. I quickly learned she doesn't take shit from anyone and I'm pretty sure she terrifies most grown men. Not me, though, I like feisty women. When Knox and Kacey left us alone for an hour, it was a blurry blend of fighting and flirting. I knew after five minutes with her I wouldn't win this challenge in a night, and that's okay, sometimes the chase is just as fun.

When Knox got hurt last fall, Jessie stepped up and took control. She made sure everyone was taken care of, that we ate, drank, and slept. Anything Knox, Kacey, or I needed, Jessie was there without fail.

Hell, I might not have gone to the arena and rode the next night if it wasn't for the verbal kick in the ass she gave me. And I was grateful for it—I wouldn't have made the National Finals without the money I won that night. I developed a new respect for her in that hospital, but I still want to rip her jeans off her and see if she fucks as good as she fights—respectfully, of course.

I slap the inside of my thighs and rock my hips back and forth, staying warm. I breathe in the familiar scent of rosin, livestock, and sweat. The arena is packed with a cheering crowd, all waiting on the next 8-second ride. Dust stirs up from the chute where my bull is pawing, amped up and ready to go.

"You got this. Don't be a pussy." Knox slaps me on the back of my helmet.

"I am what I eat." I smirk.

He shakes his head, but he's fighting a smile. "Just focus."

"Oh, come on, I've been waiting to use that one for *years*."

I'm up next, so I climb into the chute and set my rope. Once I've taken my wrap and the bull is looking forward, I nod and the gate swings open.

The bull bursts from the chute, kicking hard as he slings his head and moves to the right. I set my hips to my rope and throw my free arm over my head. I can feel my hips sliding to the inside, into the well, as he makes his next round. The way he's slinging his head, horns flying, I'm not about to fall into his trap and get the shit hooked out of me. I break at the hips and look toward his left shoulder as I wait on him for a split second before shuffling my hips back into the middle.

"Trey, you need to calm yourself. Quit getting excited and slipping into the well." Knox's words echo in my mind as we spin around and around. I feel myself relax as I find the bull's timing and start matching him move for move.

At six seconds, I feel comfortable enough to lift my outside leg and start spurring to earn myself a few extra points. When the whistle blows, I look up and point toward the section of the stands where I know Jessie is sitting, then I go to pull my tail, but I start sliding to the inside—*again*.

Son of a bitch.

With no other choice, I grab my tail as fast as I can and kick my hips, jumping right into the well, committing to the wreck my showboating has gotten me into. Thankfully, the bull fighters step in to draw the bull in the other direction at the same moment my boots hit the dirt. I walk back to the bucking chutes, waving my arms to hype up the crowd.

"How about 86.5 points to put him in second place!" the announcer bellows and the crowd cheers.

Geez, only 86.5?

They were a little hard on me tonight, but I'm sure my showboating after the whistle cost me a point or two. The judges hate that shit. But, *fuck it.* I thought it was awesome.

I should be excited about the ride, my winnings, and rise in the world standings. But I'm still wondering, *is this what will win Jessie over?*

It did not win Jessie over.

She hasn't said two words to me since we left the arena and came to this bar. Not even a simple "Good ride." All I got was a quiet "thanks" when I opened the truck door for her. And it's not like she's subdued; she's been plenty chatty with Knox and Kacey.

I need to change tactics, bring out the big guns. Kacey told me Jessie likes to dance, and I happen to be a *fantastic* swing dancer.

I wait a few minutes until the perfect song comes on before I set my beer down and round the table to her.

She's a total smokeshow tonight. With her dark auburn waves flowing down her back, almost so long they touch her perfectly-fitted dark wash jeans. Jessie is petite, but she has curves in all the right places. She's wearing boots and another one of those damn corset tops like she wore in Estes Park last year. I swear she only wears them to test my willpower and determine whether I'll glance down at her cleavage or not.

I wordlessly hold out my hand and watch her hazel eyes move from my hand to my blue ones.

"What?"

"Dance with me." It's not a question.

Silence is her only answer as she crosses her arms.

Oh, the corset is so a test.

I don't look down.

I don't know what it is about this woman that draws me in like a moth to a flame, but here I am, walking directly into the fire.

I give her my best crooked smile and say a little too loud, "Jessie Hawkins, will you please do me the honor of gracing the dance floor with your unending beauty, irresistible charm, and effortless—"

"Okay, fine. Just shut up." She slaps her hand into mine. "You're embarrassing."

I hear a snort from across the table. Knox, no doubt. He's the brother I never had and knows me well. He knows I've been obsessed with Jessie since the moment I saw her. He tells me—too often—it'll never happen, but I don't appreciate his negativity and choose to ignore him.

I lead Jessie to the floor, spin her into me and start two-stepping. I waited for a medium-tempo song, enough that we could swing dance but also have a conversation. I'm still in my cowboy hat, starched jeans, and long sleeve navy blue riding shirt—the picture of a cowboy. But the moment her hand settles on my shoulder, a jolt of heat sears straight through the fabric like it's not even there.

She moves with me like we've done this a thousand times, every step seamless. Her body molds to mine in a way that feels dangerously right. Like she was designed to fit into my arms.

"Did you see me point at you before I got off my bull?" I ask her.

"I'm not going to act like I know everything about bull riding, but I saw you showing off, then about get yourself in a wreck."

"Psh—no. I knew those bull fighters would step in. My timing was impeccable."

"Spell 'impeccable.'"

I spin her out, swinging her behind my back before stepping around and pulling her back into me. "Listen, Hawkins. I'm a bull rider, not an English teacher."

She raises a brow at me.

"As I was saying, I pointed up at you. I think you might be my good luck charm."

"I bet you say that to all the girls, don't you, stud?" she counters cheekily.

Then, the song ends. Before I know it, she winks and saunters back to our table. She's toying with me . . . and it's fucking *killing* me. I might have officially met my match. But *damn*, she looks good strutting away.

"So?" Kacey tilts her head, assessing Jessie as we approach.

"I stand by my statement," is her only reply.

"What statement?" I ask.

"You're a fuckboy," Jessie quips, looking me dead in the eyes before grabbing her beer, taking a long pull.

I prop my elbow on the table and lean toward her. "Forget what kind of man you think I am. What kind of man do you need me to be?"

She snorts a laugh, but there's a spark in her eye. "Wow. Smooth. Does that line ever work for you?"

"I don't know, you tell me."

She swallows the last of her beer. "Maybe if you would've won tonight. Second isn't a good look." With that, she turns and walks away.

But my ego isn't easily bruised. Before she's out of earshot, I call out, "Mmm, keep talking like that, and I might fall in love with you." Bringing my fist to my mouth, I bite down on my index finger as I watch her glance over her shoulder and give me a smirk.

"There is something fundamentally wrong with you," Knox says next to me.

"Mind your business, old man. I know what I'm doing." I don't take my eyes off Jessie as she works her way through the crowd to the bar.

"He has no idea what he's doing," Kacey whispers to Knox.

And she might be right.